the Arrangement

SONYA LALLI

First published in Great Britain in 2017 by Orion Books,
an imprint of The Orion Publishing Group Ltd
Carmelite House, 50 Victoria Embankment,
London EC4Y ODZ

An Hachette UK company

1 3 5 7 9 10 8 6 4 2

A CIP catalogue record for this book is
available from the British Library.

ISBN 978 1 4091 7130 0

Typeset at The Spartan Press Ltd,
Lymington, Hants

Printed and bound by CPI Group (UK) Ltd,
Croydon, CR0 4YY

MIX
Paper from
responsible sources
FSC® C104740

www.orionbooks.co.uk

For my grandparents

Chapter 1

Nani's silhouette flickered behind the tangerine-coloured curtain drawn across the front window. It was noon exactly, and the sun baked me through the glass roof of my Jeep as the suburban sounds drifted in – dogs and birds, lawn-mowers moseying across pale green lawns for the first time this year. A group of runners armed with gadgets and clad in Barbie-pink Lycra trudged down the pavement, and I followed them in the rear-view mirror as they veered out of sight, overtook the dirt path down towards the school. I looked back at the house and and saw that the front door was open a crack. I could feel Nani waiting for me, tapping her socks and sandals anxiously just out of sight. So I wiped the gloss off my lips, threw the car door open and, dragging each leg out, prepared myself for the ambush.

She opened the door as I was still crossing the lawn. Her nose twitching, she looked me up and down as I forced myself up the steps.

'Is that what you're wearing?'

I glanced down at my weekend jeans, my favourite checked shirt. 'Yes?'

She clucked her tongue as I bent over and brushed a kiss on the top of her head. She smelled the way she always smelled, like cocoa butter and roasted cumin. A touch of garlic. She stepped back and continued her evaluation, her tiny fingers pinching at the fleshy part of her chin as I kicked off my shoes.

'Did you bring anything nicer?'

I blinked slowly, adjusting to the low light. I thought of a royal-blue cardigan I'd worn camping the previous weekend. It was still in the boot, somewhere alongside a bin bag of recycling I still hadn't taken in and a spare tyre we'd tried to float on. The sweater could have been classified as 'nicer' if Shay hadn't spilled her wine on it and then tried to set it on fire.

'What, don't I look nice?'

'You always look *nice*.' Nani shrugged off her chunni and draped it around me as if it might hide the slight paunch I'd acquired since taking a desk job. She attempted to tie the crimson-red silk shawl in a knot around my waist, then shoulders, and finally, in defeat, put it back round her own neck, shaking her head as if it was my fault a chunni didn't match my outfit.

I watched her face as she reached up and studied my jaw-line with her fingers, deciding whether my too-short hair appeared more feminine in front of my ears or behind. I wondered whether to tell her that Shay had already warned me; that I'd dressed down for my own birthday on purpose. But I decided against it.

'What's going on?' I asked, trying to act surprised.

Nani winked at me. 'We have a guest!'

A *guest*. A guest implied a cup of chai and a tray of sweets quickly brought out of the freezer and defrosted. A guest was small talk and compliments. Gossip. Insisting they stayed for dinner while praying they wouldn't. A *guest* was not an unannounced blind date chaperoned by your grandmother.

I bounded up the stairs to the second floor on the pretence of finding something else to wear, knowing full well there was nothing nicer in my old room. Too-large t-shirts from summer camps and music festivals where my favourite band that year had headlined. Jogging bottoms, with black or white press studs running up the leg. My old trumpet.

It was odd how little of me I kept here. But of all the places I'd lived since moving out – shabby apartments in the Annex; a flat-share in London; and now, a new apartment with my name on the mortgage – it was this house that I'd always considered home. I heard Nani calling, her voice staccato and sweet, and I ran a brush through my hair and made my way back down.

She looked up at me expectantly. 'Nothing?'

'All my clothes are in town.'

She arched her brows. 'Anything in guest room?'

Again, I shook my head. Mom's old room. Starch-white walls and a beige linen duvet, not a trace of her left in the wardrobe. Nani sighed as I reached the bottom step, evaluating my outfit one last time. And then she shrugged, squeezed my hand and said, 'Still my pretty girl. Even in *that*.'

Anywhere Nani lived would always be home.

I tucked my shirt in and followed her through the kitchen, ducking my head beneath the cross-beam as we took the eight steps down to the lower level. To the 'entertaining room', as Nani called it: orange corduroy sofas wrapped stiffly in plastic; the walls packed with street art bought for a few hundred lire on their one trip abroad;

Lord Ganesha presiding on the mantel, a choir of porcelain Siamese cats chiming in unison. And our *guest* stood at the room's rapturous centre, awkwardly, his dark brown skin the same shade as the varnish on the wood panelling.

'Raina,' said Nani, clutching my wrist, 'meet Sachin.' She dragged me closer until the top of his forehead was square to my mouth, and I tried to ignore the dull sensation in my belly. He looked vaguely familiar. Perhaps someone I'd known as a child, or seen in the stack of pictures Nani had started leaving on the kitchen table. He was quite short, albeit symmetrical – handsome, even. He smiled and brought his palms together at his chest, bowing slightly to both of us.

'Hello, Raina,' he said, like my name was a word he'd invented.

'Hi.'

'Sachin drove far to come for your birthday lunch.'

'It's your birthday?' His face stiffened. 'I didn't mean to intrude.'

'No intrusion, dear.' She pinched his cheek. 'My Raina and I are *so* happy you joined. *Nah*, Raina?'

I nodded.

'Raina is *such* a good girl. Always coming home from her busy job to take care of her Nani.' She gasped and turned to me. 'Sachin is a busy man too. Raina, did you know he is doctor?'

'No, I didn't.' I turned to him. 'My best friend is a doc—'

'I'm a cardiologist, actually.' He glanced away. 'To be more precise.'

I clamped down on my lip. *Precise, or just plain arrogant?* I asked myself.

'Specialised at Columbia.'

'Mhm. Oh, is that right?'

He nodded, fingering his wristwatch. 'Diverse city. Beautiful campus. One of the top programmes in the country – world, even. Some might say.'

'I think I've heard of *Columbia*.' I folded my arms across my chest. 'Is that in Cleveland?'

'Actually, New York—'

'And you're the kind of doctor that cleans teeth, right?' Nani jabbed me on the arm and I tried not to laugh.

'No, no. It's—'

'*Cardio*logist. Oh! You're a sports doctor.'

He shifted from side to side. 'Actually, cardiac electrophysiology is a—'

Nani clucked her tongue, waving him off. 'Don't listen to her. She's a silly one, my Raina.' She wrapped her arms around my waist as if she were a co-conspirator in the charade.

'Oh,' said Sachin.

Evidently they didn't teach sarcasm at Columbia.

'Dear, would you like chai before lunch?'

'Chai sounds lovely, Auntie.'

She waddled up the stairs leaving me alone with him, and I sat down on one of the sofas, the plastic screeching beneath me as I settled onto the cushion. Sachin joined me a moment later, his legs spread so wide he was nearly touching me. To my dismay, he actually smelled pretty good: the way rich men tended to smell, like Dev used to smell. An understated potency that still dominated the entire room.

'Your Nani is very sweet,' he said.

'She's the best.'

'What's her name again?'

'Belinda.'

'Oh.'

I looked straight ahead, deadpan, trying not to glance at him out of the corner of my eye.

'Is that ... Bengali?'

'No,' I sighed. 'Her name is Suvali.'

'But you just said—'

'It was a joke.'

'A joke, right.' He let out a stiff laugh. 'Good one.'

Growing up, everyone referred to family friends as *auntie* or *uncle*, and names were non-essential, but I still felt mildly offended on Nani's behalf. I reclined slightly on the sofa and stared straight ahead. Lord Ganesha – eyes, trunk and all – stared back.

Upstairs I could hear Nani bustling around in the kitchen. She would be setting out her favourite teacups on the silver tray Nana had bought her as a wedding present, placing teaspoons equally spaced along the paper napkins – garish, a bold red and gold – that she'd once bought in bulk at a discount store going out of business. Fifty packets for five dollars.

'Raina, hey listen,' Sachin said after a while.

'Yes?'

He played with his rounded fingernails, picking beneath them. 'I really hate to ruin your birthday, but—'

'You have to go?' I asked, a little too eagerly.

'No.' He flashed me a smile, two rows of square white teeth. 'Don't worry. I'll stay for lunch. But I would hate to mislead you about my intentions.' He looked up at me quickly, and then back at the floor. 'I'm not interested.'

'That's fi—'

'You seem like a really nice girl, Raina. Really nice. And I don't mean to hurt you.' He sighed again. 'I'm just not in that place, you know? I'm not ready for the kind of commitment that our families – that you – seem to be after.'

I bit my tongue. The only thing I was after was for him to leave.

'I know, I know.' He stood up and paced in front of me, his hands partially shoved into his pockets. 'I'm a doctor, I get it. The biology of it all just isn't fair. It's harder for women. More pressure after they, uh, reach a certain age?'

I let out a deep, writhing sigh. 'It's *so* hard.'

'And your Nani finding you a single doctor is…' He paused and looked me dead in the eye. 'Well, it's the dream, isn't it?'

A dream? More like a nightmare.

'But really, Raina, you seem like a nice girl.' He knelt down in front of me and patted my knee. '*Really* nice. And I'm sure you will find someone soon.'

I resisted the urge to tell him what I *really* thought of him, and studied him as he crouched at my feet. Sachin was the definition of the man Shay and I had spent so many years avoiding: the *westernised* Indian. The one who used to be captain of the chess club or maths team, and although brutalised for it in high school, now threw out the stereotypes about his culture as an anecdote to make the C-cups and hair extensions laugh as he chivalrously paid for their drinks. He was the archetype who watched sports and drank beer, had the uncanny ability to mock his father's

7

accent, yet would still want his wife to learn how to make curry the way his mother did. He was the hybrid of East and West; the immigrant mentality distilled and harnessed, his arrogance a by-product – forgivable – of ambition.

Sachin looked up at me and heaved a patronising sigh. 'Are you going to be OK?'

He was also the type of man that any Nani would want her granddaughter to marry, and as I patted his shoulder reassuringly I tried to convince myself that Sachin – his type – wasn't what I was interested in either.

There seems to be a great deal of misinformation around the modern-day arranged marriage. I am often bombarded with questions by co-workers, or middle-aged women sitting next to me on long-haul flights after they've picked up on the fact that I'm half Indian – not Latina or Lebanese, as they have originally guessed. Being Indian is all the rage these days, they tell me. And in an exertion of worldliness, I am quoted anecdotes they've picked up in the frozen foods section at Costco while buying paneer, or watching twenty minutes of *Dil Chahta Hai* on the Bollywood channel that comes with their deluxe cable package. They love the bright colours and gold chains. The eccentric music. The food – oh, how they *love* the food. And, of course, they are curious about my love life. They want to know more about this whole 'arranged marriage' thing, whether I too might soon be enlisted.

But the protocol of arranged marriage in my community today is less glamorous than they might have anticipated. It is choosing from a roster of carefully vetted men: men whose family, religion, background, values and sometimes even astrology match your own. It is having parents who want their children to marry into the 'culture', who hurl them against a brick wall of blind dates until one finally sticks. It is arranged dating, really; an agreement to decide quickly whether you are in love.

I grew up with dozens of girls who went this route; women fast-tracked down the aisle, business class on a non-stop flight towards happily ever after.

And they seemed happy.

After all, they tell me – their mouths full of champagne and vanilla cream cake, cocooned in flowing bridal lenghas worth as much as a new car – what's the big deal about being set up by your family? Isn't 'today's arranged marriage' the equivalent of being set up by a friend, or an algorithm in your go-to dating app? Aren't their chances of having a successful marriage as high as the girl who ends up marrying her one-night stand? Or the one who met her leading man at college? I am one of the very few of my generation still unmarried, and I never know what to say; how much to smile. And so I help myself to another drink, sometimes another piece of cake, and reverently congratulate them on their Bollywood ending.

But I always wonder what happens after the ceremonial fire goes out and the guests go home, stuffed and slightly drunk on Johnnie Walker. Nani's marriage was arranged, and unlike today's blessed nuptials, she didn't have much of a say in the matter. Her father showed her a black and white photo of a lanky boy with round wire spectacles, and later, someone smeared red powder on her forehead and just like that – well, almost – she was married. It was simple.

9

Clear-cut. A transaction performed not out of love for a would-be spouse, but for one's own family.

But wasn't an arranged marriage beneath me? I wasn't really Indian, after all. I was Canadian. A girl who refused to feel out of place in her mostly white, middle-class suburb in West Toronto. I rollerbladed and sold lemonade on stands, rolled my eyes on 'Culture Day' at school when Shay and I were forced to wear lenghas, the other kids crowding around us for a chance to paw at the fake crystals sewn onto the sleeves. I only saw Indians when I was dragged to dinner parties, and at temple every Sunday. When we went bulk grocery-shopping in Scarborough because the corner Safeway didn't have the right brand of lentils or coconut milk. And even though Ravi Shankar always seemed to be playing, and my clothes perpetually reeked of masala, I grew up fully committed to my role in what otherwise seemed to be a white narrative. I played a girl who couldn't believe in arranged marriage, not only because of the cliché of her own family shambles but because the cynicism of her Western world, the literary fiction on her bookshelf, barely allowed her to believe in marriage at all.

So I resisted the idea of a planned union that might make me happy; that might make Nani happy.

'Did you like Sachin?' she asked after he had left. She stood beside me as I washed the dishes, the side of her head resting lightly on my shoulder.

Did I like him? I didn't *dis*like him. After he'd told me he just wasn't interested, and Nani had come back with the tea, the pressure had evaporated. It wasn't a chaperoned date, a three-hour festival I'd have to diarise so I could one day tell my daughters about all the silly things their father said the first time our eyes locked.

It was just lunch.

'Will you see him again?' Nani asked.

'No.' I shook my head. 'I don't think so.'

'Don't *think* so.'

I didn't answer, and she leaned forward on tiptoe and turned off the tap.

'You got along with him, *nah*?'

'I don't know.' I turned to face her, not quite sure how to tell her I'd already been rejected. 'What did you think of him?'

'Only you know what you need in husband, Raina. What you need to be happy.'

'I am happy.'

She wiped a fleck of foam off my neck and stared at me, attempting to read my expression the way she attempted to read English.

'I am!'

She grimaced and glanced away, as if she'd heard it too. The urgency. The insistence. I attacked the rice cooker, knuckles and steel wool, my palms burning red in the hot water. The suds washed off, I held it up, laid it sideways on the dish rack. Why did I sound like I was trying to convince myself? I was happy, wasn't I? I had everything, less the one thing that, to Nani, defined the rest. The boxes for college and career had been ticked; only one thing remained.

She rolled up her sleeves and handed me a frying pan. Staring at it, she said, 'You agreed to this.'

'I know. But I said thirty.'

'You're twenty-nine now, Raina. What difference is one year?'

'Yeah, what *is* the difference?' I squirted washing-up liquid onto the pan and put the bottle down firmly. 'What's the difference if I get married now, or in five years, or never?'

'Don't talk nonsense.'

'Really, Nani. What's the rush? Kris isn't married.'

'When he's ready, he will.'

'It's because he's a man.'

She didn't answer. She walked around me and inspected the rice cooker propped up on the drying rack. Tapping a speck of white caked onto the side, she handed it back to me.

'Just because he's been married before, or because he can have children whenever he feels like it, and his *sperm*—'

'*Beta*. Enough.'

She finally met my eye. The slight scowl that had formed on her face vanished, and she reached for my cheek. 'A husband, a family – it will bring you so much joy. You remember how happy your Nana made me?'

I wasn't so sure I agreed, but I was too tired to argue. Her hand was soft, slightly wet from the dishes, and I let my head rest against it.

'You remember, I told you when I was young, my father was in army and we had to move. Moving, moving, constantly – and I never had anything of my own.' She nodded, pressing her lips together. 'And then I had your Nana. I had *family* of my own.'

I turned back to the sink.

'And don't you want children?'

I sighed. 'I do, but—'

'*Beta*, you are getting older. Your Auntie Sarla, everyone at temple – they always ask me, why is Raina not married? Why always at that office? You cannot marry your Blueberry!'

'It's called a BlackBerry, Nani. And I'm not fussy. I'm just not ready.'

'You work and work, and life is passing by. Men are passing by. Tell me, when is the right time? When will you be ready?'

I watched the pan fill with water, bits of brown bubbling in the froth. To Nani, a man unmarried in his thirties was fine – but for me, it wouldn't be. I took a deep breath and willed myself not to fight back.

She reached for my hand, and as her slight brown fingers interlocked with my own, I realised that in my silence, I was being complicit. I recognised how much I truly loved this vivacious, slightly insane little woman, and what I would do to be the only person in her life never to break her heart. I would go along with it. I would live up to her expectations, and that promise I made her two years ago – broken-hearted and desperate for my life to make sense once again – that if I wasn't married at thirty, I'd let her make the arrangements for me.

'So we will try again?' she asked. 'We will find you someone else?'

'Sure, Nani.' I forced a smile. 'We'll try again.'

She dried her hands on her slacks and headed into the lounge. 'Good, stay there,' she called. 'I am bringing the list.' A few moments later she reappeared in the kitchen, light steps on the hardwood, a piece of loose-leaf paper fluttering like she was bidding at an auction.

Was my husband's name somewhere on that list?

She sat down at the kitchen table and pulled out the chair next to her. Dragging her thumb along the edge of the page, she muttered names under her breath.

Did I want it to be?

I abandoned the sink and sat down next to her. Looking through the list, I feigned interest as she enthusiastically explained who each of the candidates were. Going on these dates would make Nani happy, and I supposed it didn't really matter who I wanted – or whom I still wanted. *This* was happening, and with only 364 days to go, the arrangements had already begun.

Boys for my Raina

~~SACHIN — Reetu's son in Scarborough, some kind of doctor — birthday lunch??~~

JAGMOHAN — Pinky's nefew in Jodhpur (visiting Canada this summer?) — but maybe looking for immwigration

VINAY — Divya's co-worker, studies kemistry (What is that??), parents from Chennai

JAYESH — Sharon's cousin, science professor at university . . . <u>divorced</u>!!!

ROHIT — Sarla's nefew, lawyer in Boston

ARJUN — Sonia's son, pediatrishan, probly will want to have babies soon!

VISHAL — Bengali boy, also likes business things, Geeta's friend's son

KRUPAL — engineer in Vancouver, his parents at temple every Sunday — but may be too short (and dark)

RAHUL — Sarla's fisiotherapist, says he very good-looking boy ☺

AZIZ — accountant in Hamilton, Shushma's son, may have a white girlfriend??

MANJEEV — that handsome boy from temple, PhD student in computers

Chapter 2

It was light out now, when I left; summer, it seemed, was on its way. I ran most mornings before 6 a.m., before the commuters crowded the streets and the city became a mess of traffic, delivery vans and the hammering from a nearby building site. I loved the feel of bare concrete and unbreathed air, of the urban sprawl temporarily abandoned. My legs twitched and I picked up speed, nothing but the sound of my feet beating against the pavement. I headed north past the still-closed shops, St Michael's Cathedral, then cut through Queen's Park. The paths were damp and crusted with last season's leaves, and as the sun peeked through the branches and the sweet scent of dew filled my lungs, I exhaled and smiled into the light. Running was how I bore sitting upright in an office chair, sometimes for eighteen hours a day; how, as a child, I learned to survive.

I ran home through the university, the boundaries of four years of my life in bricks and mortar, paper and pencil, the glare and hum of a screen. I brushed by the buildings dotting St George's Street, each harbouring memories that became more vague with each run: the eastern brownstone where I had a class on political economy and advanced econometrics; the building perpetually under construction where I took a seminar on microfinance in the developing world.

Had it really been over ten years since I started university? I thought back to myself in those days: slightly skinnier and round-faced, commuting back and forth from Nani's house on overcrowded buses, highlighting textbooks and writing in the margins as I awkwardly stood in the aisles. There hadn't been wild frat parties with beer pong and hours of missing memories, or shots of tequila after a Monday-evening lecture.

I'd studied. I'd graduated. And, exactly according to plan, I'd got myself a well-paid job.

I was soaked by the time I completed my loop. I sprinted up the stairs of my building, each floor greeting me with a new smell. Week-old rubbish and wet dog. Compost and fresh bread. I heaved my body up the last few stairs and smelled curry – like Nani's, but tangier – from the Sri Lankan family who lived across the landing. I opened my front door and for a moment just stood in the entrance, panting as I tried to catch my breath. It never failed to strike me how, two years after moving in, my apartment still smelled of absolutely nothing.

If someone were to rifle through my things they'd extract a certain image of me, a rather banal version who did little more than sleep and bathe between scenes at the office. And it was true. Only a shadow of me lived here in this catalogue-clean apartment with two bedrooms and a view, a gallery of wicker and eggshell with midnight-blue accents. Here there were only egg whites and salsa in the fridge, vodka in the freezer, and, thanks to the previous owner, everything seemed to match but me.

I'd bought it on sight a month after flying home from London, and hadn't changed a thing except for the handful of framed photos I'd hung indiscriminately on the walls. Shay and our group of high school friends at graduation next to the fridge. A rare, complete family photo hanging in the front hall: Nani and Nana, me in a frilly dress sitting on their knee, Kris and Mom standing just behind. If asked, I wouldn't know how to explain each of these characters in a way that made sense, or my relationship to each of them. Kris is your uncle – but grew up like a brother? And your mom is alive, but didn't bring you up?

I poured myself a glass of orange juice, and leaving the empty carton on the counter, I finished it in one long swig. But no one ever asked those questions. In the two years that I'd lived here, I hadn't had anyone over who didn't already know the answers.

I showered and changed into a linen suit, and by the time I left again the city was awake. I turned south on Yonge Street towards town, manoeuvring through pedestrians and lamp posts as I answered emails on my BlackBerry. Shay was already at the diner, slumped over in our usual booth, and I slid in across from her.

'Already ordered.' She leaned back, her eyes half-closed, and I grabbed a sticky newspaper off the seat. There were mornings when neither of us spoke – when I'd read and Shay, straight from a night shift at the hospital, dozed at the table. We'd been coming to the same diner since we moved out together into a shared apartment in the building above it. At the time she was still in medical school, but tired of living with her parents, and I'd received my first big-city paycheque. I'd get home after work and find her in the diner studying her medical textbooks, not wanting to be alone in the apartment, and we'd nurse our free refills of coffee beneath the neon light of the Hollywood sign, Shay learning how to make a differential diagnosis while I kept her company and stuck straws in my nose and tried to make her laugh.

Our usuals arrived: black coffee, three fried eggs and ketchup, crunchy breakfast potatoes and four thick slices of rye bread, and for a while we ate in silence. She looked exhausted, and I waited until after she'd had her first cup of coffee, and was well on to her second, to bring it up.

'Aren't you going to ask me how it went?'

'Sorry.' She smiled groggily, then nodded her head. 'What was he like?'

I shrugged. 'He was OK, I guess.'

'Are you glad I warned you?' Shay asked, putting down her fork. She had nearly finished her plate, and she rested her elbows on the table. 'I was worried you wouldn't turn up.'

Somehow Shay's mother, Auntie Sarla, had found out Nani was inviting Sachin over – and, of course, Auntie Sarla had told Shay. Seemingly there were no secrets in our community, and nothing Auntie Sarla wouldn't involve herself in. She was my best friend's mother, and one of Nani's closest friends, but it was hard to be in the same room with her. She judged and criticised and berated, and treated Nani and me like inferiors. She was even critical of her own children, even though Shay and her brother Nikesh had lived up to every expectation.

She was a matriarch of our community, and in a way she represented everything that was wrong with our traditions.

At the same time Nani owed so much to her, making it hard to despise her.

Since moving to Toronto, Nani and Nana had made their living as restaurant owners, an Indian café they now called Saffron. But the trendy, upmarket establishment was nothing like it used to be: strip malls and empty plastic seats, Nani and Nana packing up yearly, rifling through the classified pages of the *Toronto Sun* after getting evicted. They were a homely couple, food- but not business-savvy, and intent on viewing the world the way they were themselves: honest. Business parks were re-zoned, neighbourhoods gentrified, but, more often that not, landlords took advantage. And back then, the concept of taking a slum landlord to court, asking an authority in broken English for help, was simply too foreign a concept.

It was Auntie Sarla who had turned things around for them. One of the useful features of a woman who never shut up was, well, she never shut up about their food. She and Nani became friends, and Saffron grew to be the unofficial caterer to the Indian doctors, professors and obnoxiously rich who populated Auntie Sarla's inner and outer circles. Gradually, as Nani and Nana could afford to move the business to Roncesvalles, brand their humble business as something more grandiose, they graduated from being one of Auntie's philanthropic pursuits to full members of their community.

'Did you like Sachin?' Shay asked after a moment.

'Maybe. I'm not sure. But it doesn't matter anyway.' I reached for my coffee. 'When Nani was in the other room, he said he wasn't interested.'

'In you?'

20

I nodded. 'In me.'

'Sachin, in the middle of your date, actually told you he—'

'Can we drop this?'

Shay bit her lip and then nodded slowly. 'Sure. Sachin doesn't matter.'

'Thank you.'

'Because I have someone else for you.'

'Tell me he's not a cardiologist.'

'He's one of Julien's groomsmen,' she said, her mouth full again. 'He's spent the last ten years abroad teaching, travelling – something like that.'

'You want to set me up with a drifter?'

'Asher's not a drifter. He's amazing. He's—'

'Homeless?'

'Don't be bitchy.'

'I'm not.'

'You're being sceptical, Raina. You're *single*. It's OK, but you need to start giving guys a chance. Asher, or' – she gestured to a balding man eating alone at the counter – 'that guy over there. Can't you just try and date, or do *something*, for once?'

I groaned at Shay's authoritative voice. Just because she had her own love life sorted, my best friend was allowed to control mine too?

When Shay and I had lived together, I'd never taken the men that stumbled out of her room too seriously. They were dishevelled, red-eyed boys who groggily waved to me as they slipped past the kitchen, Shay still sound asleep. At first, Julien seemed no different. But unlike the rest of them, he kept coming back, and, recently, proposed. So Shay got to skip the queue of suitable Indian men Auntie Sarla had been lining up for her since birth, opting for the debonair French Canadian boy in her class, the fellow paediatrician.

She didn't need an arrangement. So why did I?

Shay's eyes flicked back from the balding man to my plate, and I pushed my last piece of toast towards her. She lunged for it, watching my face as she stripped the edge off with her teeth.

'So Sachin's a no.' She looked up at me hopefully. 'Asher is...'

'A no.'

She took another bite of toast. 'Last week I met a few residents from South Africa. There's one who might—'

'Actually,' I said, looking at my hands, 'I've already decided to start dating.'

'Really?' Shay nearly screamed.

'Nani gave me this... list. I told her I'd look it over, maybe start making a few calls.'

'Can I see it?' She reached for my bag. 'Is it in here?'

I watched her rifle through my bag and dump its contents onto the table – tissues, pens, tampons, passport and all. She eventually found it, and started scanning the names.

'Nani knows them through the temple, or they're friends of friends, or—'

'My cousin Rohit is on here!'

'Have I met him before?'

She shook her head. 'No. He is *such* a jerk. Even Ma knows that. I don't even want him at my wedding.'

'Why would Nani put him on the list then?'

Shay shrugged. 'I guess because he's, well, *single*.'

'So she'd rather have me be with some Indian guy nobody likes than be alone.'

'She just wants you to be happy – and *open*. You don't only have to date Indian men,' she shook the paper, 'from *this* little list.'

'My birthday was *three days* ago, and do you know she's called me every day just to ask if I've met anyone from the list yet? If I've emailed or called any of these guys?' I shook my head. 'A date I find online, or one with *Asher* or that bald guy isn't going to be enough.'

'So you're really going to do this. Date and,' she hesitated, 'marry one of them?'

I didn't answer, and watched Shay as she deliberately crossed out Rohit's name with my pen.

She paused. 'So, this is … it,' she said.

'I guess so.'

'But I've never pictured you with an Indian, Raina.'

I shrugged and reached for my coffee. An Indian – one in particular – was the only man I'd ever pictured myself with.

Boys for my Raina

~~SACHIN — Reetu's son in Scarborough, some kind of doctor — birthday lunch??~~

JAGMOHAN — Pinky's nefew in Jodhpur (visiting Canada this summer?) — but maybe looking for immwigration

VINAY — Divya's co-worker, studies kemistry (What is that??), parents from Chennai

JAYESH — Sharon's cousin, science professor at university . . . <u>divorced</u>!!!

~~ROHIT — Sarla's nefew, lawyer in Boston~~ *Absolutely NOT*

ARJUN — Sonia's son, pediatrishan, probly will want to have babies soon!

VISHAL — Bengali boy, also likes business things, Geeta's friend's son

KRUPAL — engineer in Vancouver, his parents at temple every Sunday — but may be too short (and dark)

RAHUL — Sarla's fisiotherapist, says he very good-looking boy ☺

AZIZ — accountant in Hamilton, Shushma's son, may have a white girlfriend??

MANJEEV — that handsome boy from temple, PhD student in computers

Chapter 3

The humidity of early summer was starting to set in, and the air conditioners were ill-prepared as the sun arched over Bay Street and streamed in through the windows. I peeled off my suit jacket and hung it on the back of the door. I heard the usual sounds from the breakout area across the corridor; the slow drip of the coffee machine; the opening and shutting of the fridge as Emma from reception gossiped to someone in a low whisper. I sat back down at my desk, and as my wrists hovered above the keyboard, I realised that I'd completely forgotten what it was I'd been working on the moment before.

To me, work meant doing a lot of sinfully boring things that, regrettably, I'd once found interesting enough to get me through an eighty-hour minimum workweek without dabbling in self-mutilation. These days I wasn't sure what kept me going. Everything had become routine. Work meant graphing variables and predicting outcomes for clients. Analysing NASDAQ figures, Excel spreadsheets and financial statements and researching and sourcing investment products. It meant keeping your passport on hand and an extra trouser suit at the office just in case you needed to fly somewhere last minute to talk to or learn from people who did largely the same thing.

I'd once tried to explain to Nani the macroeconomic world and how exactly I fitted into it, but she'd smiled sweetly, blankly, and then turned back to the television. She enjoyed strangers' reactions when she told them her granddaughter worked at a multinational investment bank, but that was as far as her pride went. She didn't want to understand what my job really was, or why choosing this career meant I had so little time for her, let alone anyone else.

In the few weeks since my birthday, I'd started texting three of the men on Nani's approved list. It felt wrong to have more than one guy 'on the go', but Nani insisted. *Sprinkle your seeds and see which flowers grow*, as she liked to say. Arjun seemed normal, as did Vinay – although with conflicting work schedules I had yet to find a good time to meet either of them. Vishal happened to work in the building next door to my office, and so I wasn't able to find an excuse not to see him.

After a few brief, stilted texts over a weekend, Vishal and I met for coffee on the Monday afternoon in a hip café near work. When I arrived he was already sitting at the counter, adjusting his tie as he read something on his phone. I could tell it was him because he was the only Indian guy in there. I sat down, we said our hellos and how are yous. He'd already ordered a latte, and I caught him looking at his watch while I ordered mine. By the time I'd told him about my job and he'd mansplained his, I got the clear impression he was only meeting me to keep his family happy. Perhaps that was the vibe I was giving off too.

I thought I'd be nervous, but I wasn't. It was like having an awkward meet-and-greet with a client, or an interview for a job you didn't really want. Fifteen minutes later, after our glass mugs were empty and we'd run out of things to talk about, I was relieved when Vishal said he had to get back to work.

I'd kept smiling on my walk back, thinking how quickly I'd be able to prove to Nani that her arrangement wasn't going to pan out. Would all the dates be that easy? Would I be compatible with anyone on her list?

I'd overworked myself on my morning run, and my thighs and lower back throbbed. In my chair again, I reached up my arms and stretched, then closed my eyes. When I opened them, Zoey's face had appeared in the doorway.

'Got a sec?' Without waiting for me to respond, she came in and closed the door behind her. She sat down opposite my desk, stretched out both legs and drummed her stomach with her palms.

'You all right?'

She shrugged, and then glanced up at me slyly. 'I accidentally saw Alice last night.'

'Accidentally?' I laughed.

'How many weeks did I last this time?' She started counting on her fingers and then gave up.

'Six,' I said. 'It's been six weeks since you last broke up.'

'And I did so well. I didn't see her once—'

'Until last night!'

'Raina, she just showed up out of the blue. Handed me a bottle of wine and waltzed in like nothing had happened. Like we had never broken up. And then ...'

'And *then?*'

Zoey didn't reply, and I grabbed a pen and gently lobbed it at her to get her attention.

She caught it and, blushing, put the pen down beside her. 'It's fine. *I'm* fine. Really. It'll be – it'll be different this time. Won't it?'

'I may not be the best person to give you relationship advice.'

'No one's perfect. You can't be worse than anyone else.'

I laughed, trying to figure out what to say. Zoey was several years younger than me, the most junior – and the most intelligent – analyst on my team. I'd been assigned to train her on her first day, and by the time I'd showed her around the office and she'd laughed at one of my jokes, we were friends. Over a year later, she'd become more than that. We'd confided in each other quickly, and she'd told me about her life growing up in Canada's prairies, the difficulties she had experienced coming out as gay to her family, her on-again, off-again relationship with Alice, a law student she'd met in her first week in Toronto.

I'd always considered Shay to be my best friend, but these days it was Zoey who seemed to know me best and was the person alongside whom I battled each day. These days when Shay and I saw each other we talked about her wedding plans, or she analysed my text messages with Arjun or Vinay – and then she'd lecture me about how I needed to be more 'open'. But Zoey and I actually *talked*.

My mobile phone vibrated. It was an unknown number, and tentatively I answered it.

'Hi, is this Raina?' The voice paused. 'It's Sachin.'

I covered the receiver with my palm and looked up at Zoey. She'd heard all about the birthday ambush, and when, giggling, I mouthed to her who it was, she swiped the phone from my hand and put it on the desk with a thud. She pressed the speakerphone button and his voice, the tone now less formal, blared out.

'Hello? Hi? Is anyone there?'

'Hi,' I said slowly. 'It's Raina.'

'Yeah, hi! It's Sachin, the, uh—'

'Cardiologist. I remember.'

He cleared his throat, his voice scratching through the room, and I tried not to laugh as Zoey gestured vulgarities at the phone.

'And how are you today, Raina?'

'I'm fine. And you?'

'Great – great, thank you. Well, no.' He cleared his throat again. 'Actually, I lost a patient this morning.'

'I'm so sorry…'

'It happens.' His voice trailed off, and as I caught Zoey's eye, her hands dropped slowly back to her lap.

'I had a great time with you and your Nani,' he said after a moment. 'I'm sorry it's taken me so long to call.'

'I didn't know you were planning to.'

'Yeah… About that. I'm sorry I was so rude to you. My mother only told me that morning about the lunch, and I was annoyed with her. I shouldn't have taken it out on you. I'm sure you understand.'

I did understand, but I didn't say anything.

'I really shouldn't have said that I wasn't interested. I hadn't even met you, and – well, you really are a nice girl, Raina. I am interested in getting to know you.' I opened my mouth to speak but nothing came out, and after a few seconds of static, he spoke again. 'Would you like to have dinner with me?'

'Did your mother tell you to call me?' I blurted.

'No, I wanted to.'

'Really.'

'You're intelligent and forthright and attractive and – well, frankly, there's no reason why I shouldn't want to get to know you. So will you have dinner with me?' He spoke more quickly, as if he had somewhere to rush off to. 'Just dinner. With no pressure or anything. Just a normal date.'

I listened to Sachin as he breathed heavily over the speaker, to Zoey's fingernails against her BlackBerry as she seemingly grew bored waiting for my answer.

Except for my coffee with Vishal, with whom I'd had less chemistry than my toaster, I hadn't been on a date in years, and I wasn't sure I'd ever even been on a *normal* date. My brief relationships at college had started in the library, at a student party – and then there was Dev, although nothing about that date had been normal.

I could barely even remember the last time I was alone with a man. Last winter, was it? The securities seminar Zoey and I had flown to New York for at the last minute. Zoey had been on a break with Alice then, and she'd briefly disappeared with a woman she'd met in the hotel lobby a few hours before the flight home. Sitting there alone, I'd somehow become tipsy chatting to a broker from Atlanta. I could vaguely recall his hand grazing my waist next to the empty cloakroom, ignoring the longing in his glances when I refused to take a later flight home. But that was as far as it went: turning away from the kiss, forgetting the business card in a plane seat pocket. I never let it lead to normal.

I leaned forward against the desk and stared at the phone. An awkward phone call. Getting to know one another over dinner. *This* was what normal meant. Spending time together over dinners, movies and lunch dates – and then what? Months of sex and the superficial? A natural segue into the serious?

'Dinner,' I repeated slowly, conjuring up Sachin in my mind: Indian, intelligent, handsome.

Nani-approved.

If I was going to do this, *really* do this, then it might as well be Sachin. And squinting into the glare from the window, I said, 'I could do dinner.'

Boys for my Raina

~~SACHIN — Reetu's son in Scarborough, some kind of doctor — birthday lunch??~~ *Dinner 9.30pm, Tuesday @ Eldorado

JAGMOHAN — Pinky's nefew in Jodhpur (visiting Canada this summer?) — but maybe looking for immwigration

VINAY — Divya's co-worker, studies kemistry (What is that??), parents from Chennaii *after work drinks - date TBD*

JAYESH — Sharon's cousin, science professor at university ... underline{divorced}!!!

~~ROHIT — Sarla's nefew, lawyer in Boston~~ *Absolutely NOT*

ARJUN — Sonia's son, pediatrishan, probly will want to have babies soon! *Wknd coffee?*

~~VISHAL — Bengali boy, also likes business things, Geeta's friend's son~~ *Booooooring*

KRUPAL — engineer in Vancouver, his parents at temple every Sunday — but may be too short (and dark)

RAHUL — Sarla's fisiotherapist, says he very good-looking boy ☺

AZIZ — accountant in Hamilton, Shushma's son, may have a white girlfriend??

MANJEEV — that handsome boy from temple, PhD student in computers

Chapter 4

My boss Bill was pissed off that I left work early, but Nani had insisted I come and see her before my date with Sachin. After nearly an hour battling through rush hour traffic, I arrived home to find that she wasn't even there yet.

She'd left all the lights on, and I walked around the house turning them off and then put the kettle on to boil. My head throbbed, and I flopped down on Nana's side of the sofa and closed my eyes. I knew I was imagining it, but the sofa still smelled of him. I could still picture him there reading me *Little House on the Prairie*, my head resting against his knees, impatiently tugging on the cuff of his trousers whenever he stopped mid-sentence to sip his tea.

No one was home with Nana the morning he died, and I don't think Nani ever forgave herself for believing him when he claimed his chest pain was merely indigestion. Watching her lose him was harder than dealing with my own grief. Finding her collapsed sideways on the stairs clutching his parka, her wet eyes and nose buried in the garlicky tobacco scent of the goose down. She became a widow at the age of sixty. An arranged life drastically rearranged, Nani had to start over; create a life from scratch that didn't revolve around the man to whom she'd been assigned.

It took her years, but her vivacity returned, as did the

colour in her cheeks. She was always practical and homely, compassionate – most of all towards Nana and I – but these days it wasn't strange to find Nani teasing the waiters and running Saffron better than Nana ever did; driving her Mini Cooper from an afternoon tea to temple, from one charity project to another. I suppose she had to find a new balance in the equilibrium that life had imposed on her.

In a way, Nani and I grew up together. Learned each other all over again as adults. I'd learned the way she watched *The Ellen Show*, her toes wiggling in her pressure socks whenever Ellen DeGeneres and the audience danced. The way she showed she loved you through food – and then through more food. The way she only called me *beta* when she was upset or irritated. How she pronounced vegetable *–veg-ee-table*, or invented idioms like to 'take a sleep' or 'open the light'. English was her fourth language, she liked to remind me, after Bengali, her mother tongue, Hindi and Punjabi. English for her came last, not until 1969 when Nana moved his new bride across the world to Canada. To the land of opportunity.

To the land of, well, *land*.

I also learned that Nani could be vain, ignorant of what didn't concern her or her own family. I'd switch on the news, or buy her a book I thought she should read, and she'd sigh like the idea of something new tired her out. For a while I'd tried to get her interested in politics, coming home on election night – provincial, federal, American – and she'd cluck her tongue and leave the room, annoyed that I'd disrupted her favourite Hindi soap. She thought the oil sands were polluted beaches, and didn't understand

34

why Palestine and Afghanistan, and not India, was on the news so often.

Nani had never been like the other 'aunties' in the community. She wore Western clothes most of the time – Sears trouser suits and polyester sweaters – and had refused to stay at home and play house. She'd worked side by side at the restaurant with Nana and kept her chin high when her teenage daughter brought home a baby. She was *modern*, generations ahead of so many of her friends – shallow, small-minded women who gossiped and talked pettily about one another's children. But still, for Nani, getting married and having children was a woman's one true path.

Her daughter had become a mother too young, and now she feared I'd become one too old or not at all. But couldn't she try and understand how it worked now? Women didn't have to get married and have children any more – and even if they did, it didn't always mean they were happy.

I was tired of arguing with her, but at the same time maybe Nani and Shay were right: work consumed my life, and I *was* lonely. What reason did I have to resist?

I heard the back door open and I leapt up. I beat Nani to the kitchen and had the tea poured into two china mugs by the time she sat down at the table. She sighed as she brought the cup to her lips, and I watched her face, the fine lines dance and stretch as she blew on the tea.

'How was work?'

She smiled and sank back in her chair. 'I am very tired.'

'I can make dinner.'

'But you will eat with Sachin, *nah*?'

'Sure, but that's hours from now.'

'*Aacha*. Make some rice, and we will heat up *daal* I have

35

in freezer.' She took a sip of tea, and shook her head. 'But first we must discuss Sachin. I called his mother today.'

'You did *what*?'

'She is in my sewing group with temple, *nah*? I had to call anyway. And then I mentioned your dinner tonight and she grew very happy.'

I groaned. 'Nani, I asked you not to tell anyone.'

'Reetu is his mother. She has every right to know where her son is.'

'But Sachin and I said we wouldn't involve the families yet, that it wasn't any of their business until—'

'None of our business?' Nani snapped. She glared at me, and I shrank back in my chair.

'I'm sorry, I didn't mean—'

'None of *my* business.' Nani's glower tore through me and then landed on her hands. 'Manu used to say this to me.'

'I'm not like her, Nani,' I said, and for several long minutes she didn't answer.

Nani had put me in a bad mood. Her trump card for any argument: comparing me to Mom. Telling me that I, too, wasn't good enough.

I drove back into town and found the door to my apartment unlocked and Shay going through my wardrobe. I mindlessly changed in and out of outfits she selected for me. Leather pants I'd bought on a lark and never wore; skinny jeans from college that, when I sucked in, still sort of fitted. Work blouses paired with too-short skirts I hadn't worn since London; dresses Shay brought over, silky and static, tight or loose in all the wrong places.

'You look great,' Shay said as I stood in front of my mirror, only a wisp of pale peach chiffon differentiating me from a nudist. 'I'm jelly of your legs.'

I whipped round. 'My legs look like jelly?'

'No, it means *jealous*.' She bit into an apple, crunching loudly. 'It's what the kids on my ward say.'

I turned away slowly, smoothing down the dress. The evening before I'd waxed and filed and moisturised and polished, groomed and straightened. Shay, lying sideways on my bed, still in hospital scrubs, nodded or shook her head vigorously at each outfit I tried on, but still everything felt so wrong. My clothes felt like costumes, designed to impress the guy that may or may not become my husband. I just wanted to wear one of my work suits, what I felt most comfortable in and most like myself, but I had the feeling Shay wouldn't agree.

In the mirror I saw Shay lean down from the bed and smirk as she felt my smooth leg.

'You're going to sleep with him.'

'No, Shay.' I pulled at the hem of a skirt, forcing it down past my thighs. 'I'm not going to *sleep* with him.'

'It's an urban myth that men won't call you after.'

'And they've always called you?' I saw her stick out her tongue. I turned round. 'Sorry. I meant ... I meant, I don't even know if I like him.'

'Then why do you care so much?'

'Nani's the one who cares,' I grumbled.

'You did this with Dev too.' Shay got off the bed and started walking towards the bathroom. 'You built everything up in your head before you even knew him.'

'If you came over just to lecture me, you needn't have

bothered.' I turned back to the mirror and a moment later, I heard the bathroom door shut.

I sat down on my bed. I felt the skirt digging into my stomach and the sides of my thighs. I groaned and rolled over and grabbed my BlackBerry, charging on the bedside table. I had one new text message from Zoey, wishing me luck, and a handful of grumpy emails from Bill.

I could hear Shay still peeing in the bathroom, so I scrolled down to Dev's last message. It had been two weeks since I'd replied to his latest email, and I knew I'd be getting another soon. Maybe a 'little hello' from whatever city he was working in that week; a quick 'just checking in' or 'this made me think of you'; a 'remember when'.

Remember when we walked home along the Southbank from a client dinner, and we saw Elton John? Remember when I spilled espresso on my favourite tie, and you tracked down another one just like it from Harvey Nichols?

Remember our first date?

I heard the toilet flush and stuffed my phone into my bag. Shay appeared in the doorway. The irritation had disappeared from her face, and now she just looked tired, the powder blue of her hospital scrubs poking out of the top of her hoody. I wasn't sure if she'd come over straight from work or was on her way to a night shift; I'd forgotten to ask.

'How's work?'

She flopped onto the bed beside me and put her arm around my neck. 'OK. It's going really quickly.'

'When are you done with your residency again – one more year?'

She nodded. 'Just a few weeks before the wedding. It's perfect timing.'

Her arm felt heavy, and I shifted away from her on the bed.

'Raina, my Ma set the date. It's—'

'I know,' I said, holding a top against me in the mirror. 'Nani already told me. Don't worry about it.'

Auntie Sarla had confirmed Shay's wedding date. The day Shay got married to the love of her life and fulfilled her mother's wishes would be the day I turned thirty.

Thirty.

I grabbed a cardigan from the cupboard, nearly tearing the sleeve as I ripped it from the hanger, and walked back to the mirror.

Perfect timing.

I arrived early and waited outside the entrance, and at exactly 9.30 p.m. I entered the restaurant. Sachin had suggested it. It was modern-looking, all burgundy and glass, and as soon as I noticed the soft smell of roasting chicken I realised how little I'd eaten that day. I walked up to the hostess, and right behind her, to my surprise, I saw that Sachin was already there. He was seated at the end of the bar, a Scotch glass nestled between his palms, watching the news on a small flat screen on the wall.

I walked slowly towards him. His suit jacket was open, a light purple tie loosened around his neck, and when I was a few feet away he looked over and smiled.

Before I could even say 'hi', he casually hooked his finger through my belt loop and tugged me closer.

'Hi, beautiful.'

He pulled me in for a hug. He smelled good, like whisky

and paprika, and a part of me swooned. The other part of me kicked her.

'Hi yourself.'

'What's your poison?'

'Gin and tonic?'

'Josh? Double gin and tonic?' Sachin picked up his glass, drained it and then put it back on the bar. 'And another Dalmore while you're at it.'

A muscular blond behind the bar threw a dishcloth over his shoulder and rolled up the sleeves of his black collared shirt. 'Sure thing, Sach.'

'You have a preference?' Josh asked me.

'Hmm?'

He smirked. 'Of gin.'

'Oh.' I blushed, forcing myself to look back at Sachin. 'Barman's choice.'

Sachin's eyes were glossy, his smile a bit crooked, and I wondered how long he'd been sitting there; how many Dalmores he'd already drunk.

'You look amazing,' he said after a moment, as if he too had to think about what to say. His eyes flicked between my mouth and my eyes, and I tried to think of something to say in response: thank you? You too?

A heavy silence hung in the air, and when I looked up Josh was making our drinks less than a foot away. He smiled at me – laughed, almost – as if he could feel how awkward I suddenly felt.

'Don't do that,' I heard Sachin say.

'Pardon?' I looked back at him. I was playing with my bracelets, winding them rapidly around with my fingers.

'Don't be nervous.' Sachin steadied my hand with his,

traced his pinky finger in a circle around my palm. 'Do I make you nervous?'

'Why would *you* make me nervous?'

He grinned. 'Then stop acting like it.'

'I'm not acting like anything.'

After a few minutes of stilted conversation, Josh led us to a table at the back of the restaurant, and as we walked I tried to ignore the weight of Sachin's hand on my lower back. It felt good, but heavy, and I wondered whether I wanted him to move it.

We were through the first bottle of wine by the time our main course arrived. I could feel it pooling in my stomach, trickling down, and my body relaxed. The waiter brought another bottle, and as time slicked by, I tried to make a list of what I liked about Sachin; reasons that this date – that we – could be something more, maybe.

Sachin was nothing like dull, distracted Vishal. Sachin was intelligent and liberal, his views extending well past the dimension of the operating room, which I hadn't expected. We had mutual friends in banking, in medicine; had spent one of our rare holidays at the same Cancún resort; even our Nanis had been born in the same village. And with each course, each fresh bottle of wine, the list of similarities and commonalities between Sachin and me grew, and I found myself again warming to the idea of being with another Indian. He, too, had been raised with a mixed bag of expectations, straddling the cusp of Western culture and Eastern values. Like most people I knew, Sachin never felt good enough; he was always being compared to others.

Didn't I need an Indian man to understand that about me?

I looked down at my glass. It was full, but I didn't remember Sachin pouring more in. I reached for it and a wave of nausea shot through me. A dessert was sitting between us, thick chocolate and cream, and as I watched Sachin bring a spoonful to his lips, Dev's face flashed in front of me. And just as quickly, I made it disappear.

'I'm having a great time with you, Raina.'

I had to think about the words as they came out of my mouth, and I smiled. 'Me ... too.'

'You asked me if I *cleaned teeth*. Funny stuff.' Sachin pinched at a piece of stray bread on the white tablecloth until it crumbled. He looked up at me – almost past me.

Was he going to reach for my hand? I drew them down to my lap, and then made myself put them back on the table. I leaned into the table, thinking maybe he might kiss me. But we were talking again – about partition? His ex? I couldn't tell. His mouth was a blur of words, and I couldn't focus on what he was saying. Just his lips. His hands. He lifted his wine glass as if to toast me, and then put it down abruptly and reached into his pocket. 'Sorry.' He glanced down at his phone and then placed it on the table.

'You can answer it.'

Dev hated it when I asked him to keep his phone off during dinner.

Sachin waved me off. 'No, it's not important. Really.'

'Maybe it's a patient. You should answer it.'

His head swayed lazily. 'Raina, it's nothing.' And as he leaned in towards me, the phone buzzed again. I felt the vibrations pulsate across the table and through my hands, and I didn't mean to look at the screen, but I did. *Anika*.

Sachin flipped the phone over.

'Who is that?' I whispered.

'Nobody.'

'Do you have a girlfriend?'

I'd once accused Dev of having another girlfriend.

Sachin reached for my hand. I pulled it away.

'Do you?'

He pressed his hands into his thighs, looking tense, suddenly alert. 'I thought we talked about this – that we're in the same boat?'

'What boat is that?'

'That we're both at that age where our parents really want us to get married, and—'

'And?'

'I'm getting set up a lot, Raina. Just like you.' He shrugged. 'What's the big deal?'

But Dev had never cheated. He didn't have the time. Work, always work, was his priority, above his own family; above starting his future with me.

'Do you realise that Anika has probably picked out a wedding sari? And here you are, playing the field?'

'Slow down—'

'A rich and handsome guy, though, right – *Sach*? You can get away with it. You can get away with leading girls on—'

'Are you kidding me? This is our first date.'

Our first date. He was right. I didn't know him. This – he and I – meant nothing. It would never mean anything. Everything was caving in around me, and I could feel the tears brimming at the corners of my eyes, my nose starting to run.

'I should have gone with my instinct on this one,' I heard Sachin say. 'I *knew* you'd be like this.'

Vishal. Sachin. Arjun. Vinay. They were names on a list. Names to fill the page, to fill time, the gaping hole in my chest. They were nothing to me, and they would never be Dev.

I looked up, surprised suddenly to see Sachin sitting across from me. He was leaning away from me in his chair, his eyes fixed on the pepper mill. I grabbed my bag, unsteady on my feet as I stood up. I turned round, looking for the door, and flung myself forward until I felt the cool night air on my face.

Outside, Yonge Street was exactly as it had been before; exactly as it was every night. Dark shopfronts and eateries, dive bars giving off a sickening red glow. Clusters of kids on skateboards, bored stiff, slouching in their skinny jeans. I walked past them and took a deep breath, gulping for air.

Is this what Nani wanted?

For me to be the fool? To be just another Indian girl desperate to get married?

I could hear myself panting, my legs like jelly as I turned onto Emery Street, and I waited until I was around the corner – away from the kids and their faultless youth – before I let myself cry.

Chapter 5
20 May 2012

Raina turns twenty-five at 5.52 p.m. London time. Her co-workers toast her, pints of cider and lager clinking together above the wooden pub table, the stale chips someone has yet to touch. She finishes her drink in one long swig, slapping the empty glass down in celebration. Colin's ginger hair brushes hers as he leans in and asks if she'd like another. She shakes her head and glances around the room. It's unoriginal, dank and cold. Dark wood panelling wet with beer; a brick wall boasting an oil painting of the Queen. Raina reaches for her extra cardigan and Colin laughs at her – *with* her. She is always cold, it seems, and being from Canada, he teases her about this endlessly.

She has been living in London for several months in a shared third-floor flat just off Upper Street. It has an unfocused smell of damp laundry, burnt hair extensions. Heinz beans eaten cold from the can. Raina is rarely home, but when she is, they keep the flat lively with hip hop, Sunday roasts and girls' nights in. Two of her flatmates are still students at uni – bottles and books perpetually in hand – and the third is a graphic designer with the face of a model and 'Chatterbox Pink' lips. They are British girls, lovely and loud, and with them Raina feels safe.

They are a break from her sometimes sixteen-hour days,

a splash of colour in what would otherwise be a life walled in by the dreary, pale demands of working in the City of London. The girls introduce her to the real city – gigs outside Zone One, wine bars in repurposed churches – and also to the boys they know. Immature, ashy, brown-haired boys who find her witty when drunk, intimidating when sober. To them, Raina downplays her job at the investment bank, her life among the three-thousand-pound suits marching up and down Cheapside and Cannon Street. She was chosen from among fifty applicants in the Toronto, New York and Chicago offices for the secondment, but these aren't the things that interest them.

Nor do they interest her.

His name is Dev Singh, and at present, he is a mere silhouette. They have never spoken directly, yet it was his voice she noticed first. The way he gently commands a boardroom, she can tell he's humble. Dedicated. He's a man unaware of his impact on others, and this only affects her more.

She is conscious of him always. How she is slightly taller than him in heels, or the way he crosses and uncrosses his legs when he has something to say. How he stays at the office later than most – even on Fridays, never joining the rest of them at the pub across Paternoster Square. Already he is unlike any man she has ever met. He is more than the men she talks to at clubs through gritted teeth, her flatmates giggling nearby. The ones in the cash-only line at Tesco. Already he's more than either of her college boyfriends – flings so brief, so inconsequential she often forgets she had them. She is startled by the way Dev affects her. She has never been attracted to an Indian man before, and this is how she knows it must be real. She knows that Dev is different.

She has already given up hope that he might turn up at the pub that evening, when she sees him. Her heart pounds. She stiffens as he walks past her, and slyly she leans back in her chair and looks after him.

He is greeted with enthusiasm by a cluster of bankers – those more senior, sitting separate from her crowd. He leans forward against the backs of two chairs, and she struggles to hear what they are saying over the chatter, over Colin, who again asks if she'd like another pint. Dev says something she misses and it makes the group laugh – especially the woman, Becky, who heads the fixed income division. She throws her head back as she laughs, and the blond hairs of her ponytail catch on his suit.

Raina has never liked Becky.

After a moment, Dev turns and walks towards the bar. Raina exhales. This is it, she tells herself. Today is her birthday, and unlike any other day she is sure that this time she will think of something to say. Something witty, original – though not overly curated. She has been waiting for a chance to approach him. To impress him. And somehow she knows that now is the time. She counts to five before following, and as she slinks towards him, navigates through the after-work crowd, her mind once again draws a blank. Her stomach churns. She is only a few feet away, and she is considering turning back when he looks over his shoulder and smiles.

'Ah.' He leans back on the counter. 'Raina Anand. Our newest import from *Ca-nada*.'

She is giddy about the fact that he knows her name,

and bites her lip to keep from smiling. She loves how he says Canada, and her country suddenly appears elegant in her mind. She struggles not to picture him there with her, already; running to catch the streetcar on Queen Street, handing Nani a bouquet of wild flowers the first time he comes for dinner.

'That's me.'

'I've been meaning to swing by and chat, but—'

'But you're a busy man,' she says, surprised by the evenness of her voice.

'Too busy, it would seem.' He is looking at her neck. Her lips. Her hair in wisps around her shoulders. 'So,' he says, sliding a beer towards her, 'what can you tell me then, Raina?'

She smiles coyly and reaches for the beer. As she had hoped, she knows exactly what to say.

They stand there for hours. She is dizzy from the smell of his cologne, the glasses of *hefeweizen* that keep appearing in front of her. They are speaking, and, at times, she has no idea what about – redemption funds and Chelsea football team. The pub's fresco-style ceiling. She has never laughed so loud, been so inebriated by another human being. He is teasing her, enveloping her. He pinches her nose and his thumb falls slowly, parting her lips. And suddenly, they are no longer laughing.

He grabs her hand and leads her outside. Beneath the moonlit streets of St Paul's, she reminds herself that she's not supposed to believe in casual sex. But the way Dev is kissing her, his fingers lightly wound through her hair, already this doesn't feel casual. Minutes pass, and then he pulls away and tilts her chin to the side. She looks up at him and cannot meet his eye, and she prepares herself to say no when, inevitably, he asks her to go home with him. But he doesn't ask. Instead, he thumbs the leather of her bag, wonders out loud whether she happens to have her passport.

His hand stays on her knee in the taxi as they head north on Farringdon Road towards St Pancras station. Their wide smiles fill the back seat, and he apologises three, four, five times, telling her that Paris would have been more romantic, more fitting for birthday spontaneity, if only the Eurostar to Paris wasn't already booked up. Brussels is perfect, she says into his shoulder. Raina has never been to Brussels, and she senses now that she's always wanted to go.

He buys them orange juice and chicken avocado sandwiches in the cafeteria car, and as they dip beneath the English Channel, her ears pop and he tells her about growing up in West Harrow. She senses his shame as he talks about his family. She doesn't understand his resentment, but she intertwines her fingers with his and tells him that she does.

It is nearly midnight by the time they reach Gare de Bruxelles-Midi, and Dev looks surprised when Raina begins to converse with the driver, asking him in stilted French to take them anywhere he likes. He drops them off on a lively street across from La Grand Place. Brass lamp posts and cobblestones; twinkling lights and fogged-in windows. Hundreds of men stripped down to their boxers parading through the square, whipping their red, sweat-drenched football shirts around like batons, chanting *Allez la Belgique!*

Dev squeezes her hand as they manoeuvre through the crowd and onto quieter lanes. They are soon lost, and everything smells of white wine and rain. They wander past marble fountains, through alleys and impossibly green parks, and every so often he pulls her aside – against a railing or black brick wall – and kisses her. Every time, she falls further. Becomes more convinced. That rushing sensation; the inability to catch her breath. And right there, on the darkened streets of Brussels, for the first time Raina falls in love.

It's nearly dawn when they find a hotel. Dev leads her to the room and her mind races. Her body trembles. She's twenty-five now, and a virgin. Isn't she ready?

Hasn't she been waiting for this?

She sits at the foot of the bed, and Dev kneels down in front of her. Kisses both of her knees. And then he reaches up and kisses her, pulls her face down to his, and she's on the floor too, pressed hard against him.

Nani's face flashes before her eyes, and then her mother's. Every time this is what has happened, and every time it's the reason she's stopped.

She thinks about pushing Dev away, ending it before she becomes weak – before she becomes her mother. But he's kissing her neck, her collarbone. His tongue darts in and out of her ear, and then her mouth – and then it is consuming her. His hands around her waist, Dev lifts her onto the bed, pushes her down. Raina's blouse, Dev's trousers are flung to the side, and with them her doubts. With Dev, she's alive, finally, and nothing can stop her.

Chapter 6

The clear blue skies of summer seemed unending. The bodies on Bay Street were slower, stilled by the humidity, the souring heat coming off the Great Lakes. Summer had always meant studying and taking temp jobs at the library or as a research assistant. Coaching community basketball. Now summer blended into the rest of the year.

My job felt stagnant, even mindless, and at least twice a day I'd find myself lying on my keyboard staring sideways at a pile of papers, eyes blurred, until one of the senior banker's voices in the hallway startled me upright. When I'd been with Dev, I'd loved my job. Or had I? He'd travelled abroad for work every few days or weeks, and when he was in London, we both spent most of our waking hours in the office. But we'd been happy. We'd made it work, although I had no idea how. London felt so long ago, and a heavy fog seemed to block me from remembering the details.

I broke up the summer monotony as best I could. Morning breakfasts with Shay – although because of the wedding plans and conflicting work schedules I saw her less and less. When we did see each other, she was distracted by the latest wedding crisis and I'd get snappy, and one of us would end up leaving early in a huff.

But there were rooftop bars or music festivals with

colleagues after work; midnight movies alone at the cheap cinema near my flat; short weekends away at a cottage with Zoey, Alice and our friends – chopped logs and icy beer, sunbaked split ends and aloe vera for the drive home.

Zoey and Alice had got back together, which they said was for good this time. They were a brilliant couple, and brought out the best in one another. But watching them together always me wonder whether break-ups were ever really final. Because even though I'd grudgingly started to date again, somehow it still didn't feel final with Dev.

I was making progress on the list – although, according to Nani, a handful of first dates that didn't turn into first husbands didn't count as progress. Since Sachin, my dates had yet to amount to more than a few hours of wasted time, a decaf green tea after work, a lukewarm meal I insisted on paying for my share of. And every time I came home and updated Nani on the most recent failed prospect, she'd scrunch her face up as if she'd stuck lemon juice under her tongue, and say, 'Again, Raina? Not him *too*?'

After Shay had scolded me for overreacting with Sachin, and getting plain drunk on a first date, I had decided to try. To make an effort with the men Nani had selected. To try and move on from the tugging memory of Dev.

But even organic chemists like Vinay couldn't force attraction or compatibility. Krupal didn't understand my jokes. Jagmohan didn't understand English. Then there was 'call me "the Man" Manjeev', who, ten minutes after picking me up in his Dodge Charger, put my hand on his lap and asked me if I enjoyed driving stick.

'Is your Jeep not automatic?' Nani had asked. She'd failed

to see the point of the story. It felt like a betrayal to even think it, but sometimes I wondered if she failed to see me.

Nani was young enough to be my mother, but the generation between us could feel endless. Raising my mother, raising *me*, had made Nani modern quickly, unwillingly. But she still couldn't understand that women no longer needed to get married.

Was that unfair of me? Hadn't I wanted to get married? Fulfil every fantasy and stereotype? How many hours had I wasted wondering when Dev would propose, what our wedding might be like? Garlands of marigolds and traditional saris, silk drapery and bhangra music. Dev in a kurta pyjama, and, for the first time, everyone in my family sitting peacefully in the same room.

One Sunday in late August, the first day in over a month I had the option to sleep in, Nani insisted I come home and spend the day with her. I relinquished my plans to sleep off my hangover, to lounge on the balcony with a tub of ice cream and the book I'd been meaning to read for over a year, and instead Nani and I made parathas.

It had been years since I'd helped her in the kitchen, and I was proud of the result. Parathas, gold and flaky, smothered in butter, stuffed with spicy aloo. Afterwards, we ate them beneath the backyard awning, cooling ourselves down in the lazy summer breeze. Nani had slipped a disc in her back the summer before, and I'd hired a neighbour's son to mow the lawn, trim the hedges and plant while Nani pointed and prodded, sitting on a stool as she instructed him on how she wanted the beds arranged.

'Andy's doing a good job with the yard,' I said, yawning, admiring the lawn, almost a forest green now.

'What is *that*?' She reached forward and pulled at my ear, then squinted at the blue paint that rubbed off on her fingers. 'Paint?'

'Um, yes.'

'*Vhy*? Are you renovating your apartment? This is not a good colour.'

'No. I went to a, um, pride party last night.' I thought back to the evening before: Zoey, Alice, me and some of our other friends crowd-surfing, drunk on electronica music at a warehouse in the Gay Village, and decided to leave out the details.

'Pride?' she asked.

'Like, you know,' I hesitated, 'a celebration for LGBTQ—'

'Huh?'

'For gay people, Nani. It was a party celebrating gay people,' I said, trying to rack my brain for the simplest way of explaining the term. 'I went with my friends. With Zoey – you remember her, don't you?'

'Oh. Was Ellen there?'

'Ellen DeGeneres lives in Los Angeles.'

'But I thought you said you were too busy this weekend to see Jayesh. His mother is calling me *many* times.'

'I was busy,' I grumbled. 'I was at the party.'

'Raina…' She clucked her tongue. 'You are pushing luck – just like that Manu used to. Please *try*. Jayesh comes from very good family. Good Hindu family.'

'So he's automatically perfect for me?'

'I am not a silly woman.' Nani sighed and turned to face the lawn. 'His family is very educated, very stable. These things become important in raising children. *Values* are important.'

'Being Hindu. Being … Indian.' I buried my toes in the dirt in front of me, twisted them in the damp earth. 'Is that what's important to you?'

'*Nah*, Raina. Julien is Catholic, he is a white – and look, your Auntie Sarla is fine with it. Please just stop looking for things that are wrong. They are men. White, brown, yellow, blue; they all have *something* wrong with them.' Nani guffawed. 'Just pick one!'

I knew she was trying to be funny, so I laughed. But I *had* picked one – and in the end, he hadn't picked me. Now all I had to do was pick another, right? One that I liked enough, and that one day I could maybe fall in love with. We'd accept each other's faults and imperfections, and I'd retreat from the fantasy.

I watched the geraniums shudder as the sun grew fierce. I checked my watch. It was nearly noon, and our temple's Sunday service usually went on until 1 p.m.

'Nani, do you want to go to the mandir?'

'*Aacha*.' Nani smiled, and sitting forward on the lawn chair, she squeezed my chin. 'OK, let us go.'

Our temple, all limestone and Mughal-influenced architecture, was only a ten-minute drive away. It sat at the edge of a public park, its grounds clean lines of lawn and concrete. The pooja was already under way as Nani and I walked in. The altar was decorated with tin bells and displays of fruit and sweets, rose petals, shiny jewellery and garlands strung with marigolds. Nani manoeuvred her way through the crowd towards the front, where she always sat with Auntie Sarla, and I lingered near the back searching for space on the crowded floor.

I was surprised to find Shay sitting against the back wall. Both of us went to temple so rarely these days that I figured she would have texted me about it beforehand to see if I wanted to go too... to shop for outfits and gifts. She made room for me and I sat down and closed my eyes. The priest continued chanting, the room echoing him in unison. I had never had the patience to meditate, to practise yoga like Nani – but this I didn't mind; his deep voice. The long, reverberating vowels. I breathed in and out, and a few minutes later when I came to, the sharp lights lifting me back to the present, Shay was looking at me.

'Ma is making us go to India,' she said, a little too loud. An auntie in front of us coughed pointedly, her doughy back rippling out of her blouse as she whipped round to glare at us.

I leaned closer to Shay after the woman had turned back round. 'When?'

'In January,' Shay whispered. 'Shopping for outfits and gifts. Stuff for the wedding. Julien's actually looking forward to the whole thing. He cannot *wait* to see the Taj Mahal.'

'That's exciting.'

'Is it?' Shay sneered. 'No sleeping in the same room. No meat or alcohol. Having to dress like a monk. It sounds *terribly* exciting.'

I'd only been to India once – a two-week trip with Nani and Nana as a child: a quick collage of coddling distant relatives and rich goat curry; the smell of rotting rubbish and endless compliments about my fair skin, my light hair; pails of sliced mangoes and having to rinse my toothbrush

56

with boiled water. And the memory, vague as it was, polluted by the smog that seemed to settle into eyes and chests, still felt like home. The sprawling courtyard and the mango tree in Nani's village an hour outside of New Delhi. Her talcum powder scent as I fell asleep on a bed beneath the stars. It was Nani's history, Nani's home. In its own grounds, and built of baked bricks and timber, it was my home too.

But Shay hated India. It repulsed her. The people, the country, the heritage, the politics. The dichotomies of injustice: excess and poverty; humility and greed; men and, much further down, women. Growing up, Shay and her brother Nikesh had been dragged 'home' yearly to their family's estate in Rajasthan, a fortress of over thirty relatives. An extended family, an entire culture, which Shay grew to despise. She'd come over after every trip, throw both herself and a bag of gaudy souvenirs down onto my bed, and moan. Moan about her three weeks locked in a metaphorical interrogation room. The way they soaked her twine-like hair in coconut milk, stuffed her with rasmalai and then faulted her for gaining weight. How she was rarely let outside for fear of her getting a suntan, or, only slightly worse, being accosted by the local men.

Shay said the men there leered at her, smacked their lips and tried to pull down her skirt. They would drive back and forth on scooters calling her names until she'd yell at the top of her lungs for them to screw off. They didn't treat their own Indian women like that, Shay said to me, her smile limp; that even though she spoke both Hindi and Rajasthani fluently, to them she wasn't really Indian.

Neither, I suppose, was I.

The priest resumed chanting, and I spun Nani's heavy

gold bracelets round my wrists. I looked towards the front. Auntie Sarla was hovering beside the priest, assisting him as he poured holy water out of a silver tin. Shay's engagement party was only one week away, an elaborate affair in its own right, and over the past few weeks I'd spent hours on the phone with Auntie Sarla helping her organise it, answering her calls and running errands whenever she couldn't get hold of Shay.

'How did the fitting go?' I asked her.

'The lengha fitted, but Ma said not well enough.' Shay shook her head. 'I have to go back again tomorrow.'

'Do you want me to come with you?'

She looked over, as if surprised. 'Yes, oh my God, *yeah*. I need a buffer between me and Ma.' She smiled, then leaned over and kissed me on the arm. 'I wish I was getting married next week. Get it over and done with, you know?'

I nodded.

'Who needs an engagement party anyway?' Shay glanced at me. 'But at least the "drifter" will be there.'

'Who?'

'Asher. The guy I told you about, remember?' She sounded irritated. 'Julien is picking him up from the airport right now. He just flew back from Bangkok.'

The auntie sitting in front of us turned round again, her glare forcing Shay's voice down to a whisper as she nattered on about Asher. The photos he posted online of the lychee orchards on a trek near Chiang Mai. How she and Julien might now honeymoon there on his recommendation. I rolled my eyes as Shay spoke. Mom had been to Thailand when I was in high school, and none of us had known she'd been gone until she was home again, arriving at the house in the middle of the night needing a place to sleep. Tanned skin and bleached hair, a backpack the size of a small child clamped onto her shoulders. A tattoo on her calf – a Hindi phrase inked in pitch-black– one that was supposed to mean *peace*, but, Nani had claimed, meant nothing at all.

'So is that OK?' Shay nudged me again. 'I'll introduce you guys.'

'No,' I whispered, turning to Shay. 'I've been meeting enough men.'

'How was your date with Jayesh?'

'I didn't go in the end.' I shrugged. 'I postponed to next week.'

'Oh.' She sounded annoyed, like I should have already told her that detail. 'Well, have you met anyone else – anyone I *should* know about?'

I'd already told her about Manjeev the creep, and about my dinner with Jagmohan – with whom I'd had to use Google Translate to communicate. But I hadn't told Shay – or Nani, for that matter – that I'd finally met up with Arjun, who had been texting me like clockwork all summer asking me when I would have time to get together.

The weekend before, Arjun had taken me to Canada's Wonderland and we'd spent the afternoon wandering through the amusement park eating candyfloss and riding the roller coasters. It was a classic, if not a cliché, date, and I'd really enjoyed myself. I'd never been to Wonderland, despite the amusement park having been less than a forty-five minute drive away from me my whole life.

Arjun had been attentive, sweet and a good conversation-alist. And he loved his family. As we stood in the queue for the Behemoth, the park's largest roller coaster, he'd even told me he was already excited about becoming a dad. That he felt ready to take the next step.

Everything about Arjun had been suitable and appropriate, and as the attendants buckled us into the ride, it struck me that I was entirely bored. Not bored with him, but with myself. Who was I pretending to be, meeting these men? A nice Indian girl devoted to her Nani? A hard-working investment analyst with big ambitions – that is, until she became a mother?

Arjun wanted to marry a woman like the character I was playing. He wouldn't want the real me, and by the end of the dizzying ride, I was confident that I didn't want to be with him, either.

Shay poked me, and I looked down at the ground. I knew she would harass me for a blow-by-blow account if I told her about it, and would force me to explain in detail how I could be so sure after one date that Arjun and I wouldn't work. I didn't feel like another sermon, and so I shook my head.

'Nope. There's no one else.'

Boys for my Raina

SACHIN — Reetu's son in Scarborough, some kind of doctor — birthday lunch?? *Dinner 9.30pm, Tuesday @ Eldorado

JAGMOHAN — Pinky's nefew in Jodhpur (visiting Canada this summer?) — but maybe looking for immwigration

VINAY — Divya's co-worker, studies kemistry (What is that??), parents from Chennaii after work drinks - date TBD

JAYESH — Sharon's cousin, science professor at university . . . divorced!!!

ROHIT — Sarla's nefew, lawyer in Boston *Absolutely NOT*

ARJUN — Sonia's son, pediatrishan, probly will want to have babies soon! Wknd coffee?

VISHAL — Bengali boy, also likes business things, Geeta's friend's son Boooooring

KRUPAL — engineer in Vancouver, his parents at temple every Sunday — but may be too short (and dark)

RAHUL — Sarla's fisiotherapist, says he very good-looking boy ☺

AZIZ — accountant in Hamilton, Shushma's son, may have a white girlfriend??

MANJEEV — that handsome boy from temple, PhD student in computers **What a CREEP**

Chapter 7

Nani and Shay left straight after the pooja, but I stayed behind to help the volunteer caretakers water the flower beds and trees lining the temple grounds. When I arrived home I found the driveway full of cars I didn't recognise, and when I opened the front door I could hear Nani and her friends downstairs in the entertaining room.

Without saying hello, I went upstairs and stretched out on my bed. Soon after, I realised someone had started playing the harmonium, and the loud disharmony of sing-song voices carried upstairs through the vents. I focused on the glow-in-the-dark stickers I'd stamped onto the ceiling as a child, now just flecks of mild green.

Except for the dirty laundry on the floor, Nani had left everything exactly as it had looked the day I moved out. The vintage tea-stained map I had framed. My bookshelf, an antique maple hutch well stocked with Puffin classics and novels from garage sales and the clearance shelves of supermarkets. The mash-up of scatter cushions and raw silk curtains that, together, we'd sewn. I had been a hopeless student of basic domestics, and slammed my foot on the treadle as if I was a racing driver, and she'd had to undo every stitch I'd made with her Hobbycraft sewing machine.

I thought about going back into town. I had client

meetings to prepare for, recycling to take out, groceries to buy. But I knew I wouldn't do any of that. I knew that if I went back to my apartment I would just sit on the chaise longue by the window and close my eyes in the sun. Listen to the faint noises of families walking their dogs and buying ice creams. The teenagers shuffling onto the streetcar with H&M bags and neon headphones. I yawned, and before I could decide one way or the other, the doorbell woke me up.

'Nani?'

I could still hear the harmonium, Auntie Sarla's voice shrieking over the others. The doorbell rang again and I pulled myself off the bed and down the stairs. I opened the front door, and, squinting in the afternoon light, it took me a moment to realise who it was.

'Depesh?'

'Raina, hey.' Depesh was at least six inches taller than he was the last time I'd seen him, and not nearly as scrawny. His muscles were toned and filled out his shirt, his dark-wash jeans. The black, wayward curls I remembered on him as a kid were shaped and slicked behind his ears.

'Wow.' I crossed my arms. 'I haven't seen you in forever! You grew up nice.'

He rolled his eyes.

'How old are you now – sixteen, seventeen?'

'Eighteen.'

'Eighteen. God, you make me feel old.'

'Well, you look exactly the same, Raina.'

I led him into the family room and sank onto the sofa. He looked around the room, his hands on his hips, and then tentatively took a seat in Nana's armchair.

Depesh had once been like a brother to me. His mother had been diagnosed with MS when he was ten, and I'd spent the summer after my junior year of college babysitting him. His parents – a rotund lady I called Sharon Auntie and her husband, whose name I still hadn't figured out – had spent long days at the hospitals, at clinics for drug trials, three-day trips to Boston or San Jose for experimental procedures. So Depesh and I made biscuits and played Monopoly, went to the park and watched television until our eyes hurt. At the end of the summer his parents moved him to New Jersey to be closer to a specialised facility, and I hadn't seen him since.

Depesh's hands were perfectly still and straight on his lap, and he stared at them.

'Do you want some tea?'

He shook his head and looked up. 'Just picking up Ma.'

'Oh, I didn't know she was over.'

He nodded. 'Your Nani is, like, the only one who's been able to get her to leave the house.'

'Wait.' I sat up. 'You've moved back?'

He nodded. 'We've been back a month already.'

'Nani didn't tell me.' I racked my brain, trying to remember. 'Or maybe she did; shit, how did I forget that?'

'It's OK.'

'She calls me a lot. Sometimes at work I put her on speaker and drift off… God, am I a terrible person?'

'No, you're not.' He laughed nervously. 'But what do I know? I haven't heard from you in, like, a decade.'

I knew he didn't mean to make me feel guilty, but I did. Depesh had been a kind, genuine kid, and I could still see that about him; his eyes, his smile – it was impossible to

64

miss. But he was different too. He had been playful and silly. Exuberant. Brave enough to climb to the tops of the jungle gyms, face the tallest slides, while I trailed behind.

Now he seemed awkward in his own skin. Nervous, unsure of himself. I realised that I didn't know him any more, either. Over the past ten years I'd basically forgotten all about him.

'Do you want to go out and get some ice cream?'

He rolled his eyes. 'Raina, I'm not ten any more.'

'Maybe *I* want ice cream.'

He glanced over at me nervously. 'Well, you could buy me a beer.'

Nani rarely kept alcohol in the house, and the bottle of whisky Kris kept under the sink was missing. We slipped out of the front door and walked a few streets north on the wide suburban streets towards the shopping mall nearby. He waited outside while I went in and bought two large bottles of beer, and on the walk home we stopped at the park beside my old high school. A few others were around – kids about Depesh's age smoking weed by the basketball courts – and we picked a spot a fair way away in the grassy field.

I opened my bag and then reluctantly handed him the beer. 'I'm a bad influence on you. Don't tell your mother.'

He laughed. 'I'll be legal in a few months.'

He twisted the cap off the beer and brought the bottle to his lips. He stared at it for a second before taking a sip, and I saw him wince.

'Do you like beer?'

He wiped his mouth with his hand, smiling. 'Not really.

I never really drank at high school. I wasn't invited to the parties.'

'Me neither. But my best friend was, so sometimes I tagged along.'

'I didn't really have a best friend.' Depesh looked down at his beer, and with one hand started to peel back the label. 'Sorry, I'm not looking for pity or anything. I just have trouble making friends.'

I put my hand on his shoulder. He continued.

'Jersey was ... hard. And now I don't know anybody here any more, you know?' His fingers shook, and the label, part way off, split in two. 'I'm starting university in a few weeks. That will be good.'

'It will be, Depo.' I smiled at him, and then took a quick sip from my own beer. It was already warm, tasted stale, and I put it down beside me. 'And until then you know you have me, right?'

'I really don't need your pity or anything.'

'It's not pity.' I stared at him until he looked me in the eye. 'I promise. I'm glad you're back.'

He nodded and looked back at his beer.

'So, what classes are you taking?'

'Biology, chemistry, maths,' he sighed. 'You know, the usual pre-med stuff.'

'You want to be a doctor?'

'Doesn't everybody?'

'So what if everybody else does? If you want to be a doctor, then be one.'

He grew quiet, and stretched back on his elbows. It was hot, and the sun was in my eyes, scorching my face.

'I heard you're getting married.'

66

My stomach dropped, and I turned to face him. 'Who told you that?'

'My mom did.' He paused. 'Is it that British guy? I heard something a while back about a British guy.'

Nani was telling her friends that I was getting married? How many in our community had already shoved me down the aisle, selected a punchbowl on the wedding list, when I – when *Nani* – had yet to find me a husband?

I grabbed the beer and swigged it, drank until it was nearly half-gone.

'So you're not getting married?'

Slowly I put the beer back down. The aftertaste was disgusting. 'No. I'm not.'

'But there was a British guy. I'm not making that up?'

I pressed my lips together. 'There was. We broke up when I left London.'

'I'm sorry. That sucks. But London – that must have been *amazing*, hey?' Depesh's smiled brightened. 'I would love to live in Europe – or *go* to Europe, even.'

'Yeah, it was wonderful …' I trailed off. A moment later, I realised Depesh was still looking at me.

'What's London like?'

'Busy. Diverse. In some ways, entirely overwhelming.' I shrugged. 'Lonely, in other ways. Like any big city.'

'Lonely? But you had a boyfriend.'

I cleared my throat. 'So you've never been?'

'No.' He shook his head. 'I really want to, but we can never travel because Ma's treatments cost too much.' He paused. 'That's actually why we moved back. Tuition for a good uni down there was expensive.'

'Oh …'

'It's a lot here, too, though,' he said. 'I took out a loan, and I'm working part-time at Star Labs to save up.'

'Star Labs is just opposite my bank. You must drop by sometime.' I picked up my bottle. 'Like, if you need beer or something.'

He laughed.

'Or you can borrow my car if you want to take a girl out, or whatever.'

He smiled at me vaguely and put his hand out in front of his face. The sun cast a shadow across his eyes, his nose, and I couldn't tell what he was looking at. After a while he fished his phone out of his pocket and looked at the screen.

'Mom is wondering where I am.' He pushed himself up onto his knees and wiped his hands together, grass and dirt falling from his palms. 'We should probably go back.'

After I'd helped Sharon Auntie up the stairs and into Depesh's car, I lingered in the foyer. Downstairs, the harmonium-playing had stopped and I could hear Nani, Auntie Sarla and the others speaking together in Hindi: Auntie Sarla's shrill exclamations steadied by Nani's voice, low murmurs of what I sensed to be assent. I'd never learned to speak Hindi properly, and only knew the most basic nouns, verbs and phrases, but it was everything else that made the language so identifiable to me; it was a language of pitch and tone, emotive cadence and expression. As their voices ricocheted up the stairs from the entertaining room, even though they weren't saying my name I could tell they were talking about me.

I leaned against the wall and slid down onto the floor. I straightened out my legs and felt the cold linoleum on my bare calves. I leaned back and my hair caught on the fibres of the plasterboard, the way it always had when I'd sat in this spot as a girl.

What exactly was Auntie Sarla saying about me?

That every day I was letting another potential husband slip through my fingers, and not getting married like her Shaylee? That I was twenty-nine, and with each breath, each step, inching closer to thirty?

How long would it take? How long would they put me through this?

How long would I put Nani through it?

Chapter 8

'So you're Auntie Suvali's granddaughter,' he said, without standing up to greet me.

'And you must be Rahul.' I shuffled into the seat across from him. He was reading *The Paris Review*, and bookmarked his page with a peacock feather. Then, as if on purpose, laid the magazine down on the table between us facing towards me.

I was exhausted, and as I made introductory chit-chat with Rahul I realised that I was not prepared for yet another blind date. I'd worked crazy hours all week, as well as fielding panicked calls from Shay and Auntie Sarla about the engagement party – which was tonight.

I'd stayed up late the evening before with Shay's younger brother Nikesh, designing, printing and manually cutting out place cards for the table settings. I'd thought seriously about cancelling on Rahul, but Nani had called me excitedly at the crack of dawn asking me what I was wearing and where Rahul was taking me, and I didn't want to let her down again. Earlier in the week she'd wanted me to call her friend Shushma's son Aziz, about whom she 'had good feeling'.

'Nani, he has a girlfriend,' I'd said, pointing at the list. 'You wrote it down yourself.'

'Maybe you should call and check,' Nani suggested slyly, to which I replied *no*.

A waiter with grey-blue hair dropped off two jam jars of water and a wicker basket full of what appeared to be, and nearly smelled like, dog shit.

Rahul lunged for the dung and popped one in his mouth. 'What is it?'

'Gluten-free, raw vegan bread,' he said, his mouth full.

'Can bread *be* raw?'

He scowled at me as he swallowed. 'Don't you have a dehydrator?'

I shook my head.

'Wow, OK.' He looked alarmed. 'Well, it's a must-have when you're on a gluten-free, raw vegan diet. It's as indispensable to me as my NutriBullet.'

I sneaked a look at my watch. I'd been at the restaurant for only four minutes, and I was ready to leave. Rahul seemed insufferable, but maybe we had got off on the wrong foot. Maybe I was judging him too quickly.

I forced a smile, trying to make an effort. I picked up a piece of the 'bread', and nibbled on a corner. It tasted like mildew.

'Mmm,' I purred, nodding heavily. 'What's in it?'

'Vegetables, mostly. Onions, tomatoes, peppers, broccoli. Sunflower seeds, too, I think.' He chewed loudly. 'Whatever it is, it's ethically sourced. Everything here is farm-to-table fresh.'

'My Nani owns a restaurant.'

'Oh yeah? Which one?'

'Saffron. It's in Roncesvalles—'

He waved me off. 'Oh, I know it. It's quite ... popular,

71

isn't it? I imagine a lot of tourists go there. Must be in the guidebooks or something.'

'What's wrong with tourists?'

'Where you should really go is this place I know on Keele Street.' He grabbed another turd, and I thought about telling him that he still had pieces of the last one all over his teeth. 'It's less *overplayed*. You walk in, and you think it's a run-of-the-mill ciggies-and-chewing-gum convenience store, OK?'

'OK,' I dead-panned.

'And then the guy takes you through the back door and … BANG!'

'He shoots you?'

'Best Vietnamese food in the city. And *decent* virgin cocktails.'

'Naturally.'

'All in all, the evening will cost you around fifty bucks.' He eyed my handbag, which I'd hung on my chair's armrest. 'I'm guessing that's less than that bag you have there. That isn't real leather, is it?'

I glanced at it, suddenly recalling that the ebony-black tote was Shay's. I'd borrowed it the year before, swearing to give it back, but never had.

'I'm not sure …'

'Consumer culture. Am I right?'

I laughed, and it sounded about as awkward as I felt. 'I could consume a drink right now—'

'Raina, this place is alcohol-free.'

'Oh, I was joking …'

He rolled his eyes, and after handing me a menu, I resisted the temptation to hit him with it.

Rahul suggested we try the five-course lunch tasting menu, and I obliged. He ordered an aloe vera smoothie, and despite his rave reviews of the birch juice, I wasn't quite in the mood for tree. I settled on an organic root beer, and while it tasted nothing like root beer, it was actually pretty good.

We discussed the weather – hot, but not sticky-hot – and then took turns commenting on the restaurant's decor. The twinkly lights and green-brown ferns. The Persian rugs and throws in piles, as if to enforce a sense of cosiness.

Rahul had strong opinions, even on things – such as the choice between wood flooring and carpet – that you wouldn't think warranted such fervour. Everything was right or wrong, authentic or 'trying too hard'. I glanced at the hemp necklace dipping between the V of his distressed t-shirt, the twisted tuft on the top of his head that was dangerously close to man-bun territory, and wondered which category Rahul fell into.

My favourite Drake song came on, and Rahul groaned. 'Really? *Drake*?' He glanced around accusingly, as if prepared to prosecute whomever it was who had dared to play popular music.

'What's wrong with Drake?'

'Nothing, I suppose.' Rahul rolled his eyes. 'He's just so passé.'

I suppressed a smile. Authentic. Rahul was certainly authentic.

'We should have met up tonight,' he said after a moment. 'I know this hole-in-the-wall club round the corner. Great vibes, low-key – and like, you know, *fresh* beats.'

'I thought I'd mentioned already that it's my best friend's engagement party tonight.'

'Oh. Right.'

'And it's been a bit stressful, I suppose, with the planning and—'

'Ah,' he said, blinking at me. '*Stress.*'

'What about it?'

'I feel sorry for you.'

Mr Pays-Fifty-Dollars-for-Noodles-in-a-Broom-Cupboard felt sorry for *me*?

'I just don't get worked up about that kind of stuff.'

I sat up in my chair. 'What kind of stuff?'

'You know. Logistics. Details. Everyday ... *stressors* that wig everybody out – and to be honest, make life unpleasant for those around them.'

I nodded earnestly, thinking that maybe if I was unpleasant enough he'd leave, and take all the organic shit-bread with him.

'Stress. The mental, physical, sometimes even spiritual reaction to the world outside of us. Aren't they all just feelings we can control?'

'You're kind of a superhero, then, if you have the power not to feel. How do you do it?'

He smiled at me coolly. 'Meditation. Yoga. Clean eating. It's all about bringing balance to the everyday.'

'Like a Jedi.'

'Huh?'

'They bring balance to the force? *Star Wars*?' The muscles around his lips twitched, and I sat back in my chair. 'Oh, let me guess. *Star Wars* is also passé.'

'I really don't get what all the fuss is about.'

Our food arrived, if you could call it that. A vegan cheese-board. A course of dandelion salad and aubergine bacon. A bowl of blood-like broth that claimed to be puréed avocado, beetroot and tiger nut milk. (Note to self: it's not from a tiger, or a nut.)

No matter how hard I tried, Rahul shot down every topic of conversation I attempted. The Toronto Blue Jays? Too pedestrian. His favourite band? You wouldn't have heard of them.

What university did he go to?

What does it matter? We live in the present.

I let the conversation dry up, much like the prunes, figs and apricots that had gone into making our next course: a *granola bar*. At least I had chia and oat pudding to look forward to, and then a cross-examination by Nani about how the date went.

I knew she would laugh when I told her about Rahul's meat-, bread- and milk-free raw diet, and how definitively incompatible we were. But only Jayesh was left on her list. If that didn't work out, then what would she do?

'You're not enjoying the food,' Rahul said, as I poked at a loose fig with my fork.

'Sure I am,' I lied.

'Raina, one must always be true to oneself.'

Was he being serious? Did he think of himself as some kind of wise, Gandhi-like pundit? 'I'm just not used to it,' I said finally, racking my brain for something nice to say. 'But I admire your discipline.'

He laughed smugly, shaking out the elastic in his hair.

His man bun parted into a sticky inverted pyramid at the top of his head.

'It's not discipline, Raina. It's being informed.' He held out his hand, as if signalling to an oncoming vehicle to stop. 'Do you know how many pesticides you have in your body? How many you've accumulated' – he pointed at my stomach, which was still growling for food – 'that are compounding in you right *now*?'

I was about to ask him to enlighten me, but then he did anyway.

'Let me guess: for breakfast you drank coffee, which is an addictive stimulant, and had some sugar and gluten-based cereal.'

'Are you sure you're not a Jedi? Because you just read my mind!'

He smiled. Had I been too rude? I was about to apologise, but then realised he'd taken it as a compliment.

'I had Special K for breakfast today, yes.'

'See? What did I say? And I bet that when you're at home with your Nani, she makes you paratha in the morning, which is made from white flour, white potatoes and butter – which, by the way, was stolen from a helpless cow imprisoned in some industrial farm outside the city. A cow that, as a Hindu, you should be honouring.'

'Hindus honour cows because they help sustain life, and provide sustenance, like *milk*.'

'Whatever, Raina. My point is that all you need is three dates with me. Eat three of these meals, and you'll see how much better you feel and realise how much crap you've been putting in your body. You'll be happier, sleep better. Might even be able to lose some weight.'

I guffawed, audibly. Did he just tell a girl to lose weight?

His cheeks reddened. 'No, I didn't mean it like that. You look great—'

'How can I look great?' I grabbed my handbag, wondering what the hell I was still doing there. 'I had coffee for breakfast!'

'I've really put my foot in my mouth, haven't I?'

'Rahul, it's been so ... interesting to meet you, but I have an engagement party to get to, where I'll be poisoning myself with tandoori chicken and cow-y paneer.' I stood up. 'Lots of alcohol, too.'

'No, don't go.' He stood and reached for my arm. 'I'm sorry. I'm just being defensive. My whole family thinks my lifestyle is ridiculous. Most Indian people do, and—'

'Your lifestyle isn't ridiculous,' I snapped, turning to leave. 'But your manners are.'

Boys for my Raina

~~SACHIN — Reetu's son in Scarborough, some kind of doctor — birthday lunch??~~ *Dinner 9.30pm, Tuesday @ Eldorado

~~JAGMOHAN — Pinky's nefew in Jodhpur (visiting Canada this summer?) — but maybe looking for immwigration~~

~~VINAY — Divya's co-worker, studies kemistry (What is that??), parents from Chennaii~~ after work drinks - date TBD

JAYESH — Sharon's cousin, science professor at university . . . _divorced_!!!

~~ROHIT — Sarla's nefew, lawyer in Boston~~ *Absolutely NOT*

~~ARJUN — Sonia's son, pediatrishan, probly will want to have babies soon!~~ Wknd coffee?

~~VISHAL — Bengali boy, also likes business things, Geeta's friend's son~~ Boooooring

~~KRUPAL — engineer in Vancouver, his parents at temple every Sunday — but may be too short (and dark)~~

~~RAHUL — Sarla's fisiotherapist, says he very good-looking boy ☺~~ UGHHH!!!

~~AZIZ — accountant in Hamilton, Shushma's son, may have a white girlfriend??~~

~~MANJEEV — that handsome boy from temple, PhD student in computers~~ What a CREEP

Chapter 9

'Holy *shit*.' Zoey hesitated at the entrance and glanced down at her beige suit. I'd offered to let her borrow a sari, but she'd claimed to be allergic to sparkly fabric.

'Don't worry. It's just an engagement party.'

Zoey turned to face me, eyes wide. '*Just?*'

The mezzanine level of the hotel had been transformed. I had tagged along for an inspection the week before, nodding mechanically as Auntie Sarla waddled about with a tape measure, the back of her chubby arms swaying as she visualised her masterpiece. And it was. It practically wilted with decadence; an eruption of crystal and light turquoise. At its centre was Shay, gilded like a Christmas tree, and eight hundred people – mostly Auntie Sarla's own friends – milling by the open bar.

I led Zoey through the foyer, past the twenty-foot fountain of peach punch, through the clusters of families huddled at the edges: mothers and daughters in matching lenghas; men in brittle suits, their white girlfriends gowned in bodycon dresses, blissfully unaware that in this crowd, showing that much leg was the equivalent of being stark naked.

In the main hall the tables were clothed in satin, and there was a monstrous cake and a double-decker top table at the front. At Indian celebrations, the families sat at the front, I explained.

'I guess that makes sense,' said Zoey, darting into the queue for the bar. 'They're the ones paying for it.'

'*Wooow.*'

I turned round and looked down towards the voice. Nani and a few of the aunties had found us. Nani was dressed up – pink lips and shawl, a gin and tonic in hand – and when I leaned down for a hug I could smell the perfume she rarely had the courage to wear. Chanel No. 5: the last gift Nana had bought her.

'You look wonderful, Nani.'

'Me?' she exclaimed, her accent thickened with gin. 'No one is looking at me next to *this* beauty model.' She squeezed my chin and tugged until my face was level with hers, plopped kisses across my cheeks. After a moment she leaned back and then started picking imaginary lint off me like a chimp.

'Nani, stop.'

'The boys here will be lining up for you.' She winked. 'And about time too.'

'Nani, you remember Zoey?'

As if she hadn't noticed her before, Nani turned slowly to look at Zoey. She studied her oddly, looking her up and down.

'How have you been, Mrs Anand?'

'Oh, fine.' She looked between Zoey and me, and then down at the floor. 'And yourself?'

'I'm well, thank you.' Zoey touched my arm. 'Work has been surprisingly busy this summer, plus we had those weekends away.'

'We hired a cottage with friends, remember?' I looked at Nani. 'I told you, didn't I?'

She nodded slowly.

'I love your sari.' Zoey smiled eagerly. 'I'm regretting my choice of outfit, now that I can see how beautiful they look on you and Raina.'

'Thank you, dear.' Nani smiled at us faintly, and then nodded her head towards me. In a loud whisper, she said, 'You met Rahul today, *nah*?'

'Yes…'

'Tell us.' Nani winked. 'Was he a *dish*?'

I laughed. 'Yes, Nani, he was handsome. But it's *absolutely* not going to happen. First, Rahul took me to a *vegan*—'

'Enough,' she snapped, cutting me off. 'I cannot hear another of your stories. It is too much now.'

I could feel myself shrinking. I looked down at the ground. 'But Nani…'

'And here I thought, soon I would also have engagement to celebrate.'

I heard her sigh, and then felt her beside me as she brushed a kiss over my cheek.

'Zoey, maybe you have boy for her? She is so hard to please, *nah*?'

By the time I looked up again Nani had disappeared, and I felt Zoey squeeze my hand.

'Are you OK?'

I nodded, without meeting her eye. 'Yeah. Come on, let's go and find our seats.'

Our table was disguised in a garden of gerbera daisies, cream wax candles and chiffon seat covers. Zoey and I were seated across from Shay's older cousins and their husbands – women who, as girls, used to bully Shay and me. They arrived with smiles and hellos, and then seemed content to ignore us. Soon Kris arrived with Serena – Shay's good friend and bridesmaid. I hadn't seen Kris in months, and wondered whose idea it was to seat us together.

Kris was thirty-eight, halfway in age between Mom and me, and I'd never quite known what to make of him. He'd moved out to go to university when I was still a kid, and it wasn't that we weren't close; I'd just never really got to know him.

It was strange seeing him in a suit, and not in gym clothes, or his uniform of khakis and ill-fitting t-shirts that he wore as an engineering consultant. He pulled out Serena's chair and she folded herself into it, suppressing a smile, tucking her hair and sari perfectly into place.

What was he even doing here? Ever since his divorce, Kris avoided going to temple, Indian weddings or parties – anywhere he said the aunties and uncles would stare at him, judging. But as I watched Kris and Serena effortlessly interact, pour one another water, eat one another's appetisers, I realised that already they seemed to be the community's next 'it' couple.

Sitting next to Serena, the golden girl of my generation, the community must have pardoned him.

I helped myself to another glass of wine as the main course was brought out, and then another. Serena and Zoey became engrossed in a discussion about politics, and Kris and I sat together in silence. I had nothing to say. I glanced behind me, and saw Nani in fervent conversation at her table with Auntie Sarla and a few other aunties.

Had news gone round already that I'd walked out on Rahul in the middle of our date? Was this evening's gossip that Raina, yet again, was being too picky – and not that Rahul was just a complete *dick*? My wine glass emptied again, and I reached over and poured some more.

'Quite the fish tonight, aren't you?' I heard Kris say, and I didn't answer. 'I saw you talking to Ma earlier. She must be thrilled to see you all dressed up. You actually look nice, Raindrop.'

'Please don't call me that.'

He leaned in. 'Are any of them here?'

'Any of who …?' I stopped, seeing his smirk.

'She's even asking me if I have single friends for you.' He laughed. 'That would be strange, hey? My little *niece* marrying—'

'Kris, can we please not talk about this tonight?'

He brought his wine glass to his lips and winked. 'Come on. Lighten up.'

I gestured towards Serena. 'Why don't we talk about you two, then?'

'What do you want to know?'

'You seem pretty cosy.'

'So?'

'So when are you getting married?'

'Funny, Raina.' His eyes glinted. 'I was about to ask you the same thing.'

The room bustled in confusion as someone at the podium requested everyone to head back to their tables for the speeches. His voice meek, the man at the podium tapped on the microphone, coughing, trying to collect everyone's attention as if it were spilled coins.

Then someone at the back of the hall began clinking his spoon against a glass. Echoes followed, and soon the room sounded like wind chimes in a storm.

At the front of the hall, Shay and Julien stood up in front of their audience, waving and holding hands – the most public display of affection they were allowed in front of this sort of crowd. She was wearing a harvest-gold sari. Her eyes were painted, her black hair wound into a bow at the back of her neck. Julien, dressed up in an embroidered kurta pyjama, smiled down at her.

'She looks wonderful, doesn't she, Raina?' said Serena.

'Yes,' I said, wine glass in hand. I surveyed the room; everyone paired off and smiling. 'Absolutely wonderful.'

An hour later, the speeches were still going as the backlog of Shay's extended family toasted her and Julien at the podium. I was restless, my feet vibrating, and finally I couldn't take it any more. With a quick shrug to Zoey, I found my heels under the table and sneaked outside the main hall.

My throat was parched, and in the foyer I grabbed another drink and wandered around. Others had gathered outside, too, perhaps sick of the frills and gimmicks, the insincere congratulations and tears from everyone fighting for a chance at the microphone. The wedding was still eight months away, yet everyone inside was acting like they were already married, as if something was about to change. Everyone thought that Shay lived in my spare room, but the only thing in there was a rail of my winter coats, a few boxes of junk and a treadmill. Shay and Julien already lived together. They had a mortgage together. They had stupid things like a butter dish and a garlic press. Matching wardrobes they'd chosen together and bought on their joint credit card.

And what did I have? Dates with men who told me to *lose weight*. A Nani who acted like she was disappointed in me because I refused to settle.

From inside the main hall, I could hear Auntie Sarla speaking into the microphone, making a rambling speech about family and community and marriage. What did she know? What gave *her* the right to stand up and tell people what was right and what was wrong?

I moved further away out of earshot and examined the desserts. Trolleys of fruit, meringue and lemon pie; custards and salted caramel cheesecakes. Another trolley full of Indian sweets. Lassi and gulab jamun and rasmalai. My stomach felt unsettled just looking at all of it, and I grabbed a fistful of green grapes and walked on. Just behind me I saw three long tables full of small sandalwood boxes, each hand-carved with the name of a guest. Auntie Sarla had spent months organising the shipment from India, delaying the engagement party for their arrival even though surely everyone would be too drunk to remember to take one home, or would throw it in the bin as soon as it started to collect dust.

I weaved through the tables looking for my box, and just as I found it, something fierce blew in like a foghorn. She was singing. Auntie Sarla's voice crescendoed, a throaty hum traversing the scales of a traditional Indian bhajan, and I couldn't help myself. I snorted, snot dripping, as I tried to stifle my laughter.

'I saw that.'

I covered my face and whipped round. He was tall, much taller than me, his honey-brown hair clumped behind his ears, a thick beard dripping down like moss. He smirked at me and rocked back and forth on his heels.

'What? I sneezed.'

'You *sneezed*.'

'Yes, I sneezed.'

'Well,' he said, rubbing his large hands together. 'Then bless you.'

Auntie Sarla was still singing, her voice blaring through the speakers. I pressed my lips together and motioned to turn away.

'Wait,' he said. 'You're Raina. Shaylee's best friend.'

'I might be. And who are you?'

He chuckled.

'What?'

'Nothing?'

'*What?*'

'Nothing.' His eyebrows arched high. 'Although I wouldn't have thought you were that kind of bridesmaid.'

'What's that supposed to mean?'

'It just makes sense. Laughing at Sarla's singing.' He motioned around the room with his hand. 'Pretending that this entire thing is funny.'

I crossed my arms, my cheeks flushing. 'What are you trying to say?'

'I'm *saying* that while that sari looks beautiful on you, Raina, envy does not.'

'I am incredibly happy for Shay, OK?'

'Jealousy and being happy for a friend aren't mutually exclusive.'

'What are you, a bumper sticker?' I moved to brush past him, and as I did I caught hold of his scent. Like pepper and musk. Blackened green and burnt aluminium. Like Mom's winter coat, or the sixth-floor fire escape in mine and Shay's old flat.

I stopped. 'What's that smell?'

'What smell?'

'Are you *high*?'

His idiot grin gave him away.

'You can't come to a wedding high, OK? Have you no respect?'

'I wasn't the one "sneezing" at my best friend's mom.'

'Who the hell do you think you are?'

He turned away from me, eyes laughing, and picked a box up off the table. *Klein*. Asher Klein.

'Oh. Well that makes sense.'

'Seems you've heard of me.'

I uncrossed my arms.

'Come on now. Be fun. What have you heard?'

That he was Julien's oldest friend from Montreal. That he'd dropped out of teacher training college with a term left before graduation. That he'd just got back from South East Asia after ten years of travelling and doing whatever it was that his type – the *drifter* – seemed to do.

'That you existed,' I said flatly.

'And does my *existence*,' he paused, 'interest you?'

'I'll buy your story when it comes out in paperback.'

'And am I the hero in this story?' He smiled. 'Do I get the girl in the end?'

'You wrote it. You tell me.'

'I think I do.' He nodded to himself. 'Adventure. Thriller. Romance. It'll be a bestseller.'

'A regular Jack Kerouac.'

'I'm handsome like Jack, aren't I?'

'You know he died from alcoholism?'

He knocked his glass against mine. 'He died a happy man.'

I crossed my arms. 'So, Jack, what did you do while *on the road*? Bit of a drifter, were you? Bounced from hostel to hooker?' I touched his elbow. 'Tell me, have you had yourself checked lately?'

'Gossip is a powerful thing, Raina.'

I stood on tiptoe and whispered close to his ear, 'So is herpes.'

Asher laughed, and the creases round his eyes deepened. I could feel him looking at me, and my cheeks burned. Seconds passed and he was still laughing, as if I was the funniest thing in the world.

'Done?' I asked after a moment.

He nodded. 'You're—'

'Hilarious, I know. But it's so easy to be funny around you,' I said, gritting my teeth. 'After all, your life is quite the joke.'

His face stiffened.

'A thirty-something with nothing to show for himself—'

'Better than being a thirty-something drunk bridesmaid, don't you think?'

'I'm twenty-*nine*.'

'Always the bridesmaid, never the—'

But then I shoved him, hard. He wobbled, nearly regaining his balance before toppling over backwards and straight into a dessert trolley. The metal trays clanged together as they spilled onto the ground, and all over Asher. A few people standing nearby turned to look, and he picked himself up off the floor, his shirt a soppy swell of mango lassi and graham cracker crust.

'Shit.' I covered my mouth with my hands. Had I just pushed him? I wasn't sure I'd ever pushed anyone in my life. Asher slowly pulled himself onto his knees, and I put out my hand. He took it, pulling on me lightly as he stood up. I had to concentrate not to fall over, too, and I realised that Asher was right. I *was* drunk.

I ran towards the ladies'. It was all too much. Everything – Nani and Auntie Sarla, Shay, work – it was boiling up and out and I didn't want any of it. I locked myself in a cubicle, the sea-green walls spinning, and flicked down the toilet-seat lid. Sitting, I took three deep breaths and then opened my eyes.

What was happening to me? What was I *letting* happen?

I thought I might cry, but the tears refused to come. I wanted, I needed *something*, but I didn't know what. I reached into my bag and found my BlackBerry. It was dead, and I resigned myself to the fact that I'd have to leave without telling Zoey. I couldn't face going back inside the hall again. I would make it up to her.

Outside, I slipped away from the main area and found a service staircase. I took off my heels and toed my way down step by step, trying not to trip on my sari, my hand dragging behind me on the banister. I got to the last step and was about to push my way through the fire exit door when I heard rustling behind me. I whipped round, thinking Asher had followed me. But instead I saw a young, muscular blond who was vaguely familiar rolling a cigarette on the landing behind me.

He held my eyes as he licked the rolling paper. Then he slid the cigarette through his fingers and stashed it behind his left ear.

'It's Raina, right?' he said, still holding my gaze. 'I remember you.'

I pressed my lips together and shook my head.

'I used to be the barman at Eldorado. You came in a few months back with that dick, *Sachin*.'

Hazily, it came to me. The barman who had given me the eye and made me a stiff gin and tonic. I nodded in recognition. 'What's your name again?'

'Josh.'

I nodded. 'Sorry.'

'You should be. You ran off before I could steal you away.' He took a few more steps towards me, and suddenly I felt self-conscious. Woozy. I put my arm back on the rail.

'I just got off my shift. You leaving already?' Josh opened his jacket and motioned to a bottle of gin wedged into his inside pocket. 'I nicked this from the bar upstairs.'

'Don't worry. I won't tell.'

He smirked. 'Looked like a great party.'

I shrugged. 'It wasn't so great.'

'Oh?' He took another step down. He was inches away, and I could smell cigarettes, the stink of beer and wine and detergent, his meaty breath from whatever he'd had for dinner. 'Then maybe we should start another one.'

He seemed like such a cliché, but then again, wasn't I? I

held his gaze as he moved towards me, as he touched my neck with the very tips of his fingers. 'Come home with me.'

Up close, Josh was surreal. He was beyond attractive: blond, a cheeky, boyish grin and sculpted arms. He could have been a model. I would never be able to trust a man that handsome, but what he was suggesting wouldn't require that kind of trust.

My head pounded at the thought that my only prospect left was Jayesh; after I crossed him off the list, then what? What would Nani make me do? He kept calling, kept asking me to go to this new restaurant, or that art gallery, or *fishing*. But I didn't want to go fishing, or on another pressure-cooker date orchestrated by Nani. Right then, exhausted and overwhelmed, I wanted something else. I hadn't been with anyone except Dev, and just looking at Josh I thought about letting that change.

Josh leaned forward and brushed his lips against mine. For a moment I just watched him kiss me. Soppily, hungrily, the muscles expanding and contracting on his cheeks and forehead as he moved his mouth, and I in turn moved mine. He put his hands on my waist, and a second later I felt them slide down to my ass as he pinned me against the rail. His stubble ground coarse against me, his tongue prodded and his hands pulled, and eventually I closed my eyes and surrendered.

I was already standing by the door when he woke up. He lifted his face an inch off the pillow and squinted at me.

'You're leaving?'

I nodded, and his head fell back on the pillow. I was sober now, filled with guilt at having left Zoey at the party, and I noticed how his bedroom smelled like the inside of a hockey bag; how the walls were covered in creased *Lord of the Rings* posters. I vaguely remembered seeing them from just hours before – dim lighting, the bottle of expensive gin – teasing him for being a dork while admitting that I, too, used to have those same posters. Later, falling back onto the bed, laughing so loud that one of his room-mates banged on the wall and told us to shut up. Josh had smothered our faces beneath a minced-thin pillow, and, in a muffled voice, told me I was the most entertaining girl he'd ever had over.

Most entertaining *woman*, I'd reminded him.

He made a sleepy noise – a yawn, whimpering like a hungry puppy – and I sat back down on the bed. The flannel sheet crunched beneath my weight, and I wondered how long it'd been since its last wash. He rubbed his eyes and then looked up at me, smiling.

'My phone's dead. Could you call me a cab?'

He propped himself up on one elbow and I resisted the urge to rub the sleep out of his eyes. 'I can drive you,' he said, kissing me on the lips. His mouth had crusted white overnight, and when I pulled away I could still taste his morning breath.

He drove me home, the late summer wind blowing in through the windows, a strange voice singing at me through the dashboard, a single wool sock tucked into the tape deck. The passenger seat belt was missing, and I tried not to grip the seat as we sped east on Queen Street. Outside my building, he asked me for my phone number and I gave it to him knowing he'd never use it – and surely Josh knew I didn't want him to. After one more dry kiss, he left.

I took the lift and sighed as I unlocked the door. My

sari stuck to me, and I felt the grime on my teeth, my hair in greased pieces behind my ears. I found an extra charger in the kitchen and plugged in my BlackBerry, left a trail of clothing down the hall and stepped into the shower. Standing beneath the pressure of the water, I opened my mouth and drank until my stomach hurt.

I closed my eyes and tried to decide how I felt about what just had, and hadn't, happened. Damp sheets and armpits. Josh's eyelashes. Falling asleep with my head on his shoulder, both of his hands secured around my waist. The heat of a body at rest next to mine.

I lathered, and then rinsed it all away. I stepped out of the shower and wrapped a fresh towel around my body, walked through the apartment and opened all the curtains. Light flooded in. My phone had powered on, and it lit up in beeps and flashes. I grabbed it and scrolled through the alerts. A missed call from Nani. Unread texts from Zoey and Shay – even a few from Depesh. Work emails... and then I saw it.

My Raina,

It's been too long – there's so much to tell. Not sure London is right for me any more... if it ever was. There's been some rearranging, and the transfer paperwork was filed today... Will start shortly at the Toronto office. I'll see you then, darling.

Dev xo

Chapter 10

20 May 2014

Twenty-seven and alone. Twenty-seven, and starting over. She watches marathons of *Degrassi* and James Bond. *The Golden Girls* and *Star Trek*. She cries most of the day, and then again as she lies in bed trying to fall asleep. She stares at the fading star stickers taped to the ceiling of her old bedroom, thinking how, at twenty-seven, her Nani had moved to a new country, run both a business and a household.

How her mother had had an eleven-year-old daughter and the vivid life of a flight attendant. How even Shay, not quite twenty-seven, is a doctor – and has just moved in with her boyfriend.

And what do I have, Raina thinks to herself?

She has a new apartment that she'll get the keys to the following week. She has her old job at the Toronto office, one that they are anxious for her to resume. She has Nani, Shay, and other friends. But the thing she wants most of all – what she must learn to live without – she has lost. And she has no idea what to do. Raina has no memory of the woman she was before she met Dev, or how that woman managed to function. She barely eats, and moves listlessly from bed to sofa, sofa to bed. She is heartbroken and unkempt. She is carelessly adrift.

Nani bakes a cake for her birthday, and in the evening Shay arrives, still gowned in her mint-green scrubs. Raina can hear them talking about her in the kitchen.

'This is not depression,' she hears her Nani say. 'This is a break-up. She will be fine.'

'She's stopped running.' Shay's voice lowers. 'I've never seen her like this before.'

'Time will heal her. It heals all of us.'

Raina rolls her eyes and turns up the sound on the television. She is tired of them. Tired of hearing how that much passion was unhealthy; about their rage for the 'asshole' who hurt her. But Dev was not an asshole; it was Raina who walked away, and as she stares blankly at the television, she thinks maybe she shouldn't have.

Was she asking too much?

Marriage. Kids. Love. A *life* with Dev. She had grown tired of the bits and scraps he left for her to gather up, to scavenge for between work hours and out-of-town meetings, between midnight and 6 a.m. when they lay in his bed, half-undressed, beaten down from exhaustion. But did she need him to propose? They weren't that old, and it was Nani who wanted to see her married, was it not? It was Nani who *really* wanted the lavish Indian wedding, the week-long celebrations and the showing off. The expense and the traditions. Raina didn't need it, and as she feels acid spark in her stomach, she regrets having asked Dev for it.

Had it been only three weeks since she left? One day they had been lying next to one another, their ankles entwined, deciding whether to make Earl Grey or honey-lemon tea. And the next?

She plays their break-up scene over and over again in

her mind, rewinding and fast-forwarding. Agonising over every word, every look, every pause.

She had surprised him with plane tickets and a hotel reservation: a two-night stay at a resort in Tuscany for their anniversary.

'You didn't even ask,' he had said, not looking at her.

'That was the point.' She sat down next to him at the kitchen table. His head was on his hands, and she watched him stare at the surface – shiny, varnished – that neither of them ever ate on.

'I told your assistant not to book any meetings, and even Andrew was—'

'You asked my boss?' he scoffed. 'Jesus, Raina, don't you know how unprofessional that is? This is my career! Sometimes I don't get a choice about when I have to work.'

'There's always a choice—'

'It makes me look bad enough that I'm dating a co-worker.'

She stood up, tears threatening to spill, and slammed the bedroom door behind her. He came into the room seconds later and cradled her, held her until he made her believe he hadn't meant it.

Then she had asked him for the first and last time the questions that were, and still are, constantly on her mind. Was she ever going to come first? Would he ever meet her Nani?

Would he ever ask her to marry him?

When she thinks of what came next, she feels the entire world buckle around her. She was the one to make un-reasonable demands; force him to talk about the future, their plans. She had triggered everything, pushed and pulled, moulded their relationship, their unhappiness, until there was nothing left to do but leave.

And even though he didn't stop her, she knows it was all her fault.

She reaches for her laptop. With trepidation, she begins typing, drafting an email without knowing what she wants to say, or what purpose it would serve. She is clicking at the keyboard more furiously now. Meandering. Suggesting a point without wanting to make it. The pads of her fingers type and clack, and then she hears a floorboard creak.

'What the hell are you doing?'

Raina snaps the computer shut. She turns round, and Nani and Shay are standing behind her, trays of tea and cake in hand. They are glaring at her.

'Were you emailing him?' Shay shoves a cup into Raina's hand and hot tea spills onto their fingers.

Raina puts the cup down, wipes her hands on her shirt. 'No.'

'Don't lie to me.' Shay turns to Nani. 'They've been talking still. They text all the time, and *email*, and—'

'Shay!'

Nani gasps. 'Why, *beta*?'

'We love each other,' says Raina, looking down at her hands. 'I don't know if it's really ... over.'

'Oh, it's over, all right.' Shay shakes her head. 'After how he's treated you? You can't stay in contact with him. I refuse. It's masochism.'

'*You* refuse.'

'Yes, I refuse. This isn't your call any more. You have no judgement at the moment.'

97

Raina turns to Nani. 'She's being ridiculous. Are you listening to her?'

'Yes,' says Nani. 'I am listening, and Shaylee is right. It is time to move on.'

Shay has crouched down in front of Raina. She opens the laptop and skims the screen. Dramatically, slowly, she presses the delete key. 'Absolutely not.'

'Shay!'

'Don't *Shay* me.' She tugs on Raina's ankle. 'What's it going to take to get through to you?'

With birthday cake and tea comes another sermon. How Dev is now a lesson learned. How the years she gave him are not a waste; they will make her stronger. She tunes them out, still thinking of Dev. Minutes pass, and when her mind re-enters the room, she realises that Nani and Shay are discussing arranged marriages – *her* arranged marriage. They are discussing how Raina is not ready to start dating again, but how, in a few months, maybe a year, she will be.

Raina starts to resist, but Nani is adamant. She says she does not want to see Raina hurt any longer. She wants to find her a match. See her happy and settled. She wants to make an arrangement.

As much as Raina wants to please her Nani, as much as she's always wanted to, she doesn't want *this*. She wants Dev. She will always want Dev.

'A couple of years from now, Raina,' says Shay. 'If you're single at, say, thirty. Why not consider it?'

Nani smiles, rubs Raina's forearm until the fine brown hairs stand upright. *Thirty* feels infinitely far away, the destination elusive. She cannot imagine not being married by then, not having Dev in her life.

Nani and Shay are talking on either side of her about what type of man Raina might like, or rather, *should* like. Someone who is tall and handsome, says her Nani, but will provide a stable home. Shay disagrees, and says that, above all else, he must be humorous and kind; that Raina doesn't need a good match, but someone that can match *her*.

Raina tunes in and out of the chatter. She doesn't bother telling them to calm down, stop planning something that, surely, will never come to fruition. Instead she nods her head and agrees to the plan. She is suddenly famished, and cutting herself another piece of cake, she glances at the computer. Already she is crafting another email; just the thought of Dev – the mere suggestion that it's not yet over – has revived her.

Chapter 11

Autumn set in, but Nani's hot stove kept out the cold. The countertops overflowed with baking sheets of raw chicken cut into cubes marinating in the masala she had taught me how to make. Onions, ginger, cumin, turmeric. Just the right amount of fresh coriander. Standing beside me, she guided me as I stirred the biryani and turned the chicken, fried two subjis side by side on the back-burners. It had been over a month since Dev told me he was moving to Toronto, and every weekend since I'd come home to watch movies with Nani or get cooking lessons to keep myself occupied.

I still hadn't processed the news, or what it might mean. In the email he'd called me darling, and he hadn't called me that since the weekend before I left London – while we made spinach and goat's cheese omelettes – and he'd said, sipping his espresso, 'Darling, you take the one that hasn't flopped over.'

That morning had only just reappeared in my mind. Others, too – the ones I had been pushing away for two years. Mere flashes of our life in London. Kissing after hours at the office with the curtains drawn. Brunch with his friends in Covent Garden, his hand sliding up my thigh beneath the table. After months of begging, going on an afternoon date to the V&A because I'd never been; licking gelato and rolling our eyes at wedding dresses from the Renaissance. Standing next to him in a crowded lift; Dev leaning into my neck, whispering, 'You know that I love you, don't you?'

October crawled by. I jumped whenever I heard an English accent in the corridor at work, and checked my email fifty thousand times a day. I trolled through the bulletins posted by HR to see if his start date had been announced, confirm that he really was transferring. In his email, Dev hadn't mentioned what day he was coming or how long he might be staying – and I didn't know how to ask.

Was it his choice to move to Toronto?

Then there was that other question I always typed out, and always deleted.

Are you moving here for me?

I hadn't seen him in two years, but the more I thought about it, the more it made sense. Of course he was supposed to move here. I hadn't spent the happiest years of my life with a man just so that we could break up. And relationships like that, like the one Dev and I had, were never just a relationship. It was a love affair, with a screen of its own on the Central Park lawn in Mumbai's most prestigious cinema. The heartbreak had to be worth it – and suddenly I knew that Dev was going to be my happy ending.

A sputter of oil escaped the pan, and I noticed that Nani was studying my face.

'Do you want to watch a movie after this?' I asked her. 'Priyanka Chopra has a new one out, hasn't she?'

'Do you not have other plans tonight?'

Other plans. Nani's code words that suggested I should be

out on another date, trawling the streets, bars and temple for another suitable Indian.

I thought she'd lay off after I'd gone out with Jayesh, finally, and then let him down gently. Stupidly, I'd assumed that it would be over, and that I could wait for Dev in peace – once I'd met up with everyone on her list, and she'd realised her arrangement just wouldn't work.

But she continued to push, pulling eligible Indian bachelors out of some sort of magical hat. I wasn't even sure where she was finding them – whose sons, nephews or cousins they were – but they wouldn't leave me alone. She'd started to give out my phone number, and now I couldn't go more than twelve hours without receiving weird texts from guys named Billy or Harpreet, and voicemails from mouth-breathers who'd forget to leave their name.

Each time my BlackBerry lit up I'd hope it was Dev, and then get that sinking feeling in my stomach when it wasn't. He'd be here soon, wouldn't he? Surely all of this would be over soon.

'No, I don't have plans,' I said to Nani, trying to sound firm.

'Did Neil not call? He sounds very promising.'

'Please. Not today.' I gave her a pleading look. 'Work has been really busy, and right now I just want to cook and hang out with *you*.'

Nani nodded slowly, and then kissed me on the cheek. 'Well, you are natural cook. I am very proud. Manu was never good like this.'

'She liked to cook?'

Nani sneered. 'She liked to do a lot of things.'

'It's so relaxing,' I said. 'I'd never realised that before.'

'*Aacha*. When you have time, yes. But when cooking for hungry customers, hungry children – it is not so relaxing.'

Nani rarely spoke about the past, and I thought about pressing her. How did she feel about leaving her parents, one day packing her things and moving in with a husband she barely knew? What was it like getting on a plane for the first time in her life, crossing into a new country – cold, barren – and raising children in a land you knew nothing about?

I reached up to the spice rack and grabbed a small glass jar full of methi. I pinched some between my fingers, then carefully sprinkled it over the pan. With a wooden spoon I folded it in, another rich wave of aroma escaping.

'Was it hard?' I asked finally.

'Do you know I still am not sure the English word for methi?' I felt her beside me, watching me as I cooked. 'Yes, Raina. It was very hard.'

'Zoey said her grandparents were immigrants too,' I said. 'From the Ukraine. But still.'

'You spend a lot of time with Zoey, *nah*?' She paused. 'Is she—'

I heard the front door open and a beat later, slam shut. My eyes locked with Nani's as we heard a jingling of keys, the sound of the hall cupboard opening. Nani's lips were pursed as she watched the kitchen door.

'Mom?' I called out.

Footsteps dragged across the hardwood in the other room, and a moment later, we heard a deep voice. 'It's me.'

Nani's shoulders relaxed as Kris opened the kitchen door. His hair was wet and he had at least a week's worth of stubble on his face. He sat down heavily at the kitchen table, tossing his gym bag in the corner.

'I didn't know you were coming,' she said without turning round. 'Not with Serena today?'

'No.' He sat down at the table. 'We broke up.'

Nani leaned forward against the counter and massaged her temples. Eyes closed, she inhaled deeply and then exhaled like she did while meditating. It was only the week before that I'd overheard Nani and Auntie Sarla gossiping in the living room – calloused feet on the coffee table, plates of sweets on their stomachs – speculating on who, after Shay, would be the next in the community to get married. *Kris.* They'd been confident. Kris and Serena were the right age, and had established careers. What was he waiting for, Auntie Sarla had wondered aloud?

'Sorry to hear that,' I said finally. Beside me, Nani was still crouched over, slowly shaking her head. 'Nani, do you want to sit down?'

She whimpered.

'Ma, stop being so dramatic. We weren't even together that long.'

'Krishna, Serena was *nice* girl.'

'All my girlfriends have been nice. Maybe it's not—'

'Your Auntie Sarla has practically planned your wedding. And now?'

'And now you can tell your beloved Sarla to cancel it.'

'What will I say? That you again have broken up with a girl for no reason? This time with that lovely Serena? That my Krishna is refusing to settle down? Just like Manu, never considering others—'

'That, right there,' yelled Kris, staring at me. He stood up from the table and reached for his gym bag. 'That's why I never fucking come home.'

Nani didn't say another word after Kris walked out. She went upstairs, and after a few minutes I realised she wasn't coming back down. I tried to finish cooking alone, but I was frazzled, uneven, and ended up burning half the dishes.

I scraped the tray of blackened chicken into the bin, trying not to focus on how Kris had just left like that. I managed to salvage the biryani and one of the subjis, but I didn't feel like eating any of it. I put the food away in Tupperware containers, washed and dried the dishes and scrubbed down the stove and the kitchen surfaces I'd splattered.

When I was done, I found my way into the living room and slumped onto the sofa. I glanced up at the cuckoo clock. It was early evening, and it was already getting dark. I had a lot of catch-up work to do before the end of the weekend, but I didn't want to leave Nani alone. Not yet.

Her tablet was on the coffee table, and I grabbed it. I'd discovered the year before that she didn't like using the desktop computer I'd bought her because the den was too cold, so I'd given her my tablet. She'd been an infuriating student, wanting to play with it like she had with my old Nintendo before I'd even taught her what meant what, but eventually she'd learned. Now she used it to Skype her sister in India, and send emails to her friends about temple gatherings and her charity projects. I'd even seen her playing games on it, which she'd taught herself to do.

I keyed in her password – 1234 – and spotted in the bottom right-hand corner that the email icon displayed thirty-eight unread messages. I clicked on it, determined to set up a spam filter for her.

But when the emails appeared, all of them – every single one – was from IndianSingles.com.

My mouth dropped open.

I stared at the screen; was I imagining this? I blinked a couple of times, but the words didn't change. Hesitantly, I clicked on one of the emails, and I could feel the blood pumping through my stomach, my throat, my ears.

A welcome message appeared that was addressed to me, and it said I had another 'suitor' interested. I scrolled down, and a profile appeared.

Pradeep. 35. Accountant. Toronto. Hindu, olive skin, 5' 9.5". 80k salary per year, looking for educated, fair-skinned <30.

I exited the email, and without thinking clicked on another.

Neil. 32. Dentist living in Oakville. Jet-setter and avid reader. Open to meeting the love of my life.

And then another.

Nish. 27. Computer science geek, Taurus, 5' 8", searching for grl w/ good values + vegetarian chef.

I clicked through each of the emails, one after another. *Jeetu. Vinod. Baljit. Ajay. Gopal. Amar.*

Nani had made a new list, given out my number to men on the internet, and hadn't even told me. What, had I exhausted all the single men she knew? Now she had to go online to pawn me off? To make sure I found a husband before I turned thirty?

I clicked on the link in the final email and the web browser flashed to life. *IndianSingles.com*, it read: *an online destination for Indian singles living abroad searching for that special someone.*

I scrolled down, and there I was. My very own profile. My entire life. Everything a man would ever need to know.

Raina. 29. Works at investment bank in Toronto. Nice Hindu girl in search of husband.

I felt the bile rising in my throat. Was that it? Was *that* all that mattered about me?

And what about after I'd found a husband? Who was I then: a wife? A mother? Eventually a grandmother? Was that all an Indian woman would ever be? Someone defined by her relationship to others?

I stared at the photo Nani had used in my profile. She had taken the picture when I wasn't looking, at a café in Southwark. I was wearing a leather jacket, a cream and poppy-red scarf we'd bought that morning on Portobello Road. My hair was combed back into a ponytail, and I'd worn make-up that day. Mascara, blue-black liner. Even lipstick. The canvas tote bag on my shoulder was full of honey-cinnamon cashews and a piece of German chocolate cake that we'd bought at Borough Market for Dev, before we realised that he wasn't coming.

He'd been called away to Zürich, to a merger on the brink of collapsing. I didn't see him for three weeks, and Nani didn't see him at all.

I found Nani upstairs meditating at the foot of her bed. She sat cross-legged, her eyes closed on the grape-purple yoga mat I'd bought her for her last birthday. Her glasses were off, and there were clumps of screwed-up tissue on the floor beside her.

After a moment, she opened her eyes. They were red.

'There's my sweet.' With her left hand she tapped the floor next to her, and I obliged.

I lay down on the mat and rested my head in her lap. She stroked my forehead, brushing the hair out of my face, as I looked up at her. From that angle I could make out the faint lines in her neck and at the corners of her lips; her broad cheekbones, the roundness of her small, delicate nose.

'How is chicken? I smell burning.'

'That's because it's burnt,' I said curtly. Her face fell, and I was immediately filled with regret.

Nani playfully pinched my nose, looking down at me. 'Well, I would have eaten anyway. I will eat anything my Raina makes for me.'

I could feel the tears forming, the lump in my throat, a heaviness in my chest. I wanted to reply, but what was there to say?

Your son is angry with you, just like Mom is, but maybe you deserve it? Maybe it was *you* who pushed them away?

I thought about the list of men in her inbox waiting for a response. My marriage ad she'd posted online without telling me.

Nani loved me. I was her whole life. But why was she pushing me away too?

I rolled towards her, closing my eyes. Baby powder. Ginger. Paprika. I started shaking, the tears forming, and I felt her arms wrap round me.

'Don't cry, my Raina,' she whispered. 'We have each other.'

Nani and I would always have each other. But as I buried myself against her, I'd never felt so far away.

Chapter 12

'I'm sorry I haven't been around more.'

Depesh shrugged.

'I said I would, and I haven't been.' I shook my head. 'I meant to text you earlier, I just—'

'You're busy. It's OK.'

I nodded and reached for the sugar. I tore open two packets and dumped them into my coffee.

'You want to talk about it?'

'Hmm?' I looked up, taking a sip.

'Do you want to talk about what's bothering you? You look a bit frazzled.'

'That's a very polite way of saying I look *terrible*, thanks.' I laughed. 'I'm fine. Yeah, I'm *fine*, really. But I think I'm coming down with something.'

I did feel terrible. I'd barely eaten in days, and at night, no matter how tired I was, I couldn't fall asleep. I was restless, and I almost wished Dev would email me and tell me it had all been a lie. That he wasn't coming; and my life, however small it was, could get back to normal.

But what did normal even mean these days? Tackling Nani's new *online* list, the one with a seemingly infinite number of men? It had been weeks since I'd discovered her internet escapades, and still she hadn't told me about my ad on IndianSingles.com. She still pretended that the men who were calling me – men who, I told her, I was simply too busy to see – she'd somehow found through her friends.

'How are classes going?' I asked Depesh.

He nodded slowly without looking up from the table. 'Good. My mid-term exams went really well, and yeah,' he shrugged, 'so it's good. I think I've made some friends.'

'You think?'

'There's this group of guys, all pre-med too, and we're in, like, all the same classes. We study together a lot.' He shrugged again. 'You know, sometimes hang out.'

I smiled. 'That's good, Depo.'

'We're not that close, though,' he said. 'Like, we only ever talk about homework, or our professors or video games.'

'I guess those things take time,' I said. 'My best friend, Shay – you know Shaylee Patel? Auntie Sarla's daughter?'

He nodded.

'We went to school together, but it took a while to become close, even with her.' It struck me then that it had been over a week since I'd heard from Shay. But then again, I hadn't got in touch with her either.

While Depesh took another sip of his coffee I sneaked a look at my phone. I had only meant to nip out of the office to buy some aspirin, but had bumped into Depesh on the street just as he was getting off a shift at the lab. I'd told him I had time for a quick coffee, but I hadn't realised it was already past 6 p.m. I ran through the list of things I needed to do before the markets opened the next day and bit my lip. If I stayed any longer, I wouldn't be home until at least midnight.

'Anyway, tell me, what else is new, Depo? You're so quiet all the time.'

'Sorry—'

'No, don't be sorry. I just meant …' I hesitated. 'I want to get to know you better, that's all.'

He shrugged. 'Really, Raina. There's not much to tell.'

'Well, do you have a girlfriend?'

He rolled his eyes.

'Right, people don't call it dating, or girlfriends, do they? It's all about hooking up, isn't it?'

'I don't date.' He looked at me oddly. '*Or* hook up.'

'I didn't either when I was your age.'

'How old were you when you met the British guy?'

'Twenty-five.' I nodded slowly. 'We dated for two years.'

'Why did it end?'

I reached for my coffee, my hands shaking, and wished so badly I had an answer.

The next morning I woke up and just couldn't get warm. It hurt to move, to swallow. I wore my suit over my thickest wool sweaters and socks, and, swaddled in my heaviest parka on the walk to work, still the late-autumn wind tore right through me, chilling me to the bone. Most of my colleagues' offices were still empty when I arrived. My brain felt like a block of ice and I shut my door, rolled my coat into a thick pillow and put my head down on the desk. With my eyes closed, I still felt queasy, and a sickening dread washed over me.

Did I have the flu? I wanted to call Nani, but I felt too weak to reach for the phone. I kept my eyes closed, thinking

I would try in a moment, but the next thing I knew Zoey's face had appeared in front of me.

She squatted down next to my desk. A dull sunlight filled the room, and instinctively I glanced over at the clock.

'Shit!' I tried to lift my body, but couldn't.

Zoey touched my forehead, and I wasn't sure if it was my skin that was wet, or hers. 'Raina, you're super-hot.'

I closed my eyes. 'A babe, I know.'

'Raina, I'm serious.'

I noted the tone of concern in Zoey's voice. I felt her tuck my hair behind my ears and I opened my eyes again. 'How was the meeting?'

'Fine...' Her eyes hit the floor. 'Don't worry. I don't think Bill noticed you weren't there.'

'Liar.'

'Raina, you're not well.' She cushioned me as I tried to sit up again. 'You should go home.'

Sitting up, the room spun and I blinked until it stopped. 'I'm fine.'

'You look like shit.'

'Really, I'm fine.' I fumbled for the keyboard, for the button to switch on my PC. 'So how was the meeting?'

She stood up and sat on the edge of my desk, her legs waving in and out, knocking against one another. She wouldn't look up from the floor.

'What is it?'

She looked away.

'Zoey, what? Am I fired, or something?'

Her eyes darted up and around, out of the window, and by the time they finally landed on me, I already knew.

'Boardroom D,' she whispered.

I tried not to sprint, to walk at a normal pace, but I kept stumbling. My shoes refused to keep up with my feet, catching on the carpet. I let my hand drag against the wall for balance. A right. Another sharp right. The corridor seemed longer, endless, a mirage of doors and stiff suits, impractical art and sharp edges.

Then finally, I was there. And so was he.

Dev. Exactly as I'd left him. The way he still looked in my mind. The same Dev I knew, and now here – not thousands of miles away, but sitting right in front of me. Handsome and angular, a few sprigs of grey feathered into his sideburns. He was so close, only a glass wall between us; thin, sharp lines of fog. He was facing away from me, towards Bill and a few other senior bankers lined up on the opposite side of the table. Dev reclined into his chair. Crossed his right ankle over his left knee, and from where I stood, I could only just see him thumbing the silk of his tie. I knew he would turn round before he did, and sure enough, a moment later, my palm resting on the glass between us, his neck craned slowly round. He looked right at me.

It was only a moment, but that one moment dragged on and on, frozen between heartbeats. Then he waved. A small wave, his hand travelling no more than a couple of degrees, his fingers in the shape of a gun. A second later, he turned back round.

Was that it?

I turned and ran. My senses boiled up. Frothed up and out. I couldn't breathe. I felt the weight of it rising, tipping. I barely made it to the ladies' before it all came retching out.

Chapter 13

I convinced Nani not to come over. She, like everybody else, thought Shay lived with me, and that there would be someone to take care of me. I holed myself up in my flat, ordered ginger ale and crackers online. Shay came over once with soup and antibiotics, but I insisted she didn't need to come again. I didn't want company; I just wanted to sleep. Close my eyes, and have everything disappear.

I spent three days cocooned in my bed, and by the Friday, I still hadn't gone back in to work. I woke up early and glanced over at the bedside table. It was covered in tissues and magazines and stale, half-drunk cups of soup. I'd had my work BlackBerry turned off all week, and as I was staring at it, wondering what would happen if I turned it on, I heard a knock at the door.

'Shay?'

Another knock. I willed myself out of bed and dragged myself across the hardwood, as if wading through two feet of fresh snow. I tripped over my sweatpants as they slid down beneath my hip bones and, stumbling, hiked them back up. I crossed through the living room and unlocked the door. 'Did you forget your key?'

'Raina.'

His voice pinched the nerves on the back of my neck, at the base of my spine. I hadn't heard it in two years.

He leaned in and hugged me, and without meaning to, I smelled him. His hair. His cologne, the one he'd been wearing since his eighteenth birthday, the first gift he'd had from his parents that cost over ten pounds. He pulled away, leaving his hands on my shoulders. He was so close to me – and I couldn't believe it. All I could think was that I wasn't wearing a bra. That I hadn't brushed my teeth or hair in two days.

'It's so good to see you, Raina.'

'What are you doing here?'

His hands fell to his sides. 'But not like this. You look pretty vile.' He winked. 'Pretty *and* vile.'

'Dev. What are you doing here?'

'Your doorman let me in. Mac.' Dev perched himself on a stool. 'I told him I had a delivery for the sick girl in 1206. Hell of a bloke, that Mac. Talked my ear off about the pizzeria he used to work for in Napoli – some great chef, he was.'

'Also great at keeping out intruders.'

Dev took off his coat, then looked back at me like nothing had changed. Like it was the most natural thing for him to be sitting in my kitchen.

He continued. 'Turns out I've been to his old restaurant. Coincidence, or what? Amore Mio – bang on the harbour.'

I stiffened. 'You went to Italy?'

'Last Christmas. With lads from uni for a stag do – what do you call it here again? A bachelor party? The pizza; the *vino rosso*. Room was right on the beach. The sunset.' He shook his head. 'Raina, you should have seen it.'

I nodded stiffly.

'Darling, don't look at me like that.'

I didn't respond.

'Zoey told me where you lived.'

'Did she.'

'Yes. Bright girl. Heard great things from Bill.'

'Yes,' I said, icily, 'Zoey's amazing – I already know that.'

'You're angry with me.'

'I'm not angry.'

'You didn't reply to any of my emails this week.' He smiled, the corners of his lips folding up the way they did. 'I know you're angry. I still know you.'

Did he?

'I'm sorry I didn't warn you I was coming. I was in for a quick meeting. I didn't even know you'd be in the office—'

'You didn't know I'd be in the office I *work* in?'

'Literally, Raina, I got off the plane, went to the meeting, got on another plane and flew to New York.' He scratched his head. 'I knew you were pissed off when I saw you looking at me like that. I should have told you. I know that now.'

'Yes, you should have.'

'Bloody hell. Don't you think I'm nervous too? It's been ages.' He reached for me, wrapped his hands round both of my wrists. 'I only just got back this morning. And look,' he gestured to his wristwatch, 'it's still morning. And where's the first place I come?'

I felt numb, and I didn't know what to say. Or how to feel. I'd been waiting to see him – waiting for this moment – for so long, and now it felt too sudden. Sprung on me before I was ready. It all felt too fast. I shook my wrists loose and grabbed one of the glasses lined up on the counter. I sipped, choking on the dusty film that had collected on the surface, and he laughed.

'Don't drink that, silly.' He flicked the switch on the kettle and pointed towards the bedroom. 'Go and lie down. I'm right behind you.'

I didn't bother tidying my room. I crawled beneath the covers and pulled them over my head. I tried to breathe in and out the way Nani had taught me when she decided I needed to learn how to meditate. I wondered what she would say if she knew he was here, in my apartment, wedging his way back into my life. Would she be angry with him? Angry with me for being weak? Tell me I deserved better? Did I?

A few minutes later I heard footsteps, and then felt Dev sit down beside me. He peeled the duvet down beneath my chin and I opened my eyes.

'Tell me why you're here.'

'You're not well, darling.'

'No. *Here*. Canada. Where I live.' I didn't recognise my own voice. 'After you swore how much you hated the "New World" – that you didn't even want to *visit* where I was from.' My voice cracked and I closed my eyes. 'Why did you move *here*?'

'It's not exactly clear yet.'

'Of course not.'

'Corporate is doing some—'

'Rearranging, yes, you told me.'

'And I'm letting the pieces fall where they may.'

'So you being here is temporary.'

'Maybe. Well, I don't know yet.' He put the mug down

on my bedside table. 'For now it's been decided that I'll be going back and forth between here and the New York office. Others too, perhaps—'

'So you coming here had nothing to do with me.' I was fighting back tears. My eyes and glands and everything, it seemed, were swelling.

'No.' He sighed. 'But now that I'm here, Raina, now that I see you …'

'What?'

'I just don't know. Everything is so bloody *grey*.' He lay down next to me, his head only inches from mine. 'I need time. To sort things out.' He brushed the hair off my forehead. 'If it's possible, I'm even more lost than when you left.'

'Good.' I rolled away from him.

'Please, darling. I need you in my life. You've always been so good for me.' I didn't answer. I *was* good for him. Before me, he'd go for weeks without eating green vegetables. He'd forget to eat, to sleep, obsessed by a file, a problem he couldn't figure out. I'd bought him vitamins and baby aspirin, towels that didn't reek of mildew. Outside, he was tailored suits and the brick walls of a flat he could afford to buy outright; but inside, he was cavernous. Undiscoverable. A boy who played with his power like a small child played house.

He sighed. 'All right, I suppose I'll let you rest then. They'll be expecting me.'

I rolled back over. 'You're leaving?'

'Don't you want me to?'

I willed myself to say yes. *Yes*. Leave. And not just Toronto – but definitively. Get that perfect picture we had of us together out of my head, my heart and my life. *Yes.* Leave. Let me start again without you. But I didn't say yes.

I couldn't.

He stayed with me for ten more minutes, rubbing my forehead, chattering away like he always could, filling the dead air in my bedroom with titbits of his life. How the radiator in his flat in Clerkenwell Green was still on the blink. The mind-numbing delays on the Piccadilly Line; how, thanks to Transport For London, he'd nearly missed the most important meeting of his career. My head on the pillow, I watched him the way I always had. Leaning back on the headboard, his eyes lit up like a little boy's, hands gesturing wildly as he explained the new strategy for his annual targets.

Two years later, Dev was back in my life, exactly how I had left him. Still threaded with ambition. Still a man who wanted me. Still a man who needed time.

Chapter 14

I saw him through the glass door before he opened it. He hesitated, surveying everyone in the fifty-fourth-floor conference room before slowly pushing the door open. A waiter standing just inside the entrance offered him a mimosa, and Dev, startled, almost dropped it as he picked it up off the tray.

He walked closer to me, where I was sheltered just behind the edge of the bar. I was about to move towards him when a girl I didn't recognise clustered in with some of the junior analysts and waved him over. Dev smiled and then walked in their direction.

'Who's that?' I asked Zoey.

She looked up from her phone and followed my eyes across the room. 'Bridget,' she said, and then looked down again. Zoey had been cool with me ever since I'd left her alone at Shay's engagement party. I'd apologised profusely and she said she'd forgiven me, but I wasn't so sure she had.

'Are we OK?' I said after a moment.

'Yes, we're fine.'

'You're still angry—'

'I'm *not*.' Zoey looked up and sighed. 'I'm not mad. It's just hard to see you pine after him like that.'

It was hard for *her*? Pretending to Nani that I was

interested in meeting the potential husbands she was finding for me online – *that* was hard.

Having Dev back, and still not having him at all, was
hard.

It was November already, and each day the cold crept in
bit by bit. Each day, in the same way I didn't know whether
there'd be snow on the ground during my walk to work, I
didn't know whether Dev would be there when I arrived.

New York. Chicago. Santiago. He was just as likely to be
gone as he was to be in his office one floor above me. But
he emailed constantly, and when he was around, he always
dropped by and asked me for a coffee, or lunch. I forced
myself to appear disinterested and not ask questions about
when he'd be around, or when he'd be ready, even though
they were burning inside me.

'When did he get back?' Zoey asked.

I shrugged. 'I didn't even know he was coming in today.'

Human Resources had organised a sixtieth birthday
party for Bill, a Saturday brunch affair at the office, but
Dev hadn't mentioned whether or not he was coming – and
about this, too, I hadn't asked. I looked over in his direction.
He was talking to the group, and I watched Bridget flick
her long, shiny black hair. She was very pretty, and young,
with a healthy glow like she was vegetarian and never ate
junk food.

'Raina, stop it. She's just sucking up to him – she's like
that.' Zoey touched my elbow, holding it until I turned to
face her. 'Let's go and get something to eat.'

'Do you like him?'

'Who, Dev?' Zoey scrunched her mouth up, then took
a sip of her drink. 'Yeah, I do. He's been a great mentor to

all of us. All the juniors like him.' She nodded again. 'Very experienced.'

'And do you like him for *me*?'

Zoey looked annoyed again, but I didn't let up.

'Do you?'

'How am I supposed to know if he's good for you?'

I nodded, and looked back towards Dev. He was still talking to Bridget, and I wondered if Zoey was right. Was she really just trying to make a good impression? Or was she flirting – trying something with him? I shuddered. I'd looked at him like that too.

'What does Shay think?'

'About Dev being back?'

'Yeah.'

'I don't know. I haven't told her.' I turned back to Zoey. 'Don't look so surprised. She hates him.'

'Raina, she's your best friend. I understand your Nani not knowing – but Shay?'

A waiter passed with a tray of mimosas, and I wished I could reach for one. But Nani had called, again, saying that I needed to drive home after the party and help her move old boxes out of the garage.

'She doesn't need to know.' I glared back at her. 'She's busy with work. With Julien, and planning her wedding and all that.'

'Really.'

'Plus she'd probably kill him before I...'

Before I what?

I started to walk over to the buffet, ignoring Zoey's glances as she trailed behind me, knowing she wanted to ask me the same question. What *was* I doing?

I reached for two plates and handed one to Zoey. We queued behind a few bankers I recognised from Chicago. They hovered over the olives, debating the greens and blacks, chilli and salty, oiled and preserved.

I felt Zoey's hand on my wrist. 'I think you should tell Shay,' I heard her say. 'I can't help you the way she can, Raina. You're going crazy in there, I can tell. This isn't you. You need some perspective.'

'I have perspective,' I said coolly. 'It's been two years, and I still ...' I lowered my voice. 'I am still in love with him, Zoey. What am I supposed to do?'

'You're supposed to tell your best friend.'

'I can't.' I grabbed the spoon, dished olives onto her plate and then another spoonful onto mine. 'I won't. I *can*, but I won't.'

We inched forward, stopping again in front of the salads.

'Your Nani. She seems modern—'

'Zoey, try and understand.' I turned to face her. 'I'm not telling anyone he's back. So either you help me deal with that, or leave me to deal with it my own way.'

'Fine,' she said evenly. 'I'll help.'

'Thank you.'

'What do you need help with?' She reached over me for the bread. 'Besides all your work Bill keeps sending me.'

'I need Nani to stop pressuring me to find a husband. That's what I need.' We reached the end of the queue and I glanced around, looking for a free place at the tables. 'Until I figure out everything with Dev, I need her to stop forcing me to go on dates.'

I turned to look back at Dev, but he wasn't there. I searched the conference room – the buffet, the bar, the opposite edge – but he'd moved away from the crowd. He was with Bridget. They were standing near the entrance, away from everyone else. He was leaning against the wall, her hand on his shoulder, and he was laughing.

He was fucking *laughing*.

And I was the butt of the joke.

I could feel myself shaking, and I handed my plate to Zoey.

'Raina, where are you going?'

'Home,' I said, without turning round. I pushed my way through the crowd, trying to keep cool, trying to keep from crying. I had to pass them to leave. I kept my face down as I walked by, but he saw me.

'Raina, there you are.'

I had to stop. I forced my feet to slow down, to come to a deliberate halt. I looked up, tensed the muscles in my cheeks. 'Hello, Dev.' I nodded, and then glanced briefly at Bridget. 'Hi there.'

'Hello.' She had a slight Chinese accent, and perfect teeth.

'Leaving already?' Dev asked.

My heart was beating fast, too fast, and I took a deep breath. And then another. 'Yes. I have a date.'

'A date?'

I pushed through the glass door without replying. My feet sped up, and I manoeuvred down the hall, trying not to run. I pressed the lift button, two, three, four times, praying it would hurry. I pushed again, and finally it arrived. I could feel him running behind me and I flung myself into the lift, and a second later, as the doors were closing, he wedged his leg in and the doors stopped short.

'What was *that*?'

He was angry, his jaw tense, and I pushed the close button again and again, but it wouldn't shut with him there.

'I'm late. I have to go.'

'Raina, stop it.' He fought his way into the lift as a bell started to ring. He put his hands on my arms as the doors closed and we started drifting down. 'What was that?'

'What was *what*, Dev?'

'Please.' He pulled me closer as I tried to move back, to distance myself.

'I…'

But then his mouth was on mine; his body, his heat, pressed up against me. My back to the wall, he kissed me – his hands through my hair, on my neck, my waist. I was burning, my senses on overload; I wanted to push him away and bring him closer at the same time.

Another bell chimed, and he pulled himself off me just as the door opened. I was out of breath, and I stood up and away from the wall and moved forward through the door. I walked slowly through the lobby. I could feel him a few steps behind me, and just before I reached the door, I turned round to face him.

'I don't know…' I breathed out. 'I can't—'

'I didn't mean to make you jealous,' he said. He inched closer towards me. 'She's on my team. She's just young, and ambitious. That's it.'

I nodded, looking at my hands, wondering how he managed to make me feel so small and like I was his entire world in the same breath.

'Do you really have a date?'

I thought about how Nani had instructed me to come

home to move boxes at precisely 5 p.m., but how we didn't
have anything in the garage she wanted to get rid of. I did
have a date. By now, she was fed up with me refusing to
meet the new men she'd been suggesting, so tonight there'd
be another ambush. There would be an Ajit or a Prasad
or a Raj waiting for me at home, and there was nothing I
could do about it.

'It's OK if you do.' Dev crossed his arms, and I could see
on his face he was struggling, putting up a fight.

But for what? Why couldn't he give in – give in to *us*?

'I wouldn't like it.' He put his hand gently to my face,
my neck. 'But you need to do what makes you happy, love.'

Dev made me happy. He *would* make me happy.

'You're off on a date, then?'

And even though I hated myself for it, I knew that I
would keep waiting. I had to.

'No.' I shook my head. 'I don't have a date. I just ... have
to go.'

Chapter 15

I always imagined he'd take me back to Brussels to propose. Maybe at that hotel on Rue Belliard, or in the crowded square in front of the Royal Palace. At Parc d'Egmont, where he'd pretended to know how to flamenco, and guided me around the wet grass with his hands locked round my waist.

'Raina, did you hear that?'

I looked up from my food. 'Sorry?'

'Did you *hear* that?'

I looked between Nani and … I'd already forgotten his name. I shook my head.

Nani touched her napkin to her lips, as if embarrassed on my behalf. 'Neil was telling us about—'

'Auntie, it's nothing.'

'What is this *nothing* business?' She sat up proudly in her chair. 'You protected this country, like in the movies, like that man with brown hair.'

'You were in the army?' I asked him, trying to make an effort.

'Just so they would pay my fees for dental school.'

'Clever.'

Nani pressed another naan into his hand. 'More?'

'I'm good, Auntie.'

'Please. Eat more.' She lunged for the raita, ladled it onto his plate. 'You're too skinny.'

'Let me finish this, and then I'll have more.' Neil wiped his hands on a napkin and touched her hand. 'Auntie, please sit down and join us. I can't eat until you eat.'

'Nonsense.'

'I insist.' He stood up and guided her to her own chair. 'Don't tell my ma,' he said, leaning in close to her as he helped her sit. 'But this – *Auntie* – it's incredible. Much better than her cooking.'

Nani arched her eyebrows at me. 'So cute, Raina. And *so* sweet.'

Then there was that time that Dev almost proposed. Or could have. Two months before I'd left, when we took a Sunday morning off from work and caught the 55 to Chinatown for dim sum. The sun was out, and in the grey February cold we walked back, wound our way through Soho, Holborn and then right through Hatton Garden. The Jewellery Quarter. Where men like Dev went to buy a ring.

We walked by one shop and then another – endless windows of round cuts and princess cuts, gold and platinum. In their reflection I caught him staring, and I looked down at my shoes.

'What if—'

'Do you reckon—'

'You first.' He moved me out of the pavement traffic and against a shop wall. The wind had blown hair into my mouth, and he gently brushed it aside.

'No,' I breathed. 'You go.'

Was this it? I remembered thinking, hoping, as he looked at the sky, the brick walls and his shoes – anywhere but at me. He leaned in. He opened his mouth. And then, just when it could have happened – when, replayed a million times in my head, it *should* have happened – I felt a vibration through his touch, and he reached into his pocket.

It wasn't it.

'I should take this,' he'd said, darting briskly across the street, his BlackBerry wedged against his shoulder, me half a stride behind him the whole walk home. And by the time we got back to his flat, and he'd put down his keys on the coffee table with a tired clang, the moment had passed. Our laptops were back open, and our lives resumed their usual course.

Nani's voice roused me. 'The one with Tom Hanks?' she asked. She reached across the table and spooned more daal onto my plate. Eyeing me, she knocked the spoon hard against the ceramic. 'Raina, what do you think?'

'Huh?'

'*Saving Private Ryan*,' said Neil. 'Great movie.'

'I haven't seen it,' I said.

He clutched his chest. 'You haven't seen it?'

'No.'

'It is on movie channel all the time,' said Nani.

'I'll have to check it out.'

'You should.' Neil pinched off a piece of naan and dunked it in the saag. 'Maybe we should watch it sometime.'

Sometime. What Dev always liked to say when I asked him to go with me to the movies or to the theatre. To visit the Cotswolds or Brighton, or even Dorset for the weekend.

'We don't really take weekends, do we, darling?' he'd say. 'We will, though, sometime.'

'Raina loves reading too,' I heard Nani say. 'Not just movies.'

I winced, and I felt Nani and Neil looking at me.

'Don't you, Raina?'

I nodded, avoiding their glances. To Nani, was Neil the picture-perfect son-in-law, and father of my children? A man who would rouse me from my own limp life and, magically, make everything OK? Nani wanted me to fall in love with him, leap after him. Skip over Mom's generation and turn straight into her. She wanted this kitchen table full, full of hungry, smiling people, a fantasy no one in her family had ever been able to fulfil. Neil was exactly what she wanted.

But I wanted Dev.

'What do you like to read?' Neil asked.

I moved my food around with my fork. 'You know. Whatever's around.'

'And who's that written by?'

I looked up. He was smiling at me. His perfect, genuine smile. Straight teeth – unlike Dev's, pale white and splintered, hidden beneath a smirk. Was Dev still at the party, I wondered? Why wasn't *he* at our kitchen table?

'Well,' I said finally, looking at Neil, 'I have a lot of favourite books.'

'Pick one.' Neil leaned towards me.

'My friend Zoey has just lent me *Catcher in the Rye*.' I shrugged. 'I never read it when I was young. I like it.'

'That's one of my favourites.'

'Yeah, well, a lot of people like it.'

Neil grinned, and I caught him looking at my neck. I saw that familiar flaring of heat, and I winced.

'Neil,' said Nani, 'I can make you chai?'

Was it only that afternoon that Dev had finally pressed his lips against mine, the way he used to? A moment of blinding exhilaration, and then the metal doors parting, the fluorescent light pouring in. Pressure roused in me. Why wasn't *Dev* here? Why wasn't I with him? I squeezed my eyes shut. But what about Nani? I loved them both so much. *Too much*, as Shay liked to say. Loved them more than I knew how to understand. Why couldn't they fit together?

'Sure, Auntie. Would you like some help?'

'You sit. I will make.'

Nani stood up from the table, and the moment she turned round, I grabbed my phone from my back pocket. I checked the screen, and there it was. A message from Dev – from thirty-eight minutes before.

Raina – I need to know you're all right. Did you drive safely? The party is shit without you here.

Just then, another email popped up.

I can't stop thinking about that kiss.

I could feel the saliva stale on my tongue, the creases in my cheek. Dev wanted me. I *knew* he still wanted me.

Why had I left the party? Why had I run, *again*? Why hadn't I just stood there, face to face, and told him to choose? Told him to pick me – this time *really* love me – or let me go?

'Are you OK?' I heard Neil's voice. 'Raina?'

What was I doing here, with Neil? I needed Dev. I needed time. My breathing was uneven, jagged. I felt sweat sitting on my skin, my body flushing heavy and hot.

I was panting. I could feel the blood pulsing in my ears

and down my neck, through my heart. I touched my face.
It was wet.

Nani's voice, drawing closer. 'Ill again?'

'I'm sorry,' I gasped, 'I can't do this.' I stood up so suddenly my chair tipped over. 'I can't do any of this.'

I could hear her saying goodbye to Neil at the door. Making
excuses – that I was still ill, overburdened at work. Then I
heard the front door thud shut, and I'd turned face down
onto the pillow when I heard her start to climb the stairs.
I heard the door creak open, the hum of the light as she
switched it on.

'I made ginger tea.'

I felt her sit down on the edge of my bed; the shifting
of her body weight as a sigh rolled out. 'You should have
told me you were still feeling ill. I would have postponed.'

Postponed something I hadn't even agreed to? That she
and Auntie Sarla, and probably even Shay, had concocted
for their mutual benefit? So there was no Raina to worry
about?

'Tell me, where are you feeling ill?'

'I'm not *ill*.' I tugged at the covers and wrapped them
tighter around me. 'I'm not sick.'

'You didn't eat much.' I felt Nani's hand on my back and
I resisted pulling away. 'I wrapped your plate and put it in
fridge.'

I didn't answer.

'OK, so you didn't like Neil. Maybe he is a bit boring,
nah?' She laughed. 'I have found another. His name is
Chirag. He—'

'Will you just stop it?' I barked into the pillow. 'I saw my

132

profile on IndianSingles.com. I know where you're finding them now. Am I *so* undesirable you had to put up a marriage ad for me? Huh?'

I heard Nani sigh. 'I am sorry, my sweet.'

'Well, you should be.'

'I should have asked first. I can take it down, *nah*? It was silly idea your Auntie Sarla gave me. We can look elsewhere. Not online, then. I'll find others.'

Elsewhere. Others. It suddenly occurred to me that she wasn't going to stop. This was it. Until I got married, this would be my life. But what about Dev? *He* was my life.

'Sarla says she knows a nice boy in—'

'Nani. *Please.*' I was choking. I couldn't breathe. 'Please, *please* stop.' I was crying now. 'Just stop. I can't – can't take this any more.'

She didn't reply, and, my cheeks burning with shame, I buried my face deeper into the pillow. How could I tell her? Would she understand why I was waiting for Dev?

'Raina,' I heard Nani say after a moment, her voice wavering, 'I must ask you something.'

'What?' I grumbled.

'Again at dinner you mentioned this Zoey girl. You mention her often.' Nani paused. 'Is she more than friend to you?'

I opened my mouth to answer, and then realised what she meant. Was she asking me if I was in a relationship with Zoey?

'I have seen things in movies, you know. And on *Ellen*.' Her hand, momentarily frozen, had thawed, resuming its maternal massaging of my back. 'And I was thinking, it is so common now, *nah*? It is very *normal*. And I thought that maybe, maybe this is why you are resisting marriage. Maybe I am not finding you the right match because…'

She trailed off, and the silence hung thick in the air. I could hear her breathing, the hum of the lights. The sound of a car going past. The distant tick of the cuckoo clock echoing in the kitchen. Seconds passed, and it occurred to me that Nani didn't just think I was gay; she was OK with it.

'Is this why you've been unhappy with me, my sweet?' Her voice came out tentatively, and I felt her lean down and kiss me on the back of the head, her other hand brush stray hairs away from my cheek.

What had just happened? Was it really possible that the idea of me being gay didn't upset her? My breath was trapped in my lungs and my heart pounded. I knew I should say something. Letting her believe I was gay couldn't be right. But for some reason, already it made more sense than the truth. If I were gay, there'd be no marriage to arrange. If I were gay, just for a while, there'd be no more dates. No more pressure or ambushes. There'd be time. There'd be Dev.

I should have told Nani the truth. I wanted to – everything, all of it – but I couldn't.

I didn't know how. So I didn't say anything.

Chapter 16
20 May 2013

'You're getting old, love.'

Raina giggles, and rolls over to face him. 'How sweet of you to remind me.'

It is still dark outside on Clerkenwell Green, and the only light comes from the touch lamp on Dev's bedside table. In its warm, buttery glow, Raina can vaguely see the outline of his body nestled next to hers, the profile of his nose and eyelashes as he moves his head on the pillow.

'You're properly over the hill now.'

'Oh, *shush*.'

'Let me think,' he says, moving his face closer to hers. 'When I turned twenty-six, I—'

'Bawled like a baby?'

'Got promoted.'

'Well then,' whispers Raina as he kisses her nose, 'why don't you promote me?'

They hit the snooze button three, four times, and on the fifth push, Dev declares he will forgo his morning routine at the gym. Raina kisses him sleepily, and smiles. They both work long hours, but despite the demands on their time, their health – even, at times, their relationship – Raina has never been so happy. It is her birthday, the one-year anniversary with the man she loves – and she lives in *London*, a thriving, humming city that fiercely loves her back. She works in the very heart, the very centre of the world, and sometimes, lying there in a dreamlike state, Dev curled around her, it's hard to believe this is her life.

It is nothing like her Nani's; a limb of her husband's journey into a new world, working hard, with little respect for a community to which Raina never even felt she belonged. It is nothing like her mother's, either; a life disjointed and misunderstood, carelessly formed at the fringes of others'.

For the first time, Raina is finding her own way. She is doing things on her own terms, without anyone telling her who and why, how and where; she is living a life that is completely her own. These days, she is practically living at Dev's.

With him, Raina feels like a different kind of Indian.

Together, they are modern Indians. Ones who don't go to temple just to prove to others they believe in God; who can try a non-Indian cuisine – blander, with less spice – and enjoy it. Together, they command power and respect; dine, drink and travel without worrying about money the way their families did. And, Raina often muses, they will raise their children differently too. They will teach them that they don't need to be a doctor to succeed in life; they will teach them to believe that they are good enough just as they are.

Raina and Dev are kissing, and his hand is up her shirt when a phone buzzes on the bedside table. Dev removes his hand and reaches for it.

'Oh, it's yours.'

Raina grabs it, and a moment later, frowns. 'It's Nani.'

'Go on, then.'

Raina takes a deep breath and accepts the call. 'Hi, Nani.'

'Haaappy bird-*day*,' she sings, almost screams into the phone. She is loud, so loud that Raina uses her hand to cover Dev's mouth, to muffle the laughter. Raina has tried many times to teach her Nani that mobile phones these days are better than landlines; that she needn't yell into the phone just because Raina is overseas.

'Are you having a happy bird-day?' Nani asks. 'Did I wake?'

'No, no. I'm up. Just getting ready for work.'

'*Aacha.*'

Raina glances at the clock. It is past midnight in Toronto. 'Why are you up so late?'

'Oh, just missing my Raina,' says Nani. 'You are twenty-*six* now, *nah*?'

Dev mouths *so old*, and Raina lightly pushes him away. He smiles and closes his eyes, rests on his back beside her.

'How is Dev?' Nani asks.

'Good.'

'He will have a nice birthday for you? If you were home, I'd make you your favourite—'

'Yes, Nani. I'll see him at work, and then we're having dinner with friends.'

'What are you eating?'

'Turkish, I think.'

'It is not Thanksgiving—'

Raina laughs. 'No, Nani. Turkish – from Turkey, the country. Middle Eastern food. Like couscous?'

'Hah?'

'It's kind of like rice.'

'Are you eating enough? Are you being healthy?'

'Yes, Nani.'

There is a pause – long, palpable – and Raina wonders if her Nani is still there.

'I'd like to meet Dev,' she says finally.

Raina turns to look at him. His eyes are discernibly closed, and Raina pokes him until he opens them.

'He wants to meet you too.'

'When?'

'I don't know.' Raina leans back in bed, stares at her toes poking out from under the covers. 'You know you can come and visit any time.'

'He can come here?'

Raina nods into the phone, then says, 'Yeah. Maybe.'

She had asked Dev to come with her on her last trip home, but he had said he was too busy with work. Lately she has been thinking about asking him again to come home and meet Nani and Shay, to see a glimpse of her old life, but she is afraid to bring it up; afraid he'll say no again.

'*Beta*, it has been long time now. It is time for Dev to visit—'

'Nani, please, not today.'

'You are planning to marry him, and I don't know if he's nice boy. I don't know his family,' Nani continues, her voice growing louder, and Dev rolls over onto his side.

'He cannot come and meet us? He is Indian, *nah*? He does not understand how things should be—'

'*Please*, not now,' Raina whispers. She looks over at Dev, and sees that he's crawling out of bed. Without looking at her, wearing only his pyjama shorts, he walks out of the bedroom.

'Dev cannot at least *call* and tell me his intentions? His parents cannot call me—'

A panic boils up inside Raina, the warmth beside her suddenly gone.

'And you will stay in that country for *him*? You—'

This is what she fears: Dev walking away. Dev leaving her, taking everything, her whole life, away with him.

'Nani,' she says sweetly, placating. Her hand on her chest, she forces herself to calm down; forces out the words that her Nani needs to hear – that, right now, Raina herself needs to say.

Dev and Raina will get married.

Dev and Raina are in love, and there is absolutely nothing to worry about.

After a few moments, she hangs up and puts her phone back on the bedside table. The bedroom door has closed behind him, and she can't hear anything – just a dustcart outside the window, beeping, rumbling back and forth along Clerkenwell Green.

'Dev?'

She is cold, and pulls the blanket round her. Has he already hopped in the shower, started his day without her?

Is she – is her Nani – scaring him away?

They are together, committed, in love – but marriage, a life in permanency, is still far away. Together, Raina and Dev decided they wouldn't be *Indian* about their relationship: their families wouldn't be involved, and they would date and take their time. They would enjoy life, and only talk about the future in an abstract way that didn't tie them down, didn't tie them together.

They decided it *together*, didn't they?

Raina sits up. She is about to get out of bed when Dev

pushes the door open. He stands in the doorway with a sleepy smile, holding two cups of tea.

Raina's mind relaxes, her muscles unclench. He walks to the edge of the bed and places the tea on the bedside table.

She smiles at him. 'Come back to bed.'

He drops to his knees on the mattress and crawls over to her. 'Anything you say, love.'

'Sorry about that,' Raina says after a moment.

He laughs. 'I have a Nani too.'

His family live only a forty-five-minute tube journey from the city. She thinks about asking when she'll meet them, but decides against it.

Raina hears the metal gates of the shop across the road opening, and she glances at the clock. 'Wait, what time is it?'

He groans, rolls more fully on top of her.

'What time is your meeting?'

He opens one eye, then shuts it again.

'Honey, you really need to get up.' With half her strength, she tries to shift him and sit up, but he is a dead weight on top of her.

'Dev?'

Sleepily, he kisses her chest. 'Five more minutes.' He turns his head, resting on his other cheek. 'I can't make it through the day without this, Raina.'

Chapter 17

Within days of 'coming out' to Nani, strangely, I was beginning to feel like my old self. I'd started sleeping through the night. Running. Eating normal meals and not bags of chips for dinner. It was as if all the pressure was off my chest and I could finally breathe. No forced dates and looming deadline. No worrying about Nani, or whether Dev would be ready before Nani shoved me down the aisle towards some guy whose name I could barely pronounce. Finally, I had time.

'I don't see how this is a good idea,' Zoey had said, when I'd finally worked up the courage to tell her.

'You think this is a bad idea?'

'No. Not necessarily.' She scratched her head. 'But it's not a good one. Letting your Nani believe you're gay to get out of a few bad dates? It's actually the stupidest thing I have ever heard.'

'A few? I was practically getting an email every morning with her top ten matches, organised by height, weight, income tax bracket—'

'All right, I get it.' She bit her lower lip. 'Does anyone else know?'

'About Dev being back?' I shook my head. 'No.'

'Raina, no.' Zoey rolled her eyes and lowered her voice. 'Does anyone else know that that you're a "lesbian"?'

'Kris does. He came over that evening, and I kind of had to tell him.'

'And what did he say?'

'Called me a brat and then poured us both a whisky.' I shrugged. 'He's never been that interested in my life.'

Zoey nodded slowly. 'So the damage is minimal. Good. It's not too late to undo it.'

'No.' I shook my head. 'Not yet.'

'What? Why?'

I looked at the floor.

'Tell me. Why are you doing this? I want you to admit it to me.'

'I...'

'If you have to lie about him to the people you love, can he really be worth it?'

Was she right?

Dev had taken me for lunch only an hour before – a full forty-five minutes between meetings with our BlackBerries on silent. Reminiscing at the corner table over pesto and Chardonnay, it was as if nothing had changed. He was the man I had fallen for – and I was still the woman in love with him. Every time he emailed, whenever I heard his voice passing by in the corridor, my mouth curled into a smile. Dev was back in my life and I was happy again ... wasn't I?

Now that Nani's arrangement was off the table, every morning there was that same flutter in my stomach. A feeling of delight, of not being able to wait to get to the office and see if Dev was there. With every passing moment

I grew more and more sure that this – that *he* – was it. I knew that the last two years would only be one chapter of our story. Part of the plot. Dev needed time, and finally, we had it. The Bollywood struggle behind us, it was time for the third act.

'He's worth it,' I said. He had to be.

The moment I hadn't denied to Nani that I was gay, everything changed. Harder than her questions I didn't know the answers to, more disconcerting than a fresh list of potential husbands, was her concern. Her empathy. Accepting who she thought I was seemingly defied everything she had grown up to stand for. It was as if ten years of *The Ellen Show* had changed her into a woman I hadn't realised she'd become. And while it impressed me, it was downright baffling.

Shouldn't she have been angry? No one in our community was gay, or at least publicly out of the closet. It just wasn't something Indian people did. No matter how progressive she'd become in recent years, how was this acceptable to her?

The idea of me with another woman did not upset her; rather, she couldn't wrap her head around why Zoey and I were just friends. Didn't I care about her? Wouldn't *Zoey* make a great partner for me? Nani wouldn't let up, and I started to avoid her and visited her less and less often.

It was harder to put on the act face to face, and until Dev was ready – until I could face her with the truth – I didn't want to see her. I didn't know how I would 'come out' again, or how she would respond. But as I wrestled with my friendship with Dev, the few hours we spent together every time he was in town never culminating in more than a hug, sometimes a kiss, I couldn't bring myself to think about it. I couldn't even imagine what I would say, or how long – another week, or month – I would have to keep up the charade.

'Less than five months now! Can you believe?' Auntie Sarla's voice boomed from the back seat of my Jeep.

'Coming quickly, Shaylee!' said Nani, reaching forward and patting Shay on the shoulder. Shay glanced over at me, grinning, shaking her head from side to side in mock excitement.

I turned up the heat and wrapped my scarf tighter around my neck as we waited at a red light. The four of us had spent the day running wedding errands together, and even though it felt like I hadn't seen Shay in months, we'd spoken only about the wedding all day. Discussions about tiered cakes and Hindu priests, chiffon lining and perfectly timed flower deliveries were held from the back seat. Shay listened to Auntie Sarla plan her wedding with glazed disinterest, piping up only to change the radio station during the drive from one supplier to another, or to mock Auntie Sarla's accent.

After our last appointment at a ribbon stockists', we drove back towards home. It was only late afternoon and already it looked like dusk, night slowly falling over the icy roads. While Nani and Auntie Sarla were speaking in Hindi about the guest list, Shay leaned in towards me.

'Are we OK?' she whispered.

I concentrated on the road, carefully steering around a patch of ice. 'Of course, why?'

From the side, I could see Shay still looking at me, and then she looked back at the road. 'How's dating – have you met anyone you like?'

Mid-sentence, Auntie Sarla stopped talking and her face appeared between us. 'You live together and you don't *know*, Shaylee?'

Shay looked at me and then back at Auntie Sarla. 'Raina and I work different hours. Remember, Ma? I don't see her much.'

She nodded, and then slid a stubby finger across the glove box. 'Raina, do you ever clean your car?'

'Sarla,' I heard Nani say. 'Don't interfere. We're going to have accident.'

Auntie Sarla's face disappeared. 'Well, *someone* should interfere with that girl.'

'Ma,' said Shay. 'Don't start.'

'Speak to this child, Suvali. She will never get married this way.'

I pressed my foot harder against the brake pedal, wishing I could kick it.

'There is nothing to speak of, Sarla,' I heard Nani say. 'Who Raina marries is Raina's decision.'

'What marriage? There won't be a marriage if she keeps on like this. Not like my Shaylee.'

'Ma, don't bring me into this.'

'Raina is being selfish—'

'Sarla, enough!' Nani's voice prickled, and the car fell silent. 'Do not lecture us like this. I will handle my own girl.' I turned back to face the front, slowly lifted my foot off the brake as the light turned green.

'I have confidence in whatever she decides,' said Nani.

I saw Nani glancing at me in the rear-view mirror, and as I accelerated through the intersection, a wave of guilt washed through me. What exactly had I decided?

Chapter 18

No one said much on the drive back to the suburbs. We dropped Shay and Auntie Sarla off, and then I drove Nani home. She insisted I come inside for dinner, and wouldn't accept my excuse about work deadlines, my wet laundry still in the machine. After almost five minutes of bickering in the drive, her voice crawling an octave higher with each breath, I turned off the ignition and agreed to come in.

Dread washed over me as I walked into the house. I knew what was coming, and I wasn't ready to deal with it. I'd skirted round the truth before – small lies about my blind dates, and in high school about missed curfews or why my hair smelled like cigarette smoke – but never like this. I followed her into the kitchen and sat down at the table as she washed her hands and started to dice an onion. Halfway through, she put the knife down and looked at me.

'Why have you not told Shaylee?'

'Nani…'

'I am *proud* of you, Raina. She will be too, *nah*?'

'Please don't—'

'And you won't bring Zoey here for dinner? So I can get to know her properly?'

'I've told you a hundred times, we're not together. Zoey is just a *friend*.'

She wiped her hands on a dishcloth. 'You know, I read a blogger today. Do you know a Edith Windsor? She married a woman, and changed the American constitution.'

'That's not exactly how it happened.'

'This *Edith* – very strange name for a woman, but—'

'I really appreciate you trying to support me, but I just don't want…' I struggled for words. 'I don't need…'

'Yes.' Nani's voice cracked. 'You do *need*. I refuse to be one of those mothers who say it's OK for everyone else to be gay, but not their own child.' She bit down on her lips and looked away. She always looked away when she cried, even when I was young. Even when the worst had just happened.

I walked towards her, wrapped my arms around her and gave her a hug, and she turned round and pressed against me. She was so tiny in my arms, frail yet plump, her head resting beneath my shoulders. After a few moments she pulled away and, wiping her face with the backs of her hands, looked up at me.

Why was I putting up this wall between us? She loved me. She *supported* me – even with something like this. Why wouldn't she approve of me being with Dev again?

Except I wasn't with Dev, not yet. And if I told her that two years later I was still waiting for him, what would she say? Would she look at me the way she looked at Mom?

The daughter who had had a child at sixteen. The daughter who wanted nothing to do with her family, her culture or her traditions. The daughter who was seemingly living with a new man every time she called home.

'What do you need, Raina, huh?' Nani brushed my face with her hand. 'Tell me.'

It was the first time we'd talked face to face since that evening, and I couldn't look at her. I knew what her look was saying to me, and what, if I stayed in the house a moment longer, I would have to tell her.

'Right now, Nani, I just need you.'

She pressed her hand to her heart and smiled at me.

'And maybe a quick run before dinner?'

I dug through my wardrobe and found an old pair of bright pink sneakers and ratty sweatpants. Nani had chopped off the frayed edges around the ankles, and my winter-themed socks peeked out. She stopped me at the door and tucked one of Nana's old newsboy caps on my head and a vomit-brown fleece around my arms.

I stepped outside, immediately thankful for Nana's coat, which, surprisingly, fitted me perfectly. I slammed the door behind me and picked up speed as I bounced down the front steps. The air had chilled and I took a sharp breath, in and out, closing my eyes briefly as I hopped off the pavement, over a partially frozen puddle and ran towards the park. I focused on my breath, on the feel of the road. Anything but Nani, and Dev, trying to will myself once again to feel light.

I ran faster, my nose and mouth numb. I darted off the road and onto the dirt track towards the school, and the faster I ran, the lighter I felt. I ignored the sharp feeling in my lungs and pushed on. I started to sprint, the wind shrieking in my ears as I crossed onto the football field. It was close to dark, the street lights faint behind the old brick of the school. My legs were tired but I pressed on, forcing myself faster and faster, my fists clenched as I swung my arms back and forth.

I ran the long way round the field, and on the final side of the square block, it struck me that it had been fifteen years since the first day I had walked through the doors of a school where so much of consequence seemed to have happened. It was where Shay and I had gone from being the offspring of two friends to being best friends ourselves. Where I'd thrown the winning basket in the city basketball championships. It was where Mom, crying and bloated in the nurse's office, had found out she was pregnant.

I was less than fifty metres from the school, and again I picked up speed. In the distance I could see a lone silhouette shooting a basketball in the courts beside the car park. I drew closer. He looked too old to be a student, too tall, and I watched him arc the ball effortlessly through the hoop again and again. Even in the dark, I could almost see the creases on his face, the square set of his jaw. I rubbed the sweat from my eyelids with the back of my hand, and just as he went up to take another shot, right at the moment I passed him, our eyes met. He missed the shot and the ball ricocheted loudly off the rim.

'Well,' he called out to me, his arms still poised in the air. 'Look who it is.'

'Asher?' I panted, walking up to the fence. I barely recognised him without his beard. 'What are you doing here?'

'Me?' The ball rolled back to him and he grabbed it. 'What are *you* doing here?'

'This is,' I breathed, 'my school.'

'This is *my* school.'

'What, you never graduated?'

150

He ducked the ball between his legs and caught it on the other side. 'I teach here, thank you very much. It's my last term of teacher training.'

'Oh. Well, I used to go here. My grandmother's house is just over there,' I said, gesturing across the field.

'You lived with her, growing up?'

I nodded. 'Mom's in Philadelphia. But Nani is here.'

'A family saga?'

'It's not important.'

'I imagine it is quite important.'

I'd caught my breath, and I ducked through a tear in the metal fence and walked onto the court. Up close, in the shadows cast by the street lights nearby, I noticed again how different Asher looked. His wide nose and lips. The slate grey of his eyes. And even though his beard was gone, there was still something wild about him.

He caught my eye and I looked away. I bent down and tucked my laces into my red and white socks. 'What happened to your face?' I mumbled, standing back up. 'It was quite the ecosystem.'

He smirked. 'I decided to shave it. Thought the kids would take me more seriously.'

'They certainly won't take your ball skills seriously. That last shot there.' I shook my head. 'Just brutal.'

'I was frightened. Thought I had a stalker.'

I lunged forward and tipped the ball out of his arm, catching it with one hand. 'I used to play, you know. High school varsity.'

'Really? I coach the girls' team here.'

'Oh yeah?' I dribbled the ball between my knees in wide figures of eight. 'And how are they?'

'They play like a bunch of girls.'

'So they're *much* better than you.' I shot the ball. It arced too high and bounced off the backboard.

'Someone's out of practice.'

I ran for the loose ball, turned back to him and then sliced it into his chest. 'At least I'm not out of shape.'

'Is that smack talk?' He dribbled the ball towards me, and I crouched down, preparing to swat it from his hands. At the last moment he jutted out to the left, and then right again, dribbling the ball around me and up to the hoop for a layup. He caught the ball after it swished through the net, planted it slowly on his hip and winked.

'Game on.'

Asher won – by a long shot. For every point I managed – a fluke toss from the top of the key, a blind hook shot from beneath the basket – Asher scored five. He had at least fifty pounds on me, and a good six inches. I had forgotten how much I loved the game when challenged.

After I'd graduated from high school, Nana hadn't wanted me to try out for the university team; he wanted me to focus on studying. So instead I joined local leagues when it fitted into my timetable. Played pick-up games at the weekends when the girls from the team – who'd gone off to play college ball all over Canada – were home for Thanksgiving or the summer vacation. My skills stalled while theirs got better. And even though those games reminded me of what I could have been, or not been, I loved that feeling of having to work for something. Work *at* something, and having the motivation, the passion, to be better.

After over half an hour of mocking each other, Asher overpowering me, effortlessly swatting the ball down whenever I tried to shoot, I was laughing too much to keep playing. Panting, I lay down in the middle of the court and sprawled into a starfish.

'That's it?' In the shadows, I saw his smirk hovering above me. 'Did I beat the infamous Raina?'

I covered my mouth with my hand and nodded. He disappeared from my view, and a few seconds later reappeared. He sat down next to me and handed me a water bottle. I took a long sip, some of it spilling down my chin, and handed it back.

'Good game.'

I smiled. 'Shut up.'

'What?'

'You're being smug.'

'I'm not being smug. I'm being *civil*.' He knocked his knee lightly against mine. 'I think someone just isn't used to losing.'

'I let you win.'

'Really? And there was me thinking I was teaching you a lesson.'

'And what lesson is that, Mr Klein?'

'It's not over yet – I don't want to spoil it.'

'Is there going to be a test?'

He grinned at me. Crooked, almost naughty, and I blushed. I could feel Asher's eyes still on me as I sat up. I reached over him and grabbed his water bottle, and, before taking a sip, aimed it at him like a sword. 'Don't think this means we're friends.'

'Of course not,' he said. 'You and I are enemies.'

'Sworn enemies.'

'And besides,' he leaned in close, and he smelled like pepper and laundry detergent, and the sticky way boys smell after being outside, 'I don't think I can be friends with you. I don't have any sparring equipment.'

I rolled my eyes. 'I see you're still whining about that.'

'I was attacked! Pushed into some desserts – *delicious* desserts, mind you.'

'You were bruised for weeks, I'm sure.'

'Me?' Asher smiled. 'Or your ego?'

I shoved him.

'Ow!'

'As if.'

'You're so *physical*.' He massaged his shoulder. 'What did I ever do to you?'

'Besides embarrass me at my best friend's engagement party?' He didn't answer, and I glanced towards him. He was looking at me, a plain expression on his face. The muscles in his cheeks and around his eyes relaxed. Genuine.

'I shouldn't have pushed you,' I said after a moment, looking back at the pavement between my feet. 'I'm sorry.'

'Me too.'

'I'm under a lot of pressure from my Nani at the moment.' I shrugged. 'I'm not, I *wasn't*, in the greatest place.'

'It's OK. I could tell.' He smiled. 'I can read you like a book.'

'I didn't know you could read?'

He grinned, and then a second later, added, 'Could that barman read?'

'Who?'

'He looked a bit young.' Asher pressed his lips together,

as if thinking hard. 'Give him my number if he needs a tutor, would you?'

'Hang on, what?'

Asher scrunched his mouth up tight as if he was trying not to laugh, and when I caught his eye, it flickered. Then it hit me.

Josh. The barman I'd gone home with. Asher had seen us. 'Oh. My. God.'

'Please don't tell me you wore *that*,' he said, glancing down at my socks. 'Kids these days don't understand fashion.'

I hid my face in my knees and felt Asher's hand brushing the back of my head. 'I like your hat. My dad had one just like it.'

'Please. Stop talking.'

'Oh, don't worry so much. It's really not a big deal.'

My face was hot, pulsing red, and my entire body was flushed. 'I'm so embarrassed. I'm never talking to you again.'

'What?' He laughed, moving his hand to my back.

'I can't believe you saw that. I never—'

'Raina,' he said loudly. 'Look at me.' Slowly, I peeled my face up from my knees. He straightened out my shoulders with his hands and waited until I was looking him in the eye. 'I was just teasing you,' he said gently. 'Seriously, who cares?'

'I care.'

'Why?'

I turned away from him, not able to say it out loud: *because Nani would care.*

Asher dropped his hands to the pavement and leaned

back, his legs stretched out in front of him. The sweat was starting to cool on my skin, and I shivered.

'You know, I dated an Indian girl once. We were, like, twenty-one, twenty-two, maybe?' He dug the heel of his sneaker into the pavement. 'Her family was very traditional. And they put a lot of pressure on her.'

'Is this an analogy?' I asked drily.

'Anyway,' he patted his finger against his lip, shushing me, 'even though she wasn't "allowed" to date, I convinced her to go out with me. As you can imagine, she was conflicted about, you know, *sex*. Hugely conflicted. But then one afternoon after class she came over, and I thought maybe she finally liked me enough to—'

'Get it on?'

Asher laughed. 'Yeah.'

'And did she?'

'Not even close. The moment I got near her she started crying – *bawling*, actually – and then left. She refused to speak to me for the rest of term. And as I'm sure you know, I left university early and, uh, well, I never saw her again.'

'You think my problems are about *sex*?'

'No, Raina, my point is that she hated herself. I see so many kids raised to feel shame about who they are, what they want, who they love. And whether it's about sex or identity, or even just making mistakes, when people grow up, sometimes they *screw* up. Isn't that the point?'

I looked back down at the ground.

'This girl I dated, she was under so much pressure to do the right thing, she didn't even know what it felt like to make a mistake. She didn't have the courage to go out

156

and try something new, something different, and know that she'd still be OK.'

I could feel him looking at me, waiting for me to say something. His eyes bored into the side of my neck, and after a minute, I couldn't handle it. I jumped up and grabbed the ball.

'Another game?' I turned to face him and dribbled the ball, hard, down and through my legs.

He was biting his lower lip, and I turned back round. I lined up the shot and took it, and it swished through the net.

'You see that?' I ran a lap round the court, pumping my fists in the air, and then back towards Asher. 'Did you see that?'

'Yeah, I saw it.'

I extended my hand. He grabbed it, and I leaned back from his weight as he used it to pull himself off the ground.

'You know what we should do?' I asked.

'What's that?'

I glanced around the empty field. 'Smoke,' I whispered.

'You're a smoker?' He winced. 'That would explain how easily I beat—'

'No, I mean a *joint*,' I mouthed. 'Let's get high.'

'You want to smoke a joint.'

'Yeah, I haven't in years.' I grinned.

'You're kidding, right? Shaylee mentioned you liked to joke around.'

'No, I'm not joking.' I shook my head. 'I'm kind of in the mood.'

'Being here with me ... puts you in the mood?'

'Yeah.' I laughed, touched his arm. 'So, do you have any?'

'You know what, Raina, no. I don't have any on me right now.' He grabbed the ball from my hand. 'Not today.'

'Oh. OK.'

'Must have used it all up at work this week,' he said, frowning. 'Teaching *children*.'

'Asher—'

'Look, I've got to run. Dealers to meet. Things to blow up. Irresponsible stuff – you wouldn't understand.' He grabbed a beanie from his pocket and shoved it on his head, and without looking at me, turned away. 'I'll see you around.'

'Asher, I didn't mean—'

But he was gone, already jogging towards the car park, his basketball tucked under his arm.

Chapter 19
20 May 2005

Raina turns eighteen and smokes her first joint. Before this day, she has never thought seriously about smoking marijuana. Even as it billows at the edges of the school car park, on back-garden decks and at basement parties, she has never considered it. Her coaches tell her to stay away, mentioning threats of slowness and sluggishness, and Raina listens. But on her eighteenth birthday the season is already over. Basketball, volleyball, track and field – all the competitions have closed, the scores tallied. In the muddy spring schoolyard, the one round which she has jogged thousands of times, there is no one left to race. In a way she is relieved, and allows her body to slacken, but knowing that graduation is less than a month away, she is also terrified.

The final bell rings and Raina rushes out of the last period ahead of her friends. Shay told everyone it was her birthday, and they decorated her locker with dollar-store stickers and ribbons, tacked-on messages penned on hot-pink craft paper. Raina tears it all down as she throws her textbooks into her locker, then races out the front door. She is greeted by the heat of a May afternoon, the air still fresh with spring. She can smell nothing but the green of the lawn, the clipped hedges running along the pavement, and she smiles as she takes a deep breath. She is about to walk home, and she is still smiling when, right in front of the school, she sees Manavi.

Raina hasn't seen her mother in over a year. Her hair is different to the last time she visited. It is now cropped short and severe, light blond and browns like a patchwork quilt. She sits cross-legged on the bonnet of a cherry-red convertible parked in front of the school, and as Raina approaches, she looks up from the magazine open on her lap.

'Happy birthday, Raindrop.'

Raina smiles. Now that she is older, she doesn't know what to call her – Manavi, Manu, Ma? Raina has always avoided addressing her directly, but this time, when she says hello, she calls her 'Mom'. She notes how natural it feels as it leaves her lips.

Manavi slides off the bonnet and wraps her arms around Raina. She is a few inches shorter and slightly wider than Raina, and she beams as she pulls back. 'Shit, when did you grow up?'

'What are you doing here?'

'It's your birthday. Where else would I be?'

She has missed Raina's last three, maybe four, birthdays, but Raina doesn't remind her of this. Raina throws her backpack into the boot next to her mother's worn-out duffel bag and they get into the car. Manavi slides on a pair of shiny cat-eye sunglasses and smiles at herself in the rear-view mirror, pursing her lips together. Then she opens her bag and hands Raina an identical pair.

'Really?' Raina can tell they are expensive. She recognises the brand from airport billboards. Department stores that don't accept cash. She slides them onto her face. 'Thanks, Mom. I love them.' Their eyes hidden, their noses partially obscured, Raina notes how similar their mouths are. Rose-bud lips that bloom into wide, slightly crooked smiles, just a hair too close to their equally soft chins. Manavi starts the car and Raina turns to face her. 'Where are we going?'

'*C'est une surprise.*'

They snack on Dr Pepper and cheese fries Manavi buys at a transport café outside Bellville, racing down the highway with the windows down, the Top 40 blasting through the speakers. It is dusk by the time they reach Montreal, and they drive to an apartment in Laval that belongs to a friend of Manavi's. He isn't home, and she lets them in with a key. The rooms are tattered – peeling wallpaper, blue carpets with zebra patches of brown. Slits for windows that peer into a back alley. Manavi drops her bag in the middle of the hallway, steps over it as she searches for a radio. They listen to French-Canadian pop and get ready, pinched side by side in the bathroom. Raina is wearing Manavi's dress, sleek, red and short, while Manavi has put on emerald-green pleather pants, a black top that finishes beneath her ribcage. Raina realises with some surprise that her mother is thirty-four. *Only* thirty-four. Yet, as they stand next to each other, the same light brown foundation blurred on their faces, Raina can barely see the age difference; she can barely see a difference at all.

'You always look tired, kiddo,' Manavi says, sorting through her make-up kit. Raina glances sideways in the mirror as Manavi applies black paint to her lids and lashes and erases the faint circles beneath Raina's eyes with a beige pencil.

'I stayed up late last night.' Raina notes Manavi's bemused expression, then shakes her head. 'No, not that. I had a maths test today.'

Manavi rolls her eyes, and Raina feels suddenly embarrassed. She tries to think of something to say, wonders why it's so hard; and then it occurs to her that she can't remember the last time she was alone with Manavi. No Nani hovering in the background, disapproving of whatever it was they'd decided to watch on television or order for dinner. No Nana and Kris making sarcastic comments, sucking the air out of the room. No Shay filling the void whenever the silence became too much.

While waiting for a taxi, Manavi sends Raina across the road to an off-licence. She is nervous when she slides her driving licence across the counter, prepared to confirm out loud that she is eighteen, and in Montreal, finally legal. The man slides it back without looking, and Raina smiles to herself. She stuffs the bottle of expensive vodka into her bag, its flecks of gold leaf floating like a snow globe, and with her chin up, she walks back across the road to Manavi.

Raina is drunk by the time they stumble out of the cab. Over half of the gold leaf floats in her empty stomach, and Manavi buys them both a hot dog from a stand on St Catherine's. Now Raina feels like talking, and she natters pointlessly to Manavi as they eat – about the lights, the churches, the strip clubs they pass – and when a group of boys from McGill stop to talk to them, Manavi slyly wipes the crumbs off Raina's lips and winks.

The boys take them to a club that sits between a maternity-clothing store and a second-hand Rolex dealer, black metal bars stretched across the window as if in anticipation of the anxious queue outside. In the queue, Raina begins to waver, a flood of nausea passing through her every time she blinks, and she grabs onto the metal bars for support. Manavi pulls her hands away, and then the boys are leading them to the front of the queue, and Raina sees one of them shove a fistful of red bills into the bouncer's hand.

Raina can barely walk. Electronica pounds through her ears. With her eyes closed, she stumbles around aimlessly, guided by hands, breath like wet fog on her face. She can smell mould, the sweat on everyone around her, and soon she finds herself leaning on Manavi. She hands her a shot. Mindlessly, Raina drinks it, and then another, the shiny blue liquid burning the back of her mouth, trickling down. Every time she opens her eyes, Raina thinks she might be sick; she keeps pushing away the epileptic flashes of light, emerald-green pleather and clusters of faces. Raina is disorientated, and whenever she hears her mother's laugh, sees the blinking lights that blister her eyes, she thinks of her Nani.

She wants to go home.

The taste of the blue spirit rises in her throat, and then she smells Manavi's perfume and feels her tuck a stray hair behind her ear. She catches Manavi's eye and points to the door. Manavi glances at her watch, rolls her eyes and without saying goodbye to the others, they leave.

They don't speak as they turn off St Catherine's, as Manavi leads her to the Latin Quarter. They wind loosely through cobbled streets – some pitch-black between the crossroads. The sound of traffic grows more distant, and in the hollow silence, Raina can hear nothing but the even click of Manavi's heels. It strikes her that her mother knows exactly where she's going, her footsteps assured and direct, as if, without Raina ever having known, Manavi has lived in Montreal before.

Ahead, Raina sees a group of men standing on the steps of an old apartment building, and the men stop talking as they approach. Raina glances behind her. No one else is around, and she slows her walk. She feels hesitant, but Manavi's heels keep pace.

'*Mademoiselle*,' says one of them. His dark hair is groomed into thin lines around his mouth. His mouth is open, and Raina can make out his tongue as it slices across his front teeth. He is looking at Manavi. '*Tu es bien ravissante ce soir.*'

'*Merci. Toi aussi.*' Manavi smiles, flashes him her white teeth. He beckons her over, and to Raina's surprise, she walks up the stairs. They speak French to each other, quickly, effortlessly. She tries to catch what they are saying, but Raina has never been good at French, and until tonight she has always assumed Manavi wasn't, either. Every so often, one of the other men, his eyes black, glances down at Raina and gestures for her to join him. Raina shakes her head. She still feels nauseous, light-headed, and she wants to go home.

'*C'est ta sœur?*'

Manavi shakes her head and glances down the stairs. 'Come up here, Raina.'

Raina inches up the steps. She stands at the edge, watching them converse, trying not to catch the eye of the one that keeps staring at her, biting his lower lip. After a few minutes, the man with the goatee – the one whose hand is now tucked around Manavi's waist – pulls out a joint. He places it on Manavi's bottom lip, lights it and she inhales until the end glows amber. She breathes out, smoke billowing, and then offers it to Raina.

'No thanks,' Raina mumbles.

Manavi turns to her. 'Just take it.' She looks irritated, and when Raina hesitates again, she pushes it into her hand. 'Be chill, Raina. Stop worrying about everything.' She glances back at the men, mumbles something in French and everyone laughs. And they keep laughing until Raina takes a long, thick puff and her lungs start to burn.

Raina doesn't remember the rest of the night. Bits and pieces; faint smells and feelings. Coughing so hard she thinks she just might die; her cheek, cold and red, against a toilet seat reeking of shit. The night, and well into the morning, is a trance. An unfamiliar room spinning above, her eyelashes batting to a beat she makes up in her head. Vaguer memories still of falling asleep on a sofa next to the man with the black eyes, the one who, as she dips in and out of consciousness, smells like pot roast and keeps trying to touch her.

Manavi shakes Raina awake, smiles down at her weakly. It is light outside, and Raina notices that Manavi's top is inside out. Without saying a word to one another, they slip out and take a taxi back to the apartment, and ten minutes later, they climb into Manavi's hired convertible. Raina's head pounds the whole way home, made worse by the music, brash and loud, that Manavi insists on listening to. Finally, hours later, they are home. Raina swings the door open, and she is surprised that no sounds or smells are there to greet her. Nothing is cooking, and Nani's voice does not bubble out through the crack of the kitchen door, ushering her in for a cup of chai or a taste of whatever is simmering on the back-burner.

Manavi throws her bag down. 'Anyone home?'

Nana appears at the top of the stairs, the cordless phone pressed into his chest with both hands. His hands slowly drop to his sides.

'Is Ma home?'

He glances between Raina and Manavi, and, without saying anything, he turns round. Raina hears his door upstairs click shut, the lock slide into place, and she is overwhelmed with a sense of dread. She glances at Manavi, who is seemingly unchanged, and follows her into the kitchen. Nani is sitting at the kitchen table. She is motionless, her hands clenched white into two fists resting in front of her. She doesn't look up to greet them, and when Raina leans in to hug her, she shudders.

'Nani, what's wrong?' Raina steps back. She remembers that she hasn't cleaned off the make-up or brushed her teeth, and she wonders if her hair smells of smoke. 'Nani?'

Still Nani won't speak. Her fists unclench, slowly, and she places her palms lightly on the table. They are shaking.

'Yeah. About that.' Manavi has hoisted herself onto the kitchen counter. She opens a bag of crisps, and stuffs a handful into her mouth. Crunching loudly, she says, 'I took Raina to Montreal last night, for her birthday.'

Raina stiffens. She feels as if she's been punched, and she squats down beside her Nani. She searches her eyes, only to find them ice cold. 'Nani, I'm so sorry. I didn't realise you didn't know—'

'You are both adults.' Nani looks different. Her voice is changed, and Raina feels as if she is speaking to someone who has emerged from the past – a woman of whom she has heard rumours, and until now, has never had the misfortune of meeting. Nani stands up suddenly and walks

166

out of the kitchen. Raina resists the urge to follow. She can hear Manavi crunching crisps behind her, the plastic packet crackling, and she turns round. Manavi swings her legs in small circles, and when Raina finally meets her eye, her mother is grinning.

'Raindrop, pass me a bowl, would you?'

Chapter 20

Further down the office, someone in the kitchen area was starting the dishwasher, gossiping about the latest incompetent analyst Bill had hired and fired within a week. Outside, the wind tore away at the window as another snow cloud cast its shadow over the city. Was it December already?

I glanced back at Dev. He was sitting in the chair opposite my desk, right ankle over left knee, hunched slightly over his BlackBerry as he punched the keyboard with his thumbs.

'Sorry, darling. Just one more second.'

'It's fine.'

It had always been fine. I had never minded. Really, I'd been inspired. There was a certain nobility about a self-made man: the work ethic, the passion, the devotion it took to rise from beneath the tracks, defy odds and become one of the few people in the world who, rightly or wrongly, had influence on the economy; on how the world worked. He was bright and powerful, and this man in front of me, the one who had so few moments to spare but who wanted to spend them with me, was the *real* Dev.

I'd learned quickly that the man I fell for in Brussels had been on holiday. A chance glimpse, really, because he rarely took holidays. The Dev who had the inclination to read in bed with me, whisper secrets between crisp hotel sheets, was as rare as the London sun. And I was fine with it. It had always been clear what life would be like holding Dev's hand, sleeping beside his furrowed brow. Cajoling him to cheer up during dinner, his mood soured by a deal gone bad.

Life would be Dev hunting for a Wi-Fi connection, leaving me to crisp on the beaches of Corfu alone while our complimentary bottle of champagne chilled in the honeymoon suite. Dev on his phone, emailing a client during our child's Christmas concert, leaving during his solo to take a call. Dev having to keep a flat in Zone One for his late nights at the office and last-minute meetings; the rest of us in our town house in Totteridge or Haywards Heath, a sunlamp beside the davenport desk where I'd watch the clock and try to discover my life's passion.

Life would be Dev growing old and even more powerful. Meeting him for a quick bite near his office in Westminster. His hand on my waist as he avoids eye contact with the waitress our daughter's age and I massage my wrinkles, convince myself he doesn't have time for an affair. Life with Dev would be fast and slow at the same time; a waiting game between moments of bliss, between trips to Brussels. It didn't bother me. It had all been fine back then, and now, still, it was *fine*.

Wasn't it?

I stared at my computer, eyes glazed in fake concentration. He'd been sitting there emailing on his work phone for over five minutes – six, now. I tried not to look over, not to wonder how much more time he needed. Or why he kept showing up.

'Darling, sorry about that.' Dev tucked his phone into his breast pocket and then placed both his palms on the table. 'Tell me, how are you?'

'I'm just dandy, thank you.'

He glanced out of the window. 'Weather is complete shit here, isn't it? And it's twelve degrees in London today. Can you believe it? Now, why anyone would want to settle *here* is beyond me.'

'Then don't be here.'

'Raina.' He looked at me the way he always did, and I sighed.

'Let's go somewhere warm.'

'Like where?'

I shrugged. 'The equator.'

'That's quite a way, love. Might have to be more specific.'

'Brazil? I think it bisects—'

'No!' He winced 'Didn't like Brazil.'

'Uganda, then.' I rolled my eyes. 'But I doubt you have a client there.'

He smiled vaguely, and a moment later stood up.

'You're leaving?'

He nodded. 'Must do. But I wanted to come and say goodbye before I fly to New York. And from there I'll be going straight to London for Christmas, perhaps longer. It's hard to tell.'

'Are you coming back?'

'Darling,' he said, his voice low, 'of course I'm coming back.'

'When?' I cringed at the need in my own voice.

He sat down on the edge of the desk. 'Don't know exactly – whenever I can. January or February sometime. March at the latest, I reckon.'

'March?'

He extended his hand towards my cheek, and as if suddenly remembering where we were, drew it back down into his lap. 'They might want me to sit in on the division in Singapore for a few months before I make my way back here. You know how it is.'

'You couldn't have told me this sooner?'

'Raina—'

'You're back and forth, coming and going...'

'Meetings, sweetheart. Clients need—'

'Did you even want to move here?' My fingers were locked tight, and I moved them to my lap. 'Did you even want to – to see me?'

'Raina, please.'

'Please what?'

'Don't do this. You know how much stress I'm under.'

'Must be awful.'

He glanced at his watch, then back at me. 'We'll talk about this soon, yeah? When I'm back. You and me – a curry somewhere. A bottle of wine, like we used to. We'll talk about anything you want.' He touched my chin. '*Anything*.'

My heart raced.

'You know how I feel about you.'

Then why wouldn't he say it? Why couldn't he say it now? I'd been waiting years, and I could wait a few more months. But could Nani? How long could I make her wait?

'All right.' I breathed out, steadied my voice. 'Have a nice time.'

He stood up and lingered in the doorway, drumming his fingers on the wooden frame until I looked over. 'Wish I could kiss you goodbye.'

'Me too,' I lied, wishing he'd kiss me and stay, or just let me say goodbye.

Our house smelled of Christmas. Aloo gobi and mataar paneer. Milky chai, with its cinnamon sticks and whole cloves left to simmer on the froth. Burnt plastic from when Kris unpacked the silver tree and a sprig of tinsel wedged itself behind the boiler. And, of course, Vicks VapoRub, the earthy congestion of Nani's chest cold appropriating all three floors of the house.

She sat at the kitchen table with her head bent over a pot of boiling water, a crimson bath towel draped over her head. 'A facial – and good for the lungs,' she spluttered, as I brought her another cup of hot water.

Nani was always sick at Christmas. It was practically tradition. She worked long hours during December, insisting on being at Saffron to open for the lunch rush and then staying late to close. Doing paperwork in the back office until the organiser of that night's office Christmas party stumbled in, company credit card in hand, and asked to settle up.

I extended my Christmas vacation by a week and came home early to take care of her. Since Dev had left, I'd become even more lethargic about work. Zoey recommended I didn't take time off, mentioned that Bill had started to notice my poorer performance, lower output, but

I didn't care. I just needed to get out. Get away. And just by being at home and out of the town, I felt better. I felt ready for the holidays without Dev.

I established myself a routine – a suburban, more relaxed life away from the city. In the morning I'd wake up early and bring Nani her tea, two digestive biscuits resting on the saucer. I'd do her housework and then head down to Saffron, where I'd temporarily taken over. In the evenings I cooked dinner, and Nani and I watched TV huddled together on the sofa, and after she fell asleep, I'd go for a run, sometimes past the school's basketball courts. Once I saw the girls' team practising – running drills, shuttles and layups. Asher was standing in the corner with a clipboard, and I'd slowed down and waved as I jogged past. But he didn't see me – either that, or he purposely turned and looked away.

Living at home again, I got a sense of what it was like to be Nani. How much energy it took to run a thriving business. Everyone enquired after her health, making sure she was keeping well, that I was taking good care of the 'boss'. They *adored* her – customers, suppliers and staff alike. Watching Nani on the sofa, piled beneath shawls and camping blankets, looking as fragile as a newborn, I wondered how she did it all; how effortlessly she managed to be everyone's Nani.

She was getting older, and ignoring this fact was seemingly the only thing Kris and I had in common. Being at home, I started to notice the little things. How it took her a few seconds longer to march up the stairs. The way she sat down – often, sometimes in the middle of what she was doing. She'd always refused to let me hire her a cleaner, yet the house was always in perfect order. Not a speck of dust or grime; everything in its place. As I took over her routines for her, I wondered who did it all when I wasn't here. Who reached up to the top shelf to fetch a light bulb, or for a packet of sweetener when she ran out? Who unloaded the groceries after her trips to Costco, carried in the twenty-two-pound bag of basmati rice?

Because watching her recover – as she read magazines, watched TV or played around on her tablet – I found myself worrying what she would do without me. Then Nani would cough, or I'd notice her shiver, and I was overcome with the more selfish, more unshakeable of fears.

What would I do without her?

As December wore on, Nani's health slowly improved, and as her spirits rose, unfortunately so did the number of questions.

Why were Zoey and I not together?

Did I have a different girlfriend?

Would I have natural children or adopt?

How did I define my sexual orientation, and was that different from my gender identity?

It wasn't until Christmas Eve, while surfing on Nani's tablet after she'd gone to bed, that I found out where those questions were coming from. And surely, from where the questions would keep on coming.

Her browser history was littered with LGBTQ websites. Organisations, support groups, blogs, chat forums. Terminologies, ideologies – tips on *how to set aside your feelings on homosexuality*, and *how to redefine your relationship with your gay child*. There was even a link to some gay porn (which, I gathered, she'd stumbled across by mistake). I laughed out loud at first, as I made my way through the websites – the new *list* – feeling rather proud of my progressive Nani.

But then I imagined her on the sofa, her doughy, wrinkled brow mouthing along with the words, and I realised that maybe it wasn't so funny. I kept scrolling, and more websites appeared. Ones outlining in layman's terms same-sex civil marriages, how Canada had been the fourth country in the world to legalise. Sites with advice on raising kids of gay parents – for *grandparents* of kids raised by gay parents. Sites on adoption. Donor insemination. IVF treatment. Another on adoption. Then it hit me like a frying pan to the skull. Nani didn't just support me being interested in women.

She wanted me to marry one.

Chapter 21

Nani and I both pretended not to notice that Kris didn't come home on Christmas morning, or that Mom hadn't even called. We spent the day cooking together and watching old movies, and then got ready for Auntie Sarla's party. She first invited us over for Christmas dinner after Nana died. It had started out of sympathy – just for our family and Shay's – but over the years the numbers had grown, and these days Christmas dinner felt like just another one of Auntie Sarla's famous parties. Her two dining tables became a hodgepodge of salads, curries and daals, shrimp fried rice and over-salted stuffing. And in true potluck style, sometimes there were six turkeys – and other years there were none.

Their marble foyer was already littered with winter boots by the time we arrived for dinner. The house was all extravagance and no taste, a house of horrors and oversaturated colours. Rose-water-pink carpets and blindingly gold walls; an indoor swimming pool only the dog used; a six-foot statue in the middle of the living room – just because.

Since their engagement, Shay and Julien had decided to alternate holidays with their families, and this year was Shay's first Christmas away from home. It felt odd being in her house without her; usually we'd sneak upstairs away from the party, hide in her old bedroom with a bowl of stolen desserts, ignoring everyone until Auntie Sarla found us and insisted we come back down and socialise. I thought about going up to her room alone, but it felt too strange. I wasn't sure how it happened, or when, but these days Shay and I barely spoke.

When was it that we started growing apart? Sure, I'd become more distant since Dev moved to Toronto, and avoided seeing her for fear of letting the lie slip, but I wondered whether it had started before then. Things hadn't been right since she'd got engaged and become fixated with the wedding. Maybe there'd be time over the New Year to talk things out, at her bachelorette party in New York City. Julien and his groomsmen would be there, too. Ironically, they'd both be spending their last 'singles trip' together – a group holiday I'd had planned for months. But ever since my misunderstanding with Asher I wasn't looking forward to it.

The house was packed with new faces – the old and the much too young. Most of the girls Shay and I had grown up with had moved away – to Los Angeles, Vancouver, Calgary – or were off on holiday with families of their own. The few I did know sat in clumps in one of the living rooms, holding hands with their husbands or boyfriends, chasing after toddlers dressed up like reindeer, in tiny novelty onesies bought specifically for the occasion. I quickly said my hellos, my congratulations, and then moved towards the kitchen.

I peered round the corner and saw Nani and Auntie Sarla arguing in front of the stainless steel oven, their faces flushed. Quietly, I drew closer, coming within earshot.

'This is not right, *ji*.'

'Suvali. I am helping her. I am helping *you*. Raina needs a husband.'

'Raina doesn't need—'

'You know what everyone is saying? They are saying none of the men she meets likes her, that she is too difficult to please.'

'Why are you making up lies?'

'Suvali, why would I lie?'

'Raina doesn't need a husband, and – and—'

Nani's voice tailed off, and they both turned to look at me.

'What's going on?' I asked slowly.

'Nothing.' Auntie Sarla turned back to the stove. 'Have you eaten?'

'Not yet.'

'*Jao*. Go and make up a plate.' She nodded at me, and then threw Nani a glare. 'Take your Nani with you. She is looking pale.'

I led Nani into the empty hallway. She was perspiring, fanning her face with a folded piece of paper towel. I found a table nearby with fresh glasses of champagne and thrust one into her hand.

'What's going on?' I asked.

'That woman is going on and on – always talking, talking.' Nani tapped her fingers together. 'She knows nothing, and still? Always talking.' Nani scrunched up her face. 'Who is that woman to talk like that about my Raina? We need to tell them. Band Aid' – she flicked her hand like a conductor – 'off.'

I put my hands on Nani's shoulders and took a deep

breath, trying not to imagine what would happen if everyone found out. Another scandal in the Anand family. Another daughter who hadn't lived up to expectations. What would Nani have to endure if everyone thought I was a lesbian? Most of Nani's friends couldn't even pronounce homosexuality, let alone support it.

'Should we tell them?' Nani reached up and stroked the side of my cheek. 'I am *OK*.'

I shook my head.

'Raina, please—'

'No, Nani. Not yet.' I looked her straight in the eye. 'Promise me you won't tell anyone. Not until…'

Until when? Until Dev was back from London or Singapore, or wherever the hell he was going? Until I could admit that it was *him* I wanted to marry, and not another woman? The man who had humiliated me? Who had humiliated Nani?

'Just promise me you won't say anything yet. Please?' I took a deep breath. I would come clean when Dev was back. I would tell Nani everything. Dev would be back, and we would get back together and I would make Nani realise.

I would make them both realise.

'OK.' Nani sighed, and her hand slid to my chin. 'But Raina, eventually you will have to face them.'

No, Nani, I thought, my stomach wrenching. Eventually I will have to face you.

Chapter 22

I worked the next five days straight to make up for my 'ill-timed Christmas holiday', as Bill had called it, and then just before 5 a.m. on New Year's Eve I took a taxi to the airport for the first flight out to LaGuardia. Serena was already there, a cappuccino in her hand and a crime thriller tucked between the thighs of her skinny jeans.

I sat down beside her hesitantly. I hadn't seen her since she and Kris had broken up, but she seemed happy to see me. Slowly, the rest of the group started to trickle in – Shay's twin cousins, Nikki and Niti, who I remembered as toddlers, but who now apparently had jobs in brand management and social media. Then came Julien's co-resident in paediatrics, Matt, and Julien's younger brother Victor, who'd sworn that his fake ID would work.

Finally Shay and Julien arrived, hugging us all through fatigued smiles. I hadn't made time to see her since they'd got back from Quebec, and I couldn't remember the last time we'd seen each other, or even spoken on the phone. Lately our only contact had been brief texts, hours apart, which were always about plans for the wedding, for the trip to New York.

Shay eyed me oddly as she drew closer. I thought she

was going to lean in and hug me, but then she stopped and patted me on the arm. 'You look good.'

'You too.'

Did she know I was avoiding her? That I was hiding something?

'Good Christmas?' she asked.

I nodded. 'You?'

She didn't reply as she looked around the terminal, and after surveying the crowd, looked back at me. 'Where's Asher?'

I shrugged, and a moment later I saw him.

'There he is,' said Julien.

Asher jogged towards us, a duffel bag swinging in his hand. He'd let some of his beard grow back, a soft scruff on his chin and cheeks, and instead of a suit or sweatpants, he was wearing loose jeans and a faded leather jacket, with a white t-shirt and trainers. Almost exactly the same outfit that I was wearing. He slowed down as he approached us, and, without looking at me, smiled broadly and wrapped an arm round both Julien and Shay and steered them towards security.

He avoided me as we waited, and then, at the front of the queue, when Shay bent over and took her time unclasping the buckles on her boots, I veered in front of her, angling myself behind him.

'Hi, Asher,' I said.

Whether he heard me or not, he didn't answer.

'How was your Christmas?' I said a little louder.

He retrieved his passport from his back pocket. 'Festive.'

'Were you with family?'

'Sure was.'

'Did you guys have fun?' I paused. 'Play any basketball?'

'Guess that depends on your definition of fun.' He leaned on the metal rail and slid off his shoes. 'My nephews prefer Sponge Bob over, you know, *weed*.'

'I am really sorry about that.'

He tossed his wallet and keys into the plastic bin.

'Asher, come on. I said I was sorry.'

But he walked away through the metal detector without turning round.

There were only a handful of others on board, and after take-off we spread out sideways on the seats. I blinked in and out of sleep, and it felt like only minutes before we started our descent into New York City. I sat up and peered out of my window, watching the clouds feathered above The Rockaways. Snow was sprinkled over the city like icing sugar.

I had booked ahead, and a square black van was waiting for us outside the airport. I sat in the front seat chatting with our driver, Ramone, about the state's public school system, the newest speakeasy that had just opened beneath a pho takeaway in the Lower East Side, camouflaged in strings of red and yellow lights, and we drove down the expressway towards Manhattan. I'd been to New York often, either with Shay or other friends for weekend shopping trips or music festivals; on a dozen conferences with colleagues, the days spent at the office on East 55th, the nights in the hotel bar on Lexington in a black pencil skirt, charging the Grey Goose martinis to the expense account. It was one way to live. It was Dev's way. As the chalky grey peaks of Midtown rose on the horizon, I tried to push

Dev out of my mind. Where he was. What he was doing for New Year. Whether, on those countless autumn trips to New York, winding around that last bend on the Long Island Expressway, he had thought of me too.

On the other side of the Midtown Tunnel we hit traffic, and after thirty minutes of crawling, block by block, Ramone muttering about tourists and the traffic diversions around Times Square, we reached our hotel. I'd booked us two suites at a hotel in Hell's Kitchen the week after Shay got engaged. She'd turned up at my apartment, drunk, with two butter chicken burritos and told me I was her maid of honour, and that instead of Vegas, or some cheesy night doing the limbo with a tanned stripper, she wanted her bachelorette party to be during the New Year. And she wanted to share it with Julien.

We said goodbye to the boys, dumped our things in the room and set out for Fifth Avenue. It was still early, the shops and pavements almost empty, and Shay was acting unlike herself. Bubbly, almost, and she couldn't stop smiling, picking up clothes and holding them against herself, her eyes shining as she walked past a shopfront, exclaiming at something showcased in the window, and then hustled in to buy it. She chatted ruthlessly with the girls working at Chanel, Mango or BCBG, trying everything on as she stood in front of the mirror and surveyed the room for an opinion.

'So, what do you think?' she asked us, her fingers playing with the sequins of a stiff black dress. 'Is it too much?'

Everyone chimed their approval as Shay turned this way and that in front of the mirror, sucked in her stomach and elongated her arms behind her. Surprisingly, she had the

perfect figure: petite and curvy from a diet of hospital cafeteria food and from the exercise of running from patient
to patient.

'No.' Shay shook her head and pouted at the salesgirl
texting on her phone. 'I can't.'

'Come on,' said Serena. 'You *have* to.'

'I can't. What if Ma sees the pictures?' Shay shrugged and
turned away from the mirror. 'She'd hate it.'

The four of us bought it anyway when she wasn't looking, and when we stopped for glühwein at the German
Christmas market, Serena handed her the bag. Shay eyed
me suspiciously.

'I told you guys not to get me anything.'

'Just open it,' I said, and when she did, she started to cry.

'You guys,' she spluttered. 'I can't believe it.'

'Calm down.' I rolled my eyes. 'It's just a dress.'

'It's not just a dress,' said Shay, wiping away snot with her
wrist. 'It might be the only thing in this whole wedding I
actually choose for myself.'

'We love you, sweetie,' said Serena, hugging her, and the
rest of us joined in, and soon we were all clumped madly
together in the middle of Union Square, shopping bags and
scarves flung to the side, pigeons knocking at our feet, the
tourists walking by, nodding and smiling at us like we were
some interesting occurrence that made up the landscape of
the city.

'Should we take a picture here?' I asked Shay.

Shay nodded, and her eyes landed on a miniature wooden
lodge selling wicker crafts and discount Christmas wreaths.
'Yeah. Over there in the light. Raina, do you have him?'

I nodded, tapping the side of my bag. 'I have him.'

Him was Draco, and as maid of honour, or, perhaps, because he didn't fit in Shay's clutch, I was in charge of lugging around the stuffed teddy bear Julien had bought for her on their first real date. Ever since, Julien and Shay had carried him around like a child, ready for every photo op: Draco perched on one of their shoulders at the CN Tower or Niagara Falls; in the operating room with a clinical white mask over his face; in sunglasses on the beach, or riding the neck of an alpaca at Machu Picchu. The last time I'd seen him was the weekend before my twenty-ninth birthday when Shay, Draco and I went camping, and we took pictures of the three of us canoeing on Lake Nipissing, drinking beers by the campfire. By now, Shay had accumulated enough Draco photos to warrant his own slideshow at the wedding, and although Auntie Sarla had originally vetoed the idea, it was the one thing Shay insisted on.

Afterwards, we caught the 4 train uptown and took more pictures with Draco at Trump Rink in Central Park, in Christopher's shadow on the steps of Columbus Circle and, later, propped on a velvet chair at the Ritz. High tea was a surprise. We walked into the hotel on the pretence of looking around, and when I took them up to the hostess and told her we had a reservation for a 'Shaylee Patel', Shay looked at me and again started to cry.

'You remembered.'

Being in New York City on an over-chaperoned class trip at high school. Sneaking off to the Ritz just for a moment to take a look. The dining room of old men and money. The decor of another century, the wine-red carpet and classical music. Fantasising about the lives of the people who were allowed inside – what they ate, what they did. Promising each other that one day we would get there, wherever *there* was.

I handed Shay a tissue. 'Of course I remembered.'

After tea, we went back to the hotel to change – Shay into her new dress – and we were still full of foie gras and lavender macaroons by the time we arrived at our reservation in Chelsea: a jazz-themed seafood grill where all the waiters – like any fine city establishment – appeared to moonlight as models. An Italian with side-swept hair flirted with Shay as he took our order, and she giggled in response, played with her hair, and ordered everyone the chef's tasting menu and several bottles of wine.

The table was large and we were spread out. I was at the end, Shay sitting closest to me, and as the other girls chatted, Shay and I looked at each other. I realised that neither of us knew what to say.

'Did your Ma tell you?' I finally asked. 'She booked that band from Vancouver for the wedding. They'll fly in before the sangeet—'

'Are you seeing anybody?' she asked suddenly. 'Is there anyone you haven't told me about?'

'No. Why?'

'Where have you been, then?'

'I'm right here.'

'No,' she said. 'Where have you *been*?'

I shrugged. 'Working.'

'And before?'

'And before …' I trailed off. 'Well, I've just been busy. I've been working, Shay. Same as ever.'

'Is this about Asher?'

'What?'

'This morning,' she paused and looked away from me, 'it looked like something was going on with you two.'

'Oh, *that*.' I shrugged. 'It was nothing.'

'Nothing.' She nodded, and by the way she bit her lip and dropped the subject, promptly engaging herself in conversation with the other girls, I knew she was hurt. Whether it was the offhand comment some guy in a history class had made, or how few edamame beans the bitch at the salad bar had put in our order – with us, it was never *nothing*.

But what was I supposed to say to her? Nani thinks I'm a lesbian, and, oh, yeah, Dev's moved to Toronto and we might get back together, but he's still not quite sure? Just like you would have predicted? I knew what she would say, and I didn't want a lecture. Not from her – not from a girl who could memorise an algorithm or an amino acid structure in the blink of an eye. Not from a girl whose fiancé had fallen into her lap; who, it seemed, never had to work hard for anything. Shay was my best friend. She always had been. But some things she just didn't – *couldn't* – understand.

I felt queasy throughout dinner. Unsettled. When I poured my wine into Nikki's glass, everyone had drunk too much of their own to notice, most of all Shay. The waiter kept flirting with her throughout dinner, sneaking her shots of ouzo from the back room, and I had to peel his hands off her waist as he helped her into her coat. She was practically catatonic. Outside I ducked into a minimart and bought her water, and then we walked towards Hudson Street, with me supporting most of her weight.

The guys were waiting for us outside the club. I saw

Asher first, almost a foot taller than everyone else, leaning against a handrail with his coat open, a charcoal-grey suit beneath. Shay unfastened herself from me and stumbled straight into Julien, but somehow we managed to get her into the bar without attracting too much attention.

The hostess led us towards our reserved area at the back. We were seated in a corner section with two long plush bench seats facing each other, a table full of glass bottles of vodka and gin, cranberry and Coke lined up in between. We were at the edge of the dance floor, just in front of a terrace. The doors were wide open, and each gust of wind brought in the citrusy smell of perfume, the diesel waft of the heat lamps. I sat at the end of the group, disengaged, at the fringes of the conversation, as Victor told the girls about the all-you-can-eat brunch at the strip club just off Washington Square Park.

Asher was sitting across from me, and I kept catching his eye. But every time I turned to face him, he looked away. Annoyed, I finally waved at him, and to my surprise, he waved back.

'How was your day?' I yelled over the music.

'What?'

'How was your day?'

'Great.' He smiled. 'Smoked *loads* of weed—'

'OK. Stop it.'

He grinned. 'Stop *what*, princess?'

I leaned forward. 'You know what? I said I was sorry – three times now. And I'm done. So if you don't want to—'

'See, the thing is,' he walked round the table and perched himself on the armrest beside me, 'you don't even know what you're apologising *for*.'

'Yes I do.'

'Do you? Because you're *hilarious*, Raina. Always making jokes. And you can't offend anyone if you're kidding.'

'I didn't mean to offend you, I just thought—'

'You just *thought* I smoked weed because you smelled it on me at the engagement party – which, by the way, you were wrong about. I was outside on the phone to my sister, and some kids were smoking it right next to me, so that's why I smelled like it. I haven't touched weed since college.'

'Oh.'

'And you also assumed that I had drugs on me at my workplace.' He grabbed his drink from the table. 'I mean, I'm just some shaggy guy who hangs around in a high school field, so I must be—'

'Look,' I took a deep breath, 'I knew you'd been travelling, and that you'd barely been back since you left, and everyone I know like that also—'

'Well, obviously, I'm just like them.'

'Yes, OK, I made an assumption. Sue me. I know your type. My own mother is your type. And people like you don't give a shit about anyone but themselves. I mean, who leaves their family for ten years?' The lights around the dance floor kept slicing me in the eyes, and I blinked hard. 'But it's all fine, isn't it? You've been "finding" yourself. Learning about the world. Not really having to deal with how selfish you are.'

'Sounds like you've got me all worked out.'

'Haven't I?' I snapped. 'And don't *you* have *me* all worked out?'

'All I did was try to get to know you.'

'But you *did* know me, didn't you? You knew that I was

189

twenty-nine and that my best friend was getting married before me.' I coughed, my voice catching. 'So obviously I'm desperate to get married, right? I take bar staff home because all I really need is some validation.' He had looked away, and I glared at him, shaking, until he looked back. 'Go ahead. Validate me. I *really* need it.'

He rubbed his lips together, and then his hands, and when he looked back at me as if he might say something, I heard Shay calling my name. I looked over. She had hoisted herself off Julien's lap and was inching towards us.

'What's going on here?' she asked, leaning down between us. She dipped and planted a wet kiss on my cheek. She moved for the other cheek and missed, hitting my chin.

'Do you want some more water?' I asked.

She shook her head, her hair falling onto her chest as she wavered in front of us. 'No. It's picture time.'

'Now?'

She nodded. 'Group shot.'

'Sure. I'll bring Draco in a minute.'

'OK,' she said, slurring her words. 'Let me know when you're ready.'

She stumbled back towards Julien, and I grabbed my coat from the back of the bench.

'Are you leaving?' asked Asher.

I nodded.

'Why?'

'It's nothing.'

'Who's Draco?' He followed me as I cut through the dance floor trying to lose him, and then up the stairs towards the club's entrance. Outside on the pavement, I stopped. Trying to catch my breath, I felt him behind me, his hand on my shoulder.

'Raina, who's Draco?'

I rolled my eyes. 'Oh, you know, just another guy who won't marry me.'

Chapter 23

'Shit.' I stepped back onto the kerb as another cab drove past me. I let my arm fall to my side and turned round. Asher was still leaning against a lamp post, his left foot hitched up, his arms folded across his chest.

'What time is it?'

He glanced at his watch. 'Eleven twenty. Do you want a hand?'

'No thanks.' I raised both my arms and waved frantically at another cab as it whizzed past.

'You know,' I heard Asher say, 'if the light's off it means it's taken.'

'You're being a nuisance.'

'That's because you're not letting me be helpful.' He uncrossed his arms, then crossed them the other way.

'Fine.' I gestured to the street. 'Be my guest.'

Asher pushed himself off the lamp post, and as he walked towards the edge of the pavement a cab pulled up. The door opened and three girls in stilettos and long parkas filed out. Asher placed his hand on the roof of the car as he helped them out, and then looked at me smugly.

'Lucky bastard.' I got into the cab, and before I realised what was happening, Asher slid in next to me and pulled the door shut.

'Thirty-eighth and Tenth, please.'

'Wait, what?'

'No problem,' said the driver, steering sharply into the traffic.

Asher reclined in his seat and drummed his fingers on the window frame, and a moment later, looked over at me. He smiled. 'What?'

'What are you – why are you—?'

'It's eleven' – he glanced back at his watch – 'twenty-two. In New York City. On New Year's Eve. I'm not letting you go alone.'

'So, you're being chivalrous, are you?'

'Something like that.'

We made it to the hotel in good time, and Asher waited in the lobby while I ran upstairs and grabbed Draco, who was still sitting on the windowsill where I'd left him. I stuffed him into my bag and ran back downstairs. Asher was talking to someone at concierge, and as I approached, he shook the man's hand and walked briskly towards me.

'They can call us a black car, but it will take a while to get here. Or we can walk over to Eighth and try and catch a cab there. Apparently we won't find one around here.'

I reached for his hand and rotated his wide wrist until I could see the face of his watch. Eleven thirty-five.

'Subway?'

He shook his head, looking at his wrist where I'd touched him. 'It's out of the way, walking there and then back again – we might as well just walk down.'

'Well, why don't we?'

'Walk?'

'Yeah. We'll go fast.' I lifted up my right boot, the flat edges covered in salt. 'We might even make midnight.'

We cut towards Ninth Avenue and then turned south. Our strides long and brisk, we walked silently, in step, the faint smell of salt and fuel hanging in the air. We passed ninety-nine-cent delis and experimental tapas restaurants, low-income housing and upscale apartments alike, the windows light and dark like a chessboard. The crowd thickened outside Penn Station, and we darted through the throngs of pedestrians and delivery boys on bikes, pizza boxes and steaming white paper bags strapped over the back wheel. After a few blocks, the pavements thinned out again, and the silence between us once more became palpable.

I looked at him out of the corner of my eye. 'Are you still, uh, angry with me?'

'Not really.' He dodged to the right of a couple walking their dog while I curved round to the left, and when we'd passed them, he said, 'Are you still angry with *me*?'

I shook my head. 'No.'

'Good.' He smiled. 'Your apology is officially accepted.'

'I haven't apologised...'

'But you're about to.'

I laughed, hopping over a broken beer bottle. 'Yes, I guess I was.'

'Go on then.'

I sighed. 'I'm sorry I misjudged you. I'm sorry I assumed you were a stoner and an irresponsible drifter. And a nuisance. And, um, implied you were a slut.'

'Ouch.' He raised his eyebrows. 'When you say it like that, I'm not sure if I've forgiven you yet.'

'Oh, calm down,' I teased. 'You're fine.'

'Raina,' he said after a moment, in a tone I couldn't quite read. 'Did you really think that badly of me? I know I've led an unconventional life, but I'm just not as scandalous as some may think.'

'No Thai ladyboys during your travels?'

He laughed.

'Because I hear you can never be quite sure.'

'Nope,' he said, grinning. 'And no bastard children, either.'

We dashed through another intersection, the streets dirty with melted snow, the malty smell of engine oil converging with something sweet, like a bakery. I looked down at my boots. Mud had caked onto the edges, and with each step I tried to rub some of it off.

'Did I say something wrong?'

I shook my head.

'Tell me, Raina,' he said softly.

'Really, it's nothing.' I shrugged, and as his pace slowed, so did mine. 'But I guess, technically, *I* am a bastard child.'

'Oh.'

'It happens all the time, doesn't it? Same story, different characters. I never knew my dad, and Mom's kind of all over the place. He had blue eyes and blond hair – and was *tall*. That's all she ever told me.' I shrugged. 'She was too young.'

I felt Asher's hand on my shoulder.

'My grandmother – my Nani – was different back then. Different with my Mom. She wasn't allowed to do anything, not even take swimming lessons because a swimsuit was too revealing. She rebelled, she had me – and then when I was young I guess she'd had enough. Mom left, and has barely been back since.'

'So are we all allowed to blame everything on our childhood? Forever?'

'She's still finding herself, I think.' I glanced at him. 'She travels, she switches jobs when she feels like it – kind of like you did. We all find ourselves in different ways, although I suppose your way has been far more interesting than mine.'

'Interesting – sure.' Asher kicked at a loose stone. 'But being away from everything and everyone you've ever known, it's so easy to get lost.' He shrugged. 'You can lose your perspective on life, rather than find it.'

'Is that what happened to you?'

'Who knows? I've been everywhere, tried everything,' he winked at me, 'almost. And I don't regret much. Except that I wasn't at home when I was needed.'

'What did you miss?'

'My sister's wedding, for one. It's taken her a long time to forgive me.'

'But she forgave you.'

'Of course; she's my sister. But she has kids now. I'm an *uncle*, and a pretty great one too. And I know that when I have kids I would need Anna to be around for them. So now I want to be around for her. It's a small family.' His voice grew quiet. 'Our parents are dead.'

'Asher, I'm so sorry.'

He smiled. 'I was at university – my last term, actually. Their car slid off the road.'

'Was that why you left uni?'

'It's life, you know?'

I felt his hand brush against mine, and I squeezed it. '*Life* doesn't make living through that any easier.'

His fingers stayed intertwined with mine until the lights changed. On the other side, people had started to gather on the pavement in front of a yellowing sign with 'Punjabi Hut' painted on it in dark blue lettering. I'd seen shops like this in New York before: twenty-four-hour Indian eateries with platters of authentic veg or non-veg served on styrofoam plates for a five-dollar bill. Never more than three rickety tables inside, yet always full, always ready for the next wave of customers dashing in and out for a quick taste of home.

'What's going on?' asked Asher as we walked towards them. More were arriving, from the handful of cabs parked halfway up the kerb, pouring out of the restaurant, the scent of spices and oil trickling outside as they propped open the door. Someone was setting up a speaker, and we gathered at the edge of the growing crowd, watching everyone speaking excitedly in Hindi or Punjabi, buttoning up their coats over saris and kurta pyjamas.

The speaker pulsed to a start. Bhangra. Asher smiled at me in recognition, like he'd heard the lively, low, swinging beat before. Soon, everyone around us was dancing, old and young, their hands clapping or twisting, their hips moving as fluid as a belly dancer's. A woman who reminded me of Nani, petite and with a kind face, walked by with a Tupperware box full of ladoo, popping the sweets into people's mouths at random. She walked up to Asher and tapped his stomach. He opened his mouth and she plopped the whole thing in, and part of it crumbled off his lips. He caught it, laughing. 'What is this?'

I wiped the crumbs off his chin. 'It's a blessing.'

'It's good!'

The crowd formed a circle on the pavement, and everyone took turns dipping in and out of the middle, bobbing their shoulders with the beat, dancing with such vigour Asher and I couldn't stop watching. On impulse, I dragged Asher inside, and, laughing, I taught him the lehira step, and he jerked his arms from side to side, a silly, childish grin painted on his face. We danced and spun, and the saris swished, the smell of masala overflowed and being there – right *there* – with Asher, I felt something I hadn't in such a long time.

Happiness.

The music swelled, and in a chaos of shouts and laughs, the countdown began. I could feel Asher looking at me. Bodies pressed and clumped together. I was sober, but suddenly woozy, drunk on pepper, on the scent of aftershave.

'We're missing midnight.'

He was inches away, and it was like the crowd was pushing us closer. My ears rang, and I swallowed the saliva that had staled in my mouth. I could feel the heat of his body as it neared, and my neck prickled.

'No, we're not.'

As the numbers fell away, reverberating through the street, the mass, I couldn't breathe. I couldn't move. My hands were so close to Asher's, and his fingers brushed against me.

'Five ... four ...'

I could smell him. Pepper, earth, aftershave. Our fingers locked together, and I looked up.

'Three ... two ...'

And I couldn't look away.

'One.'

Then, in the middle of New York City, as I thought of nothing and no one else, he kissed me.

Chapter 24

I woke up alert, ready to hop out of bed and grab my trainers. I peeled back the covers, and then I noticed the floor-
to-ceiling window with a view of the West Side Highway,
the bleached white linen, and remembered where I was. I
stretched my arms high above my head, and then let them
tumble back onto the pillow. I looked over. Shay's side of
the bed was empty, the evidence of the rest of last night
scattered around the room: our boots and coats and dresses
in scattered piles on the chairs and dresser; wine and water
glasses still half full of champagne or chocolate milk. An
empty carton of Chinese takeaway on the bedside table, the
grease dripping onto the hotel's copy of the Bible. I sat up
and wiped it off with a napkin, and then scrambled for my
phone. I had a handful of work emails – from Bill, mostly
– sent just after midnight about a file I hadn't finished on
time. One new voicemail from Nani, and a text from Asher.

Good morning :-)

I smiled until my cheeks hurt, and rolled sideways onto
the duvet. *Asher*. Who would have thought ... and what
was I thinking?

I wasn't thinking. I still wasn't. But, for whatever reason,
I couldn't stop smiling. The rest of the night had passed in
a blur, even though I'd barely had a sip to drink. No one

had even noticed that Asher and I had disappeared, and after taking the photo with Draco, we carried on partying with the group, dancing to old-school R&B. Then, after a quick hug at the end of the evening, the bride and groom's parties had gone their separate ways.

I lay there, staring at the ceiling, wondering what to text back. A simple good morning? A mention of last night? But what *was* last night?

Would there be time to talk about it in New York? We were flying home that afternoon, and most likely wouldn't have a moment alone together until we were back in Toronto. I wondered where Asher lived, whether he'd want to see me again. But what did it matter? I had to go back to work, go back and wait for Dev … didn't I?

I swung my feet over the edge of the bed and pulled on a bathrobe hanging behind the door. Shay was sprawled across the futon in the main room, her morning-after hair tied in a bun on top of her head. She had an ice pack on her forehead, her mobile phone on her stomach, and Nikki and Niti were limp on the other sofa, half-dressed, their eyes half-closed. Serena was in the kitchen pouring coffee, and she pushed a full cup towards me as I sat down at the counter.

'Coffee?'

'Thanks.' I took a sip, and then glanced back at Shay. She was glaring at me now, and I wondered if she'd figured out what had happened with Asher.

'How was everyone's night?' I asked no one in particular. I took another sip, and then glanced over at the twins. 'Nikki? You seemed to be having fun.'

She groaned, lifting her head slightly before letting it

flop back down on the pillow. I heard Serena laugh behind me, but Shay's face hadn't changed; she was still staring me.

'Shay, you feeling OK?'

She didn't blink. 'I talked to Ma this morning.'

'Oh yeah?' I crossed my arms. 'How was her New Year's Eve party?'

'It seems she had a nice little chat with your Nani.' Shay sat up slowly, curling her fingers over the edge of the futon. 'Want to guess what it was about?'

I laughed. 'Did your dad get drunk and sing again?' I caught her eye, her icy glare, and when seconds passed and she hadn't said anything, I knew. My stomach dropped. 'I…'

'Is this all some kind of elaborate *joke*?'

'Shay—' I stopped. I glanced at Serena, coffee cup frozen halfway to her mouth, a blank expression on her face.

'Look,' I said, turning to face Shay. 'I can explain. Can we talk in private for a second?'

'In private?'

'Shay, come on.'

'What the fuck is going on, Raina?'

I hopped off the stool, walked past the twins and started to pull her up by her wrist. 'Please, let's just talk.'

'No—'

'In private. Shay, please.'

'Get off me, you *dyke*.'

'Shaylee? What's—'

'Stay out of this, Serena,' Shay growled. The air in the room had gone flat; soured. Nobody spoke, and I could hear my heart beating furiously. Homophobes used that word. And as I looked at Shay, at my best friend, I couldn't understand why she was too.

'So,' she continued, 'you have an audience now. Always begging to be the centre of attention. Well, here you are, Raina. We all want to hear your joke now. We all want to hear from the *dyke*.'

'Don't say that word.'

'What word?' She crossed her arms and stood up to face me. 'A *dy*—'

'Don't you *dare* say that word, ever again. Do you understand me?'

'No, Raina. I don't fucking understand you. Since when does your Nani think you're a lesbian?'

I heard a shuffle behind me and turned round. Nikki and Niti were off the sofa, one behind the other, walking towards the door. Serena had already gone. A moment later, the door clicked shut, and all I could hear was the hum of the fridge, the door still slightly ajar.

'Well?'

I looked back at Shay. She was standing there staring at me, panting almost, with anger I'd never seen in her before.

'What's going on with you?'

I sat down on the sofa. I couldn't breathe, and I wished that I could open the window. Everything felt trapped inside me, and I didn't know how to let it out.

'Unbelievable.' She threw her hands in the air. 'You're going to sit there, and not even look at me? After everything we've been through, you're going to keep *lying* to me?'

I concentrated on my toes – dry, cracking – trying to steady my breath. But what was the truth? That I wasn't as strong as her? That I hated myself; that I hated the way Dev treated me, yet I couldn't stop? That I was ashamed, and alone?

'Fine,' I heard her say. 'Lie to me. Let's go with that. Let's go with you being a fucking *lesbian*.'

My mouth was dry, and I swallowed, trying to find words – *any* words.

'You, coming out to your Nani.' Shay's voice cracked. '*You*, a lesbian – the same girl who became a doormat for the first guy to really look at you, some guy who didn't give two shits—'

'Shut up.'

'And now you're telling people you've given up on men? Want to try the *ladies* for a while?' She laughed cruelly. 'Good fucking luck.'

I looked up at her. 'I said, shut up.'

'You know what?' She shook out her hair. 'I'm not going to shut up, not like I did when Dev turned you into a puddle and *I* had to deal with the mess.'

'Shay—'

'It was pathetic, and *this*,' she threw out her hand, 'whatever it is you're doing now, is *really* pathetic.'

'You know, I always thought that I was the judgemental one, not you.' I scratched my chin, and I heard my voice grow cold. 'I wonder if Julien would still marry you if he knew what a slut you used to be.'

Her mouth dropped open.

'Who knows? Maybe you still are.'

'You know I would never cheat on Julien,' whispered Shay.

I stood up. 'How would I know that, *Shaylee*? Maybe I don't know you at all. After all, you didn't know I was *gay*.'

'Raina, you're not gay.'

'How the hell would you know?' I screamed. 'You haven't

204

been around. You've been off with the man of your dreams, lecturing me about my problems whenever—'

'*I'm* not around? You're the one that keeps disappearing, that keeps shutting me out.'

'If, one day, you and Julien were finished – *finished* – would you want me to tell you just to "get over it"? Tell you to grow a pair, and be strong?'

'I never said that! I was always there—'

'You didn't even try and understand what I was going through. You lectured. You sat up on your high horse telling me what to do, telling me to move on, telling me I could fix it all by screwing guys like *you* did—'

'How long was I supposed to let you sulk? Look at you. How long has it been, and you're still not over that jerk?'

'He's not a jerk—'

'Your Nani flew all the way to London and he wouldn't even meet her.'

'It wasn't like that. He was called to Zürich, and then he—'

'Dev and you are *over*, Raina, and you're still defending him. Why? You need to delete that picture in your head. That guy who rolls in cash and runs marathons, and runs the world, because guess what?' She poked me. 'You've already dated him. And he never had time for you. He didn't even—'

'Just *shut up*. You don't even know what you're talking about. You with your perfect family and job, your perfect fiancé. You growing up with Auntie Sarla's silver spoon stuffed down your throat.'

'Right, because only *your* mother was the fuck-up. No

one else gets to screw up their child.' Shay had tears in her eyes. She took a step backward.

'So I'm screwed up,' I said softly. I was crying too, now. 'I'm pathetic, and screwed-up, and *gay*—'

'You're not gay!'

'Maybe I *am*. Maybe I—'

'You won't tell me what's going on.'

'And why do you think that is, eh?' I walked towards the bedroom door and, getting ready to slam it behind me, screamed, 'Because you're so *fucking* understanding.'

Chapter 25
20 May 2003

The girls are spread out around the room, in threes and fours on each sofa, some flopped down or cross-legged on the shag carpet, others with their knees up, their backs against the brightly papered wall. They take turns switching their favourite CDs into Raina's portable player – Macy Gray and Destiny's Child, Missy Elliott and Creed. The coffee table is full of kettle corn and fuzzy-peach candies, ketchup and salt and vinegar crisps. Birthday cake. Sprite – although some of the girls have brought cans of beer, water bottles full of vodka and lemonade powder, and they drink this instead.

It's Raina's birthday, and it's decidedly a girls' night. Who decided it, Raina cannot remember, but nonetheless, Nani's entertaining room is now full of them. Girls from the team. Girls with bad haircuts who play the clarinet or the trumpet. Ones who run track, or who have met Shay in Chemistry Club. They are all shuffled in together at random, high on sugar, on each other, and they are giggling about boys.

Boys, thinks Raina, listening to them; the only thing of any concern on a girls' night.

Shay stands on the sofa cushion, and everyone watches her body wriggle as she talks about Theo. He is a senior, and after class, Shay recounts, he drove her home in his dad's Mercedes, first parking the car behind the hockey rink. Raina is anxious to learn more when she hears the door open. Shay slinks down into her seat, slides her can of beer beneath it, just before Nani shuffles into the room. She puts down a tray of pakoras and samosas, along with tamarind and mint chutney in little clay bowls, and smiles to the girls. Everyone murmurs their thanks, and Nani hovers expectantly as they examine the food.

All the girls in the room except for Shay are white, and they follow her lead, carefully selecting one of the flaky fried chunks like a chimp with a new toy, biting off tiny pieces. Taking the smallest of morsels to place on their tongues. It is a success. Their eyes pop and they shiver in thanks. Raina suspects most have never tried Indian food before, and they lick their fingers clean.

'Thanks, Mrs Anand!' they cry, as Nani turns to leave.

'Please,' she replies, heading back up the stairs. 'Call me Nani.'

Shay waits until the door clicks shut, then turns back to the group. She is smiling from ear to ear, and, Raina knows, waiting for someone to prompt her.

'So,' says the girl beside her. 'What happened with Theo? Did you ...'

Shay smiles coyly. 'Did I what?'

'Just tell us!'

'Come on, Shaylee,' says another.

'What happened?'

Shay squeals and topples off the sofa, rolls back and forth on the floor. Then she sits up, arcing one arm high in the air. 'OK, OK, I'll tell you.' She is breathless. 'We didn't do *it*, but he …' She smiles, and points between her legs, and there is a chorus of gasps around the room.

'Down *there*?'

Shay nods, and another girl chants, 'Shaylee, no way!'

'Did it feel good?'

She screws up her nose like she's about to sneeze. 'I think so.'

'You think so?'

She nods again. 'He said he knew what he was doing.'

'Of course Theo knows what he's doing,' says one of the girls from track. 'He always knows what he's doing,' and two other girls laugh.

'Shay,' says Raina. 'You never told me that.' And after Shay turns to her and shrugs, Raina asks, 'Is he your boyfriend?'

Shay glares at her, as if she is irritated. 'I don't care about things like that.'

'Do you think you'll have *sex* with him?'

But Shay has already turned away, has turned her attention to another girl, another question, and they launch into a discussion about things Raina has never done – things she can barely fathom. Shay reaches into her backpack and pulls out a *Cosmopolitan* magazine, bright yellow and pink, with Sarah Michelle Gellar posing on the front cover. Everyone leans in, and as they paw over the glossy pages, shrieking, Raina slips out of the room unnoticed.

Upstairs, Nani is splayed out on the sofa, her calloused feet resting on Nana's lap. And although he appears to be asleep sitting up, eyes closed, his fleshy chin pillowed onto his neck, his hands are awake, softly stroking Nani's feet.

'What are you doing?' asks Raina, watching them from the hallway.

Nani looks over, and Nana snorts himself awake. 'Raina.' His yawn lands in a wide smile. 'How is the party?'

'Good.' Raina walks over to them as Nani slides her feet off the sofa and Raina wedges herself between them. She sinks into the cushion. 'What are you watching?'

'*Mohabbatein*,' says Nana, wrapping his arm around her shoulder.

'Again?'

He nods towards the TV. 'Your Nani loves this one.'

'Should we start it again?' asks Nani. 'Your friends want to watch?'

Raina shakes her head and stares at the screen. The actors are in a market throwing coloured powder into the air, dancing beneath the festive debris. It seems like the DVD has been on a loop ever since Nana brought home a pirate copy from the restaurant, and from time to time, Raina has watched it with them. The characters are in their first year of college, falling in love for the first time, and as Raina watches them, her stomach drops. Their lives, their experiences – it all seems like an eternity away. But Raina is now sixteen, and college is not so far off in the future.

Raina cannot imagine having to decide what to do with her life. What or whose path she should follow. Shay already knows she will be a doctor, but Raina is not strong like her, and she cannot see herself in a hospital, in the witness box of death and decay. Kris studies engineering, but Raina does not know what that means. She likes maths, physics even, and wants to know more, but these days Kris rarely sleeps at home. Nani despised his Sri Lankan girlfriend, a nutritionist with buck teeth and giant breasts, but she convinced him to propose, and now talks excitedly about the wedding even though a date has yet to be set.

Her Nana tells her that she would make a good lawyer, but Raina has never met one before, and other than episodes of *Law and Order*, she has no idea what lawyers actually do. Often she wonders if she should go to university at all. Nani didn't, and neither did Manavi. The last time her mother lived at home, instead of a degree hanging above her desk, she had a map. Tea-stained and bristling with red and blue pins. All the places Manavi had been – or wanted to go. Places that Raina knows nothing about.

'Are you OK, my sweet?' Nani brushes Raina's cheeks with both hands. 'Are you having fun?'

Raina nods. 'Yes, thank you. Everyone loves the food.'

Nani wiggles her eyebrows. 'Don't worry. I saved spicy ones for you.' She grabs a plate of pakoras from the end table and hands them to Raina, and Raina pops two in her mouth at once. She smiles, crunches the spicy warmth between her teeth.

'Now,' says Nani, putting the plate back down, 'go and have fun.'

Raina stands to leave, but lingers by the doorway. 'Hey, guys?'

They both look at her.

'Manavi had just turned sixteen.' Raina looks at her socks, traces the lines in the hardwood with her toes. 'She was sixteen when I was born.' Her lips quiver, and inexplicably, she wants to cry.

'Raina.' Nana's voice is strong and sweet, and it draws closer. Raina feels him, both of them, as they stand on either side of her, looking up at her intently. Nani takes Raina's hand in hers.

'Listen to me.' Nani squeezes her hand. 'You are such a capable girl.'

'A *good* girl,' adds Nana. 'With such bright future ahead.'

A tear falls, and Nani wipes it away. 'You are *nothing* like your mother.'

'Do you understand?'

Raina nods. She forces out a smile, says, 'I understand.'

Raina rejoins the party. Her seat has been taken, and so she curls up on the floor by the coffee table. The girls have moved on from the magazine. They are sillier now, passing cans and bottles around to one another, giggling, already thinking they are drunk. A bottle of beer reaches Raina. It has gone warm, and her hand sticks to the green glass. She takes a deep breath, wraps her mouth round the lip of the bottle and throws back her head. As she drinks, Raina cannot stop thinking, what if Nani is wrong? What if she actually is like her mother? What if Raina, too, is a disappointment?

Chapter 26

For the first time ever, I was grateful for the long hours and sleepless nights at the office, the distraction of the cutting-edge, thankless world of banking. Winter churned on outside my window, and I sat in my twelve-square-foot cell poring over financial statements and market data, working and reworking a balance sheet. Dissecting a cash flow problem, an economic implication. I worked without really working; absorbed and spat out what I was supposed to, and as I sat there on the phone with a client discussing pharmaceutical investments and market shares, and made notes on a risk analysis, I was thankful for the diversion. The disturbance. Thankful that I didn't really have to think. I tore through reports faster than they were assigned, and Bill warmed up to me again, happy to see that I was 'back to my old self'. Ironically, although predictably so, I felt further away from myself than I'd ever been.

January and then February dragged on, and still the winds sliced brisk and sharp, the sleet and snow creeping in through the revolving doors, at the edges of frosted windowpanes. It seemed as if spring would never rear its willowy horns and fill the city with light and sun. It seemed that Dev would never show up, either. He'd been temporarily assigned to a project in Jakarta now – something about an emerging market, heading up a risk analysis. These days he called often, and his texts and emails were flowered in 'darlings' and 'missing you's, constant reassurances that he'd be 'be back in a jiff'. But even when – even *if* – he came back, I wasn't sure what I'd do or say, or how he'd fit into the spectacular mess I'd created and, with each passing day, obstinately ignored.

I mean, it wasn't every day that someone managed single-handedly to divide a community.

After New York, I'd gone straight home and asked Nani what had happened, and she'd simply apologised and collapsed soundlessly onto the sofa. I prodded, but she couldn't remember all that much about Auntie Sarla's New Year's Eve party, except that she'd reacted when Auntie Sarla made a derogatory remark about two men kissing on television. And then, part way through the argument, Nani had told Auntie Sarla – told *everyone* – what she thought to be the truth.

Nani outed me to a roomful of people born in a country where homosexuality was still a crime, a roomful of people who quickly took sides. Overnight everyone knew, half of them disgusted with Auntie Sarla, the other half disgusted by me. And in the months that followed, Nani cut ties with at least half of her friends. She disinvited herself to dinner parties and to the movie club, to any social gathering organised by someone on 'Team Sarla'; anyone who believed homosexuality was wrong.

'You should have *seen* her reaction, Raina. Terrible!' Nani had sobbed, clutching me in her arms. 'But if you saw, you would have done the same. In front of everyone, she *screamed* at me, asking me how I could allow this—'

Nani panted, exhausted from the dramatisation, and then continued. 'And I reply, "What is there to allow?" Then that *voman*, she told me to leave the party. Told me, of course I would make all my girls turn strange.'

I'd ignited a war between them: Auntie Sarla, a social pillar of West Toronto's Indian community, wife of a neurosurgeon and mother of two successful children, and Suvali Anand: a blue-collar, social-climbing widow. Mother of rebels. Grandmother of, apparently, a lesbian.

I sat in my office, my belly full of a Vietnamese noodle bowl Zoey had brought me for lunch, and I let my face fall onto my desk. My forehead stuck to the varnish, and I could smell my hair and sweat as I breathed against the hard surface. I was bored, and restless; it was becoming harder and harder not to think about Shay. She'd gone to India with Auntie Sarla and Julien, and had already been back for a week, Nani had told me. She'd seen Auntie Sarla back at yoga classes, but she'd refused to turn round and look at her as she attempted the chair pose at the front of the temple recreation room.

'That woman is so inflexible – it is not *stool* pose,' Nani had said cattily, waiting for me to laugh.

For the millionth time, I flicked through my phone, scrolling back to my last message from Shay. It was dated from over a month before: New Year's Eve, 11.51 p.m.

Where are you Raaaaaina

I peeled my head off the desk and stared out of the window. It was the middle of the afternoon, dark and miserable, and I missed Shay.

I missed my best friend.

I looked back at my computer screen, inundated with numbers, formulas, and I tried not to think about her. Concentrating, narrowing in on my work, there was something else I tried not to think about; someone else I hadn't seen since New Year's Eve.

My intercom buzzed, and I hit the button. 'Yes?'

'Raina, you have a, uh, visitor here.'

My stomach fluttered. 'Who is it?'

'A Dep-oosh Sax-ee-na?'

'Oh.' I caught my breath. 'All right, thanks Emma. Send him up.'

I opened my office door and waited out in the corridor. A minute later, the lift doors opened and Depesh appeared; fresh-faced, even taller it seemed than when I'd seen him at Christmas.

He followed me into my office and sat down in Zoey's usual chair, crossing his legs tight.

'How've you been?' I asked. 'Haven't heard from you in a while.'

'Haven't heard from you either.'

'Yeah, you're right.' I sat down beside him. 'Sorry again.'

He shrugged.

'Want some coffee?'

'Hmm?'

'Coffee.'

'Oh.' He shrugged, then looked down at his feet. 'Nah, it's all right. I'm fine.'

'OK…'

He went silent, and I watched him as he shook his foot wildly, refusing to meet my eye.

'Is everything OK?' I paused. 'Is it Auntie Sharon?'

He shook his head. 'Ma is fine.'

'And you don't want coffee.'

He shook his head.

'Er, tea?'

'No.' He stood up and started pacing the office. 'I don't want tea, all right?'

'Depo?'

He stood by the door, and when he put his hand on the knob I thought he might leave. But then he closed the door and sat back down.

'That British guy. Did you even love him?'

'Pardon?'

'I don't get it, Raina, I—'

'Depo, slow down. What on earth are we talking about?'

He paused, and then said, 'You're gay.'

'Oh.' I sank back onto the chair. '*That.*'

'I heard it, like, *weeks* ago.' He glared at me. 'Thanks for telling me, by the way. And what are you, like, thirty?'

I blew air out through my teeth. 'Nearly.'

'Everybody knows now, do you even know that? Like, *everybody* is talking about it.'

'Yeah, thanks.' I scratched my head. 'I am acutely aware.'

'Why did you have to tell everyone? *Now?*' He looked at me like I'd done something wrong, like I was being ridiculous. 'Why couldn't you just keep it a secret?'

'Excuse me?'

'Like, after all these years. What made you come out?' He shook his head. 'You hid it this long, and now you just didn't want to, *what*, explain it to me?'

'Explain what, exactly?'

217

'You knew it would cause a scene with everyone, our whole community, and still—'

'Listen, I really don't have time for a lecture.'

'Raina, please just explain it to me, OK?' His voice came out softer now, pleading. 'I need you to explain it to me, because . . .' He paused. 'I am, too.'

'Come again?'

'I'm gay, Raina. Just like you.' He slumped forward, and put his head in his hands. 'And I have no idea what to do.'

We waited in the cocktail bar on the ground floor of my office building, and I sat there playing with my hands, watching Depesh drink his second whisky and Coke in ten minutes. He'd slurped down the first in three clean sips and noisily chewed the ice cubes until a waiter came back and asked if he wanted another. At first I was surprised they hadn't asked for his ID – Depo, a kid in Converse trainers and a t-shirt, here on Bay Street; a kid who, to me, still looked like the ten-year-old I used to babysit; who I'd seen cry after I let him watch a horror movie. Whose eyes lit up whenever I suggested ice cream.

But then I looked again. He had stubble on his chin and above his lip, and the baby fat had been sucked from his cheeks, exposing a chiselled jaw and brown bone, a beaky nose. He wasn't the kid I knew any more. He was eighteen – nineteen, now – and I struggled with what to say. I could feel my heart pounding in my stomach.

He was gay?

It was the middle of the afternoon, and the bar was empty except for us. All the waiting staff were clustered behind the bar unloading glasses and chatting about whether this year, finally, the Leafs would make it into the play-offs.

'You sure you don't want a drink?' Depesh asked after a while.

'No,' I said. 'I have to go back to work after.'

He nodded. 'You're sure you have time?'

'Of course, Depo. I have time.' I glanced at the door. 'Sorry, I don't know where she could – ah.' I saw Zoey waft through the entrance and my stomach unclenched in relief. 'There she is.'

We were at a booth by the window, and she pulled up a chair at the end. She looked at Depo curiously and then extended her hand towards him.

'I'm Zoey.'

'Depesh,' he said. He shook her hand and then drew his own back into his lap.

'Hi, Depesh.' She glanced between us, and her eyes landed on me. 'You texted that this was some sort of emergency.'

'Not quite …' I looked at Depesh. 'You're sure?'

He nodded, and I looked back at Zoey.

'Zoey, my friend Depesh wants to talk to us about something.' I swallowed. 'He's … gay.'

'Also,' he said, his eyes flicking between us, 'Raina says you guys are too.'

'*Also* gay,' repeated Zoey, her eyes still on me. I saw her press her lips together, and I could feel my cheeks flush.

What was I *doing*? This boy, who'd been like a little brother to me, was gay, and I was going to lie to him? Tell him I was gay too?

For a few seconds – what seemed like eternity – nobody spoke. Depesh stared at his hands, Zoey stared at me, and all I could hear was the barman's ignorant position on which Leafs players deserved to be in the Hall of Fame, the elevator jazz drifting from a distant speaker.

'Sorry,' I heard Depesh mumble, and I looked up at him.

'What on earth are you sorry for?' I asked.

Looking as if he might cry, he shrugged his shoulders.

'No, *we're* sorry.' Zoey flicked her eyes at me, then back to him. 'Just a little stunned, that's all.' Smiling, she pulled her chair closer to him. 'Is there anything in particular you'd like to talk about?'

He shrugged.

'Raina, do you want a drink?'

'I'm good.'

She flagged down the waiter and ordered a small glass of Chardonnay. While he walked away, and lingered chattily behind the bar, then sauntered back with the wine, none of us said a word. Zoey lifted the glass to her lips and took a slow sip.

'Perfect.' She set it back down, wiping off her lip print with her thumb. 'What are you studying, Depesh?'

'Biochemistry.' He shrugged. 'I'm going to apply to study medicine.'

'That's pretty cool.'

'Not really. Like, everyone wants to be a doctor.'

'Well, why do you?'

He looked at me as if he was expecting me to answer for him, and when I didn't he glanced back at the table. 'My mom is ill.'

'I'm sorry to hear that.'

'Don't be.' He chewed another ice cube. 'You didn't give her MS.'

Zoey nodded her head slowly.

'We're close, you know? I'm the only son. The only *child*, and I've got to help out a lot. My dad has to work a lot more now too.' He glanced at me again, like he was surprised I wasn't interrupting, offering my own version of events. 'We used to live in New Jersey but her treatment got too expensive. Gotta love American healthcare.'

'No kidding,' Zoey chuckled. 'How long have you been back?'

'Six months or so.'

She nodded again.

'And there's treatments here, too, but,' he shrugged, 'there's just not a lot anyone can do. It's secondary progressive, and sometimes between attacks she's back to normal, almost, but it's a waiting game. Like, you never know who or what the trigger is going to be.' His voice grew quiet. 'Whether *I* would be the trigger.'

Zoey nodded, and as I sensed what was happening, what she was doing, I fought the urge to leap over the table and hug her. She was patient. Empathetic. She knew people, how to read them and what they needed, and I felt an overwhelming sense of gratitude to her for being there for me; for being there for Depesh.

Tentatively, she said, 'Did Raina tell you my coming out story, Depesh?'

He shook his head.

'Well, it's a pretty standard story. I was about your age, and I'd known for a while.' Zoey stared intently at her wine glass. 'And because I'd figured myself out so easily, I just assumed everyone else would, too, and,' she paused, 'that my parents would someday just work it out.'

He nodded.

'So I just didn't think about it. I didn't think about the fact that I was always hiding, or lying, or making excuses about why I never had a boyfriend. Of course, my best friends knew, and I dated, well, I *slept* with women. And then one day I met a girl, a girl who turned out to be pretty special to me. This girl was *gorgeous*, intelligent and sassy as hell. And, of course, she went on to break my heart, but in retrospect, I swear to you, Depesh, it was still worth it.'

He nodded, his eyes still looking at the table.

'I told my parents about her. And they screamed and they cried, and they threw shit—'

'Did they forgive you?'

'Depesh, there was nothing to forgive. I am who I am, and they simply can't or won't accept that. Don't get me wrong; I sacrificed my relationship with them for a new relationship, but those feelings are part of who I am. They're a part of all of us. Love and heartbreak – it's everywhere, its universal and there's no shame in any of it.'

I thought of Dev, and how this whole mess had started because I was ashamed.

As if she knew what I was thinking, Zoey reached for my hand under the table. I grabbed it, and it gave me strength.

'And,' I continued, looking Depo in the eye, 'if there's one thing Zoey and I can impress upon you, it's that *you* have absolutely nothing to feel ashamed about.'

Chapter 27

A young Rani Mukerji danced in a train station wearing a blue boob tube, shaking her hips, lip-synching to a voice possibly a full octave higher than her own. An actor I didn't recognise – aviators, dressed like a sailor – appeared behind her, sang to her as he did push-ups and made the street children laugh.

I looked over at Nani. She had her feet on the coffee table, one toe bouncing along with the beat, but her eyes were glued to her tablet, her finger tracing long, slim lines across the surface.

'If you're not watching this, can I put something else on?' I grabbed a cushion from the floor and wedged it behind my back. '*Anything* else?'

Nani didn't reply. She pushed her glasses up her nose with the back of her hand and resumed her finger-positioning at the tablet.

'What are you doing?'

'Candy Crash.'

'Candy *Crush*?'

She smiled at the screen, then let out a mild shriek. 'I *von*! I beat the level.' Turning to me, she winked. 'Pretty good for old woman, *nah*?'

I laughed. 'Good job.'

She put the tablet down on the coffee table and turned her attention to the television. I watched her, studied her face. Was she really watching? What was she thinking? Why was her granddaughter – supposedly successful, in the prime of her life – home with her, watching Hindi movies, on a Friday night?

And then I shuddered. Because for as long as I could remember, Nani had never been at home on a Friday night either. She had dinner parties, temple gatherings and poojas; helped out at festivals and volunteered.

'Why are you staring, *beta*?'

I sat up and leaned closer to her. 'Have you spoken to Auntie Sarla recently?'

She pressed her lips together, and then after a moment looked back at the screen.

What had I done? Had I ruined Nani's life too? Ousted her from the community she'd helped build?

I wanted to say something, to come clean. It felt as if a wall had been built between us, and I'd never been so far away. And I knew that no matter how many evenings per week I came to visit, no matter how many new subjis I learned to cook, I couldn't fix this without telling the truth.

But what was the truth?

Depesh needed my help. That was the truth. And every time I saw Nani, every time I tried to speak up, he held me back.

He was a kid, a kid who texted or called me almost every day now because he didn't have anyone else to talk to about who he was. A kid who had trouble making friends, opening up and confiding in people – especially his own parents. It was getting warmer now; we were on the verge of spring, and sometimes after work he would drop by the office and we'd go for walks along the harbour – sometimes with Zoey too.

He didn't need a matchmaker or a mother or some sort of gay mentor; he just needed a friend. Someone to listen to him talk about his latest exam, or the pressure he felt from his father to be perfect, the guilt he felt about his mother's illness. He'd been so brave to come out to me – and now what was I supposed to do? Come out *again*, to make it easier on myself?

All this had started because of Dev: the man of my dreams. The man I had to lie for. The man who was working half a world away, but still called, still emailed. Still wouldn't leave me alone.

I loved him, didn't I? And I *knew* he loved me, even if he didn't say it. But how could this all have been worth it? Dev coming back wouldn't fix anything any more. *I* had to fix it. I'd been selfish – I'd thought only of myself – and now it was my turn to face the consequences.

I looked back at Nani, and watched the TV glow flicker across her face. Yes, I thought. Depesh needed me now, and I was going to be there for him. For now, even if it meant not being there for Nani.

The phone rang, and Nani reached for the cordless handset between us. Deliberately, she pressed the button and then held it to her face.

'This is Mrs Ah-Nund. Hello, who is speaking?' She made a face into the phone, and then looked at me. 'Raina, for you.'

I reached for it. 'Hello?'

'Raina, it's Julien.'

225

I breathed out. 'How did you get this number?'

'From Shay's phone, when she wasn't looking.'

I looked over at Nani, staring at me curiously. 'Work,' I mouthed to her, hopping off the sofa.

'You didn't try my mobile?'

'If you saw my number, I wasn't sure you'd pick up.' He paused, and then said, 'I saw your car there when I was driving home from Sarla's tonight.'

'Ah.' I walked into the kitchen, the door swinging closed behind me. 'How was *that*?'

'All right.' I heard the faint whirr of a coffee machine, a few echoing voices, and I could tell he was in the doctors' lounge Shay used to call me from. 'I was over there for dinner.'

'I see.'

'You know we went to India?'

'I heard.'

'We've been home for weeks already,' he said. 'I was hoping you guys would have made up by now.'

'Yeah, well, I wouldn't hold your breath.' I sat down at the table, slumped my body onto its hard, cold surface. I could hear him breathing into the phone, and as I waited for him to say something, anger surged through me. She was getting her *fiancé* to call for her?

'Raina, listen…'

A moment passed. 'I'm listening.'

'OK, here it goes.' He sighed noisily. 'I wasn't going to say anything about this, but… to hell with it. Look, Raina, I'm Catholic, so I guess I understand why some people reacted the way they did—'

'Are you really defending your mother-in-law?'

'No, of course not – that isn't even why I called.'

'Why did you call?'

'Let me start again.' Another sigh. 'Something has happened with you and Shaylee, and I'm not even going to pretend I know what that is, or even what's going on with *you*, for that matter. You haven't exactly been there for her.'

'Helping plan the wedding, organising the trip to New York? That wasn't being there for her?'

'You know what I mean, Raina. Things have been off with you and Shaylee for a while. Well before New York. And I won't even claim to understand women.'

I could almost picture Julien sitting there, brow furrowed, chewing his lip on those hideous orange couches Shay had described to me a thousand times, her hand buried beneath the cushions while we guessed how much change she would find, what gadgets she might excavate.

'Whatever's happened between you and Shaylee, she won't talk to me about it. She won't say a word. But I know her – and she feels terrible.'

'Good. She should.'

'Whoever's fault it is, whatever it was that caused this, don't you think it's time to make up?' He laughed. 'For Christ's sake. She still brought you home a bridesmaid's outfit.'

I didn't respond. In the other room I heard the cuckoo clock start to chime, and a shiver crept down my spine.

'I don't know if I can forgive her, Julien. I honestly don't know.'

'Don't you want to try? Don't tell me that you of all people haven't said anything in the heat of the moment!

There's nothing you wish you could take back – something you took too far?'

I bit my lip.

'You have been best friends – you've been *sisters* – for over twenty years. You know her better than anyone in the entire world. Whatever you fought about, ask yourself – is it really worth it?'

'I'll talk to her,' I said slowly. 'But she has to apologise first.'

'Funny, that's exactly what she said.'

I rolled my eyes. 'Well, we were best friends.'

'You *are* best friends. And Shaylee needs you right now, what with the wedding coming up. And I know that Sarla is driving her crazier than usual because of—'

'Because of all the drama I've caused?'

'You said it, not me.'

I smiled, and realised that even though they'd been together for nearly five years, this was the first time Julien and I had ever spoken on the phone. Indeed, it was the longest conversation we'd ever had.

'Will you think about talking to her?'

I nodded slowly. 'I'll think about it.'

'Good. And just so you know, Raina, you may be Shaylee's best friend, but she's *my* best friend. And I know everything about her. Everything.' He paused. 'And I love her just the same.'

I thought about it. I thought about all the terrible things I wanted to say to Shay. About how awful she'd made me feel; how disappointed I was in her. But the more I thought about her, the less angry I became.

I just wanted to know how Shay was doing; if she'd liked India this time, and what it was like visiting her family now that she was *finally* getting married. I wanted to be filled in on the wedding plans; on her favourite patients at the hospital; find out if she ever bought that phallic-shaped figurine – of what, exactly, we never figured out – that we once saw at Urban Barn.

I wanted to know if she missed me too.

And so, the next weekend, when Julien asked me to meet them at the diner, and told me he was sending Asher to escort me there, I reluctantly agreed.

I had only an hour's notice. I showered and changed and tried to style my hair – curled, jutting out at the back – the way Shay had once said suited me. I found my make-up bag beneath the sink and outlined my eyes. Curled my lashes.

The buzzer rang. I let Asher up, and then waited in the doorway. I hadn't seen or heard from him since New York, and I could feel my heart beating in my stomach.

Did he still think about New Year's Eve too? Did he think about me at all? So much had happened since. In a way that night – that *kiss* – felt so far away, so surreal, I often wondered if it'd even happened.

The lift doors parted and Asher stepped out. He was wearing his leather jacket again, a grey hoody underneath the same colour as his eyes. His hands were deep in his pockets as he walked towards me.

'Hi.'

'Raina.'

The ease between us had shifted, and it felt oddly formal as he avoided my eyes and followed me inside.

'Nice place.'

'Thanks.'

He scanned my living room, and I wished that I'd cleaned a bit more. But his eyes skimmed past the piles of newspapers and the dirty dishes, and he squinted out of the window.

'That Allan Gardens?'

'I think so.'

'It's beautiful there. Especially in summer.' He cleared his throat. 'My mom loved gardening – she used to take me to the greenhouse all the time.'

'Asher...'

He turned to face me. 'Do you ever go?'

'To the greenhouse?' I shook my head.

'You should check it out. It's beautiful.' He smiled, glanced down at his shoes. 'But I've already said that, haven't I?'

It was only a quick walk to the diner. We didn't speak, and as we dodged our way along the crowded pavements in town, I tried not to focus on him looming beside me, his body briefly touching mine as we stood waiting for the traffic light. Instead, I tried to focus on Shay. What I would say; what *she* might say. And with each step I grew more nervous and less confident about what the hell I was doing, or what the right thing was *to* do. Why should I be nervous? It was Shay who owed me the apology, wasn't it?

I pushed open the front door of the diner, and saw Shay and Julien sitting in our usual booth at the far corner, right underneath the neon Hollywood sign. They were both in powder-blue scrubs, hoodies open over the top, and as I walked towards them, I started to panic.

'I can't do this.' I spun round and ran head first into Asher's chest. For a moment, barely, I was pressed up against him. The peppery soap smell clung to me, and I held my breath. I felt his hands on my shoulder blades, and he gently steered me back round and guided me across the linoleum floor until we were standing right in front of them.

Julien glanced up, and a moment later, Shay stopped speaking. She followed his gaze to the side, and looked up at me like she was waking up from a dream. I blinked, and she snapped her head back towards Julien.

'I *knew* you didn't want to eat here.'

'Wait,' I said, dumbfounded. 'She doesn't know?'

Julien smiled at us sheepishly and scooted out of the booth, and mechanically, guided by Asher's palms, I slid into his spot.

'I'm not staying.'

'Me neither,' said Shay.

'Babe, yes you are.'

'*Her* babe, or me babe?' said Shay, cuffing Julien on the arm. 'Traitor.'

'You're the traitor,' I mumbled.

'Julien, can you please tell her I'm not speaking to her?'

'Shay, she's right there.'

'I'm not staying.'

'Yes you are,' said Julien.

'And since when do you tell me what to do?'

'Since now.' Julien drummed the table with both palms. 'You are both going to talk. Right now. This is enough.'

Julien brushed a flyaway hair from Shay's forehead, and when she slapped his hand away, he laughed. 'We're going to be outside guarding the door, so don't even think about leaving.' He took a step backward, Asher in stride, and said, 'That means you, too, Raina.'

After they'd gone, Shay wouldn't look at me. Instead, she rolled her eyes and leaned her head back against the seat. She stuffed a French fry into her mouth, chewed it purposefully, and still she wouldn't look at me.

'Child,' I muttered.

She looked up at me, stuck her tongue out and took out her phone.

'Typical *Shay*.'

Another moment passed, and then she put down her phone, dug in her bag and retrieved a copy of *White Teeth*. My copy of *White Teeth*. She flicked roughly through the pages and lifted the book up so it blocked out her face.

I slid her plate towards me – three-quarters of a chicken burger, a fistful of fries – and then reached to the side for a bottle of mustard and noisily opened the lid. She moved the book down an inch. I smiled as I slowly tipped the bottle up and then squeezed it as hard as I could, mustard in thick swirls covering the entire plate.

Shay hated mustard.

'What the hell?' She tossed the book to one side. 'I was eating that.'

'I'm sorry.' I stuffed three fries into my mouth, mustard dripping off my lips. 'Did you just speak to me?'

'You're such a child.'

'Yes.' I nodded. '*I* am the child.'

'A child. And a liar.' She reached for the plate and I swatted her hand away. 'And a brat. You're—'

'Shay!' I pulled the plate back, so hard that she rose off the seat. 'Let go!'

'You let go!' She tugged at it, and then I tugged back, and just then, the plate flipped over and everything toppled onto the table in a big angry flop. 'Look what you've done!' cried Shay.

'Me?'

'Yes, *you*.' Her voice was hoarse, and as we used the paper-thin napkins to scoop the mashed yellow fries back onto the plate, I looked up at her and saw that she was crying, thick tears rolling down her cheeks. I handed her a napkin, and she roughly wiped her face.

After a moment, she stopped crying. She screwed the napkin up in her palms and then tossed it at me. It ricocheted off my shoulder and dropped into my lap. I picked it up and threw it back at her, hitting her square in the nose.

She smiled, and then her smile disappeared.

What had happened to us?

A waitress came by and glared at both of us as she grabbed the dirty plate, and then we were left in silence. The diner was mostly empty, a few quiet tables closer to the front seating children and grandparents, teenagers on daytime dates. A speaker above us was playing an easy-listening radio station, the tune and lyrics barely audible but entirely familiar.

Shay stared at her hands, and I knew she was working up the courage to apologise. That face, sheepish, red and sullen – I'd seen it a hundred times; Shay facing up to her mistakes, Shay acknowledging when she was wrong and trying to make amends.

But this time, was it really her fault?

Was it so awful that my best friend fell in love before I did? Even after she'd started dating Julien, hadn't Shay always been there for me? Hadn't she always supported me whenever Mom came home, and when Nana died? And when Dev and I ended, how many times had she shown up in the middle of the night with half a caramel cheesecake and a bag of popcorn, determined to cheer me up? Belted out Coldplay until my sobs turned to laughter and the neighbours complained?

And what had I done for her?

I'd been too busy making sure my calendar matched Dev's to invite her to visit me in London. I'd pushed her away whenever she tried to help. I'd distanced myself as her wedding approached, as her residency drew to a close; whenever her life went right, and, seemingly, mine went wrong. I'd lied to her, abandoned her when she needed me.

It was my fault, the fight. The lie, ballooning by the day. It was all my fault.

'I'm sorry,' I said finally.

Shay looked at me, a surprised look on her face. Her smile reappeared, and then she shrugged. 'I'm sorry too.'

'No, really, I'm sorry.'

'I was such a bitch to you.'

'What I said was horrible too, Shay.'

'I was just so angry, you know? I was angry, and I didn't – I *don't* – understand what's going on with you, why you're lying to everyone. I don't even *like* saying that word, the "d" word.'

'It's OK.'

234

'And I can't believe I called you out in front of everyone, called you that word. You know I didn't mean it, don't you?'

'I know you didn't mean it.' I paused and took a deep breath. 'And I guess … I just couldn't believe you're getting married.'

I looked away, embarrassed by the blunt and bitter truth: I couldn't believe Shay was getting married, and I couldn't believe it wasn't me.

Shay reached across the table and found my hand. 'It's OK.'

I blinked, trying to force away the tears, and she squeezed my hand until I looked her in the eye.

'Are you ready to tell me the truth now?'

Wasn't this why I came? Wasn't I ready?

'What can be so bad, Raina, that you're lying to everyone about *this*?'

I told her. Over two pieces of fresh pecan pie and cups of coffee, the whole story came out. I told her how Dev was back in my life, sort of, and how I still didn't know what to do or what it meant. I told her about Nani – the dates, the pressure, the slip-of-the-tongue lie – and how annoyingly supportive she was being. I told her about Depesh, that I'd been talking to or texting him almost every day. How we'd talk about his feelings of isolation and disappointment, of having to lie about who he was to everyone he knew.

I told her that I had no idea how to fix this without hurting him, without hurting Nani, and that I needed her help; I needed my best friend's help.

When I finally stopped talking, I was close to tears. Shay hadn't said a word the whole time, her face expressionless.

'Well?' I asked.

'Well ...' She paused, and pressed her lips together. 'Truth is, Raina, I don't know what the hell we are going to do.'

Despite everything, I smiled. *We*. Shay and I were back.

'Jesus, don't cry,' she said. She stood up in the booth, walked round the table and sat down next to me. She wrapped an arm tightly around my shoulder, and I let my head fall onto hers. I could smell her shampoo, her soothing tang of sweat and hospital plastic.

'You OK?'

I shook my head. 'What am I going to do?'

Abruptly, she pushed me off her and then angled her body so that she was facing me on the seat.

'We're not going to tell anyone, that's what we're going to do.'

'Really?'

She nodded. 'Can you see any alternative? If we tell anyone – and I mean *anyone* – we have to assume it's going to get back to Depesh. You said so yourself. And he *trusts* you, Raina. You can't abandon him.'

I looked at my hands and nodded. I knew that. This was about Depesh now, and I couldn't betray him. Besides Zoey, and now Shay, I was the only person who knew; the only person he trusted.

'But you can't go on pretending forever, either,' Shay added. 'At some point, this is all going to come out; we're just delaying the inevitable. At some point you're going to have to tell your Nani and my Ma – and boy, I do *not* want to be there for that. And you're going to have to tell Depesh.'

I looked up at her and nodded. I knew that too.

'But now is not the right time.'

'When is the right time?'

'Down the road, after he comes out? After he's more, I don't know, comfortable with himself?'

Shay sighed and wrapped her hand around her coffee cup. 'At some point – whenever that is, whenever you tell him the truth – you're going to hurt him, and he may never trust you again. There's no way round that.'

I'd racked my brain so many times; conjured up a million scenarios where he, and my Nani, didn't get hurt. But none of them worked.

'And your Nani …' Shay sipped her coffee and then put it back down. 'She'll be OK, I think. She's resilient.'

'Everyone thinks I'm gay,' I blurted. 'How is it going to be OK? How is anyone ever going to look at me – at *her* – the same way after the truth comes out?' I laughed, despite myself. 'I've seen her browser history. You know, she's been so supportive I think she might actually want me to marry a woman, have children with a woman. I don't know how I let it get this far.'

'You'd do anything for her, Raina. Everyone knows that.' Shay shrugged. 'And she'd do anything for you, even accept—'

'That her granddaughter isn't actually a lesbian?'

'That her granddaughter's just a bit of a liar,' said Shay, rolling her head back onto the booth. 'Shit, I should really go.'

'Already?'

Shay nodded. 'I have to train the new residents, and then go and help Ma with, I don't know, *something*.'

'How are the wedding plans?'

Shay groaned. 'She has been such a pain. The three of us brought home eleven suitcases from India. *Eleven*. Can you believe it?' She reached for her coffee cup. It was empty, and she slammed it back down on the table. 'I don't even know what's in the stupid things. It's turning into such a spectacle – ugh – and to think, Julien and his family wanted a tiny church wedding.'

'And what did you want?'

She shrugged, and then in the clearest of voices, 'I just wanted him.'

I turned round in the booth and glanced out of the front window. Julien and Asher were still standing on the pavement outside, arms crossed, talking to one another. I looked back at Shay.

'Do they know I'm ...'

Shay smiled. 'Julien thinks whatever Ma has been telling him. I haven't said anything about this; that muppet can't keep his mouth shut. Did you know they have dinner together when I work late?'

'I did know, actually.'

'And Asher – well, he thinks it was a damn good kiss for a lesbian.'

'You know about that?'

'Of course I know.' She glanced at her watch, and then reached across the table for her bag. 'But I have to get back to work. And you're going to call me tonight and tell me what the hell has happened between you two, OK?'

'Promise.'

She stood up, fumbling with her coat, her scarf. When she was all wrapped up, I clambered out of the booth and stood beside her. She came up to my nose.

'Shay...' I paused, struggling to find the words. 'All this time, you've never told anyone I was lying. Not Auntie Sarla, not Julien or Asher... Why?'

'I was *angry*,' she said, rolling her eyes. 'But I'm still your best friend. I was never *not* going to cover your ass.'

Chapter 28

After she'd disappeared from the diner, I took my time finishing my pie, my coffee. When I finally left, I saw Asher standing across the road, leaning against a lamp post, waiting for me. For some reason, I wasn't surprised he was still there. I put on my sunglasses, and through their shelter, took in his broad, shadowy physique. The strong line of his jaw; the upturned corners of his mouth. He smiled as I crossed the road towards him, and I found myself smiling back.

We wandered aimlessly, wrestling our way along the city pavements. It was one of those rare winter days that almost felt like spring, and the whole city, shoulder to shoulder, felt alive; everyone seemed to be outdoors, their winter parkas tied hastily around their waists; shopping or sports bags flung over one shoulder.

It wasn't until we'd walked past my office building that I realised that, some twenty floors above, Bill and Zoey were probably waiting for me; that I'd told him I'd come in and help with the next report. I looked behind me as the skyscrapers fell away and followed Asher towards the lake, resolving not to think about it. Resolving, for now, not to care.

Cherry Beach was spotted with snow, and as we walked westwards along the lake, a breeze picked up and I shivered.

'Are you cold?' he asked. 'Do you want my coat?'

I shook my head. He took off his sunglasses and squinted at me for a moment, and then, smiling, put them back on.

'Have you and Shaylee made up?'

I nodded.

'In New York she didn't take your news well, I gather.'

I didn't say anything; timed my footsteps with his.

'People don't always understand what isn't right in front of them.' Asher's feet kicked sand up onto mine. 'Not right away, at least. And how much can we really blame people for not knowing better? But then, when they do know better, I think we can blame them for not trying.'

I swallowed loudly. Asher thought I was gay; he thought the fight was about me being gay.

'I think she's trying.' I felt him looking at me, and after a moment, he continued. 'I haven't told you about my sister Anna, have I?'

I kicked a loose stone. 'Have you?'

'About the time she swallowed everything in the bathroom cabinet and had to have her stomach pumped?'

'Asher, that's horrible.'

'It was. She's OK now, thank God. But at the time Anna was just a kid who needed help.' He shrugged. 'She's gay, and she didn't know how to deal with it – not even in a family like ours. I can't imagine what it would have been like for someone growing up somewhere less ... tolerant.'

He looked over at me expectantly, and my stomach felt as if it might tear in two.

Asher's sister was gay?

'Anyway, Anna's happily married now,' he said. 'Jess is great. They have two kids in the suburbs. Piano lessons, bake sales, the whole deal. But it just terrifies me to think how easily none of that could have happened.' He glanced at me. 'Actually, it's one of the reasons I wanted to be a teacher. Kids should be happy, you know? I never want to see what happened to Anna happen to anyone else.'

I nodded, staring furiously at my shoes as we toed our way across the sand. Asher's sister was gay, and, like Depesh, it had been a struggle for her to accept it. I was making light of that. I was making a mockery of everything.

And for what? Not for Dev. It wasn't about him any more. I knew that. It was about Depesh. And right now, he needed me. He needed a role model; he needed a gay Indian to be strong, stand up, hold her head high. And even if I had to lie, even if I had to go about it all the wrong way, I was going to be that person for him.

Would Asher understand? I wanted to tell him the truth too. I barely knew him, but I already sensed that I could trust him, that despite everything, he would understand. We stopped at a part of the sandbar that jutted out into the lake, a small peninsula of granulated rock and glass, and I stared across the water.

'I hear you're teaching now?'

'Yeah, I got a full-time position at your old high school. I'm teaching history, English, politics ...'

'Basketball?'

He grinned. 'Of course.'

My stomach tightened. 'Asher, look,' I breathed out. 'I need to talk to you about something.'

He glanced away. 'If it's all the same to you, I'd rather not.'

'But—'

'In New York, I...' He hesitated. 'I got carried away. That's all.'

Was that all?

'It's all behind us, for better or worse. I've thought about you a lot since New York. And in hindsight, it really does make sense.'

'What does?' I whispered.

'Maybe it's growing up with Anna, or travelling and meeting so many other – I guess you could say – lost souls. You have that same look. Like you feel completely inadequate, despite your accomplishments. Like you're struggling to fit in, searching for something else, and—'

He paused, looked me straight in the eye, and I knew this was my chance to tell him the truth. Tell him that I had lied, and dug myself into a hole so deep that I needed help getting out. That I *was* searching for something else – and that even though I wasn't quite sure what it was, or how my life might ever make sense, that maybe, around him, it didn't need to make sense.

He was looking at me, his breathing deep, but I didn't know what to say or how to say it. His gaze was too heavy. His longing – I felt it; then it snapped, and it was too much. The moment passed, and I didn't say anything.

'And, I suppose,' continued Asher, glancing back at the water, 'what you were looking for ... I just never guessed it was this.'

Chapter 29

'You want to let that woman *win*?' Nani had asked me, when I announced I'd invited Auntie Sarla and Shay over for tea.

I'd never understood their rivalry. Auntie Sarla had been Nani's saving grace when our family had moved to Toronto. She'd helped Nani grow the restaurant, and had supported her after Mom got pregnant. Yet her friendship had come at a cost. Criticisms. Judgement. Sarla was everything negative about our Indian traditions incarnate, yet she and Nani had remained friends all these years. And it was only now that Nani had withdrawn.

Nani was 'losing' because of me. I was the one standing between them, and even though I would never forgive Auntie Sarla for her judgement, I wanted Nani to.

It took a few weeks to get both of them to agree, and Shay and I planned for the reconciliation to occur over chai and ladoo while the four of us finalised wedding plans. Before they arrived, Nani opened all the windows and doors, and the chilled air of early spring billowed through the house. She bustled about the rooms like a bee faltering in the crosswind: red-faced, tripping on the hem of her sari, running past me with a burning stick of incense, trying to mask the pungent stench of bleach. I walked into the living room and stopped in my tracks, because draped over the mantelpiece like a splashy Christmas stocking was a giant rainbow flag.

'Nani! What is *that*?'

She swatted the incense smoke like a wayward mosquito, but didn't respond.

I took three more steps into the room and stopped again. 'Is that a, uh, a pride flag?'

'Amazon sent it to me.'

'You know,' I frowned at the flag, 'it doesn't exactly match the room. Maybe you want to take it down?'

'It matches perfectly.' She sprouted up from the floor like a flower. 'Don't you think it's nice to have it out for,' she smiled sweetly, 'our *guest*?'

Auntie Sarla and Shay were an hour late. She came through the front door and marched in like she lived there, Shay following, her eyes rolling at me as she sat down on the sofa opposite us. Nani turned off the television, and as Auntie Sarla stood in front of the three of us, her hands planted firmly on her hips, no one said a word. Shay and I looked at each other, trying not to laugh, as Nani and Auntie Sarla stared at each other in silence. Finally, Auntie Sarla sighed and dramatically folded herself onto the sofa next to Shay.

'Sarla,' Nani smiled at the ground, 'do you like our new decorations?'

Without looking up, Auntie Sarla growled, 'Suvali, I am saying this once. I am here against my will. Shaylee is the one who insisted—'

'Ma, please—'

'No, no.' Auntie Sarla cut her off, waving a hand. '*She*

should know. I am not OK with this. I am not OK with either of you, but' – Auntie Sarla cleared her throat and glared around the room accusingly – 'Shaylee *insisted* that we all get on.'

'I threatened to cancel the wedding.' Shay smiled at me as she reached for the bowl of cashews. 'And I was serious too.'

Through gritted teeth, Nani and Auntie Sarla spent the next hour discussing preparations for the sangeet. The billeting of various relatives and friends flying in from Jaipur, Singapore and Dubai; where they would stay and what they would eat. It was almost back to normal, and Nani and Auntie Sarla were bickering about something inconsequential when Shay sidled over to my sofa.

'I need to tell you something,' she whispered.

'What?' I glanced over at Nani and Auntie Sarla. They were still discussing Shay's great-uncle's dietary restrictions, and weren't listening to us. I looked back at Shay. 'What is it?'

'Asher is seeing someone.'

I felt my heart drop.

'Thought you might want to know.'

I nodded, and wondered why I cared so much. Asher and I had kissed, but it hadn't meant anything. Had it?

'She's another teacher at his school. I'm sorry...' Shay kissed me on the forehead. 'But she's a bit of an idiot, so I wouldn't worry.' Her head turned. '*What*, Ma?'

I looked up, and Auntie Sarla was staring at us, her mouth frozen mid-sentence.

'What, am I not allowed to kiss my best friend?' Shay snapped.

Auntie Sarla growled, and then she tore her eyes away from us. 'Disgusting.'

'Stop it.' Shay's voice shook. 'Raina's no different than before.'

'This is true. Raina was *never* a good girl.'

'Sarla,' said Nani. 'Do not speak about Raina like that. Not in my house.'

Auntie Sarla laughed, and gestured to Nani. 'But what could we expect? Another one raised by *her*.'

'Ma,' said Shay unsteadily. 'I'm warning you. You think I'm joking, but so help me if you don't stop—'

'Fine, fine.' Auntie Sarla smiled and reached for her tea. 'It's all fine.' She glanced pointedly at Nani, and then towards me. 'I am sorry.' She smiled, and spoke slowly. 'I am very, *very* sorry.'

Nani's face was bright red, and I could tell she was breathing heavily. I tried to catch her eye, but she just kept staring at Auntie Sarla.

'Would you like some water?' I asked Nani. She didn't answer. 'Nani?'

'I am not taking this – I am not taking *you* – any longer,' said Nani, as if to herself. She stood up and pointed to the door. 'Leave, Sarla. Right now. This is not acceptable treatment. You have been an interference too long.'

'I am being honest. Are friends not honest?' Auntie Sarla stood up too, face to face with Nani. 'We have been friends *twenty* years, Suvali—'

'You insult us. You insult Raina. She is a wonderful girl, and I am proud of her.' Nani reached for the phone. 'Let's call her girlfriend. I'll show you, you ignorant woman. This Zoey girl is more decent than—'

247

'Nani, Zoey and I are just friends.'

'—some of these boys she could have married. She is more decent than your husband, than *my* husband—'

'Can Zoey give her children? No. It is *wrong*, Suvali. I am trying to help. Have I not always helped you?'

'No, you—'

But then the phone rang, a shrill, piercing reminder that silenced us all.

It was Depesh.

Sharon Auntie was in hospital.

Chapter 30

The waiting room was full, and I crouched down on top of a vent in the hallway opposite. It was chock-full of Indians – some I recognised, some I didn't – and I kept my eyes low. Beneath the white fluorescent lights, my hands looked ghostly pale. I picked at a sliver of dirt beneath my fingernail.

Shay had used her ID badge to sneak Nani and Auntie Sarla into ICU, past the barricade of nurses and attendants who refused to let Sharon Auntie's other friends through. I checked my phone again. Shay hadn't responded to my last text, but as I scrolled through my alerts I saw another email from Dev.

These days his messages were often, and verbose, but said absolutely nothing. And every time I read one, and sent him back a half-hearted reply, I tried not to wonder what my life would have been like if I'd listened to Nani and Shay when they first told me I should cut contact. What my life would have been like if I'd given myself the chance to move on.

'Raina? Is that *you*?'

I looked up. An auntie was standing just in front of me, and I stood up to hug her. She smelled like old clothes and soured perfume, and I racked my brains for her name.

Poonam? Vish-*mi*? She was in one of Nani's temple community groups, but I couldn't remember which one. I smiled at her and we made brief, stilted small talk – in English, with whatever Hindi words I knew thrown in – and then she continued on her way.

I watched her as she found a free seat at the far end of the waiting room. She sat down between some other aunties I recognised, and a moment later I saw them all turn and look in my direction.

I looked back at my hands. It was the first time I'd seen any of them since Christmas. What were they saying? Which ones cared that I was supposedly gay, and which ones didn't?

Did it matter?

I looked up and saw Shay walking towards me, and I stood up.

'How is she?'

'She's good.' Shay smiled. 'Completely fine. It's not a relapse. She just fainted, and Depesh brought her in to be safe. They're going to keep her in overnight.'

'Is Depesh in there?'

'He said he was going down to the cafeteria. Ma and your Nani took over the room the instant they got in there. I'm surprised the doctors are letting them stay.'

'What are they doing?'

'They're coordinating a phone tree to raise money for her home care, and figuring out who gets to cook Depesh dinner.' Shay rolled her eyes. 'Arguing over whose Tupperware they should use.'

'Wow.'

'Yeah,' said Shay. 'Looks like the gruesome twosome are back together.'

I nodded, and looked back down the hall.

Within the hour, the news had travelled and dozens in the community had shown up in support of Sharon Auntie. It was strange how connected we were; an invisible safety net that I'd never really stopped to think about. As frustrating as they could be, I knew they'd be there for Nani and me too. They always had.

'Who are you looking at?'

I shrugged.

'It's embarrassing, isn't it,' Shay said. 'The way some of them are acting.'

'And what are we supposed to do? Accept them for how they are, and blame it on their upbringing? Appreciate everything that's good,' I turned back to Shay, 'and try not to focus on the bad?'

'I guess so, yeah.' She pushed her hair out of her eyes. 'But I don't know, Raina. I don't know if I have an answer for that.'

There was good and bad, light and dark, yin and yang to everything, wasn't there? Their homophobia, their reluctance to accept what they didn't understand – wasn't that just a relic of tradition? Something bound to be trampled on in time?

I heard Shay sigh and glanced back at her.

'I don't know if I've ever explicitly said it to you – if I've ever *said* – but I'm sorry for the way my mother has treated you and your Nani.'

'I've brought it on myself, haven't I?'

Shay crossed her arms, and I knew exactly what she was about to say.

'Depesh hasn't.'

I found him at the furthest table in the cafeteria. His hair was greasy, and he had dark rings under his eyes. He was staring out of the window, a dark sliver peering out into the car park, and he didn't see me until I was right next to him.

'Mind if I join you?'

He shook his head and dropped his legs off the chair next to him. I sat down and he leaned in, hunched over the table. His eyes and the tip of his nose were red.

'How are you doing?'

He didn't answer, just smiled half-heartedly at the table.

'Your mom can go home tomorrow,' I said. 'Have you heard? She's completely fine.'

He wouldn't meet my eye.

'Depesh, what are you thinking?' I whispered. 'You can tell me.'

'I don't know, Raina.' He sighed, an exasperated, frustrated sigh. 'My mom is in hospital, she has a disease that one day might actually kill her, and all I can think about right now is a guy.' He shrugged. 'A *guy*.'

'You've met someone?'

He nodded.

I smiled and poked him in the arm. He didn't look up, and I kept poking him until he smiled too.

'Tell me about him.' I leaned back in my chair. 'But only if you want to.'

'His name is Caleb, and we met in human biology a while ago ... He's one of the friends I told you about.'

'So he's a friend?'

Depesh smiled, shaking his head. 'Not any more. Yesterday we ...' He paused. 'Raina, I'm falling for him. I want to be with him. The same way everyone else is.'

'Depo, you *can* be with him.'

'No.' He shook his head. 'I can't. Not the same way everyone else is.'

'What do you mean?'

'I want to hold his hand. Like, I want to show him the house I grew up in, and bring him as my date to ... I don't know, Thanksgiving dinner with my family. I'll never be able to do any of that stuff.'

'You don't know that. Remember what Zoey said?' I sat up straighter in my chair. 'You have to work up to telling your parents, work *yourself* up to it. Besides Caleb, you've talked to people, right? You told me some of your new friends know now?'

Depesh nodded.

'And how was that?'

He shrugged. 'It was fine. They were great about it. But my parents ... Ma is sick, and – and—'

'Your mom is getting the treatment she needs. She's getting stronger, overall.' I leaned closer. 'There's never going to be a right time, Depesh. If you want to come out to them, then—'

'They think I'm some kind of dream child, Raina. They respect me and love me, and rely on me – how am I supposed to take that away?' Depesh shook his head. 'Raina, you think Auntie Sarla is bad. You should have heard what they said about you.'

I pressed my lips together.

'They are who they are, and if they can't, or *won't*, change, how are they ever going to look at me the same way again?'

A strange silence passed between us, and I became conscious of the wind-like rustling in the vent along the wall; a vacuum roaring faintly in another wing of the hospital.

'People are talking about me – *looking* at me.' I paused. 'Do you remember how they used to look at me?'

He rolled his head slightly to face me. 'What do you mean?'

'When I was younger – maybe you were too young to remember – but you should have seen the way they used to look at me when I was little, before my mother moved out. You should have seen how they looked at my whole family.' My breath caught. 'Do you know she was *sixteen* when I was born?'

He shook his head.

'And do you remember Vikram Prasad's wedding, about ten years ago?'

Again, he shook his head.

'Half his family didn't show up for the wedding because he didn't marry a Hindu.'

'Really?'

I nodded. 'And now? I'm all grown up, and does anyone care about how I was born? Does Auntie Sarla – does anyone in this community – care that Shay is marrying a white Catholic guy?'

He shook his head. 'No, they don't.'

'A lot of them are behind the times. It's going to be hard for the first person to do anything different.' I smiled. 'But as much as Auntie Sarla, as much as everyone talks shit and bickers, they stick together. Yes, they're judgemental. And yes, it's fucking frustrating when they don't see things the way we do. But this community is a family, and it's always stuck together.'

I heard him swallow.

'And whether your parents kick you out, cut you off, cry, scream, disown you – they're still your family. And they're still going to love you.'

He nodded.

'If you tell them, it's going to be hard, Depesh. I'm sorry that I can't change that for you. But – but you're brave enough to be that person, OK? I know you. I know that you're the one who's supposed to do this.'

'You did it, Raina – you're doing it now.'

I swallowed hard and the guilt flooded over me.

'But maybe you're right.' He took a deep breath and looked me in the eye. 'Maybe I can be brave too.'

Chapter 31

A few days later, I found myself parked outside Depesh's house. He was sitting on the front step, elbows on knees.

I hadn't been to his house since the summer I babysat for him, when we used to sit on that same porch step and wait for his parents to come home from the hospital; where we'd eat ice cream or grape ice lollies and wash our sticky hands and faces with the garden hose before going back inside. He was a kid then ... and now? I got out of the car and walked towards him, hopped over the cracked cement and realised that he wasn't a kid any more. He was going to face the truth about himself with the people he loved; he was going to do what most adults, gay or straight, never have the courage to do. What I didn't have the courage to do.

I sat down beside him. The block was more run-down than it had been the decade before; trees and shrubs were overgrown, taking over the pavements and fences; graffiti decorated the lamp posts and the fire hydrants.

'I'm so proud of you, Depo.'

He didn't reply, and then he whispered, 'They won't be.'

'No,' I said. 'Probably not.' I turned to face him, waited until his eyes met mine. 'But you'll be proud of you.'

'You don't know that.'

'If you respect yourself, your own choices,' I looked back out towards the road, 'isn't that what matters?'

A group of kids walked by, laden down with skipping ropes and plastic cones, soccerballs and netting, giggling, stamping along the pavement in a tight pack. They were oblivious in their own happiness. We watched them pass in silence, and I wondered how many of them would one day have to go through what Depesh was going through right now.

As they grew up, as they discovered life in its imperfection, weren't there greater problems to dwell on, to agonise over, far greater than fearing the implications of one's own sexuality? The world was disturbing enough as it was; not just across the world, deserts and oceans away, but right here at home. And before anyone could grow up, grow the courage to change any of it, surely *home* was where it had to start.

The kids disappeared round the corner, and after their high-pitched voices had faded behind them, I could hear Depesh breathing heavily beside me.

'I've never disappointed them before, Raina. I've never not been what they wanted me to be.'

I turned to him and steadied his hand in my own. 'Who do you want to be, Depesh?'

It went exactly how one might have expected it to go. Yelling and crying. Complete and unabashed outrage. Blame: that Depesh had turned gay somehow under my mentorship. Depesh defended me, and, his voice calm and level, he defended himself. And when Sharon Auntie didn't drop dead in front of us, and his father's yells became more hoarse, Depesh suggested that I leave; told me he wanted to handle the rest of it on his own.

I drove back into town on autopilot, replaying the scene over and over again in my mind. He had been brave and calm. He had been an adult. The kid he was less than a year before had grown up before my eyes, and I was so proud of him.

It was dark by the time I got back to my apartment, and I flopped down on my bed. I texted Depesh, asking him how he was doing, and then opened my laptop. I stared at the home screen, blinking, trying to figure out what it was I needed to do. Since I'd started helping Shay with the wedding plans again, I'd been missing more and more work, but I knew I wouldn't be able to concentrate. Just as I was about to shut my laptop, I got a notification from Dev requesting a video chat.

I don't know why I answered. He was in Hong Kong, and I lay face up on my bed as Dev nattered away to me about the politics of our foreign office, even though all I wanted to do was tell him to shut up, eat a jar of peanut butter and fall asleep with the television on.

He steered his webcam around the patio of his suite, out towards the view of the harbour.

'Look what's just cropped up there – the Central Plaza. See it?'

I nodded, and then realised he wasn't looking at me. 'Yes, I can see it.'

'Huge, innit?'

He turned the camera back to face him. He was wearing sunglasses and a tangerine polo shirt with the top two buttons undone, and as his pixelated smile filled up my screen, I felt that familiar surge. The shortness of breath. That smile – the way he could wield it as both shield and sword.

'It's great, Dev. Looks like you're having a great time.'

I didn't recognise the shirt. Had a woman bought it for him? I wondered whether he even had time for women with the hours he worked – and it was me he had been calling whenever he had a spare moment, wasn't it? A part of me wanted to scream, ask him who had bought that shirt, and what we were, and why he couldn't just make up his mind already.

The other part of me was just too exhausted to care.

'Your work all right, darling?'

'It's been all right. Busy, but all right.'

'That's the beauty of it, though. The busyness, the rush, don't you reckon?'

'Yeah, sure.'

'Complacency, Raina. It doesn't suit you.'

'Yeah, well . . .' I thought about what to say next: that neither does this job; that after you, it has lost its last redeemable feature. Dev glanced behind him and out onto the harbour. The image wasn't clear, but it was clear enough, and I could tell from his tensed chin, the set of his jaw, that his mind had already wandered. He wasn't looking at the morning blues, yellows and greys of the skyline, enjoying the few minutes he would spend outdoors. He was already thinking about that day's agenda; the intense session at the gym he'd fit in between client meetings; the conference call in the back seat of the 5 Series on the drive back to the office.

Dev had travelled constantly while we were together.

Direct flights from Heathrow, gone for two days, or two weeks – then the fast train to Paddington and back to the office. After each business trip abroad, I'd swing by his office with two coffees and pastries from Pret, and he'd have nothing to say about the observation deck on the Burj Khalifa, or the white sands of Copacabana. Wiping the crumbs from his chin, he'd tell me about the swanky boardrooms in our Dubai office, the portfolio he'd sorted out in Rio, complaining about what went wrong, or what they had but we didn't. Dev wanted it all: to be a part of the whole world. But going that fast, I always wondered if he'd end up missing out on everything.

I heard my mobile buzz on the end table.

'Where'd you go, love?'

'Hmm?' I said to the screen. Dev's picture had frozen – his mouth open, tongue slightly curled – and I waved my hand.

A second later, his screen unfroze. I picked up my phone. It was Depesh, telling me he was all right, and that he'd call me soon. I sighed in relief.

'I have only twenty minutes, and you're going to chat with someone else?' I heard Dev say.

'Excuse me? You can run off for however many months, but I can't look at a *text*?'

'Raina, please don't.'

'You call me when it's a good time for you, but did you even ask whether now is a good time for me? Did you ask me how my day was, except for *work*? Do you even know what else is happening in my life? Have you once asked me how Nani is doing?'

He held up a hand to the screen and I heard him sigh.

'Sorry, you're right. I don't want to fight, darling. I'm knack-ered. I slept like shit last night, and—'

'And it's always about you, isn't it?' I pressed my lips together. He repositioned his screen, and his face was closer now.

Was this the man I was waiting for? Was I, months later, still waiting for *him*?

'I need to know,' I said, looking at my hands. 'Are you coming back to Toronto?'

'Soon, Raina.'

'What does *soon* mean? In a week, a few months? Maybe never?'

'Where is this coming from?'

'You're a smart guy, Dev. It's not that difficult.'

'Raina, we've never played games with each other. Yes, I'll be the first to admit I wasn't – I *haven't* been – great to you.' He ran his hands through his hair. 'But being away, bouncing around between offices... It's been hard for me too.'

'I'm so sorry this has been hard on *you*. Truly sorry.'

'I've never led you on, darling. I've always been honest. *We've* been clear about the situation between us. You knew when I came to Toronto that we weren't quite sure whether I could... that I was still...' He trailed off, and I could feel my ears burn.

He was right. I'd gone along with what he said, what he wanted, desperate to make him happy; convinced that it would make me happy too. But what for? When had I become this woman – weak, desperate, my everything dependent on him? I'd lied; I'd created this whole mess because I loved him, but I was so tired of it.

All of a sudden I was so fucking tired of him.

'You know how I feel about you. I just don't know what else to—'

'Dev,' I said, interrupting him. 'Let *me* be clear then. Crystal clear.' I took a deep breath and stared straight into his pixelated eyes. 'Come back. Don't come back. It doesn't matter any more.'

'Darling, you can't mean that.'

Didn't I mean it, though?

'I mean it,' I said, slowly, firmly.

'Raina—'

'Because I'm done waiting for you.'

I slammed the laptop shut. My bedroom was silent. Murky-dark, except for the sliver of light coming in from beneath the door. I got off the bed and opened the curtains, stared out into the dark night.

And then I closed my eyes and let the tears drop, and let it all fall away.

Chapter 32

Spring fluttered by, and suddenly Shay's wedding was just over one week away. In anticipation of the half-dozen events leading up to the big day, with all of her parents' friends, Shay had organised a kick-off party for their own friends, and had hired the back room of a club she and Julien used to frequent as medical students.

I spent the afternoon on my balcony – sunglasses, a wool sweater for the wind – and tried to read a book. But I kept getting distracted, a nervous feeling rising in my stomach. I knew Asher would be there, and I wondered if his new girlfriend would be coming too. After twenty pages I gave up and went back inside. I showered and found a charcoal-coloured dress that had been hanging in my wardrobe, unworn, for months. I curled my hair and put on make-up. Staring at myself in the mirror, I took a wet towel and wiped most of it off.

I was restless, and I fell back onto my bed to keep myself from pacing. I could feel my heart beating in my stomach, and I took a deep breath, trying to calm myself down. Why was I so nervous? Why did it even matter – Asher had moved on, hadn't he?

My phone buzzed, and I lunged for it. I thought it might be Depesh, but it was just another email from Dev. I pressed delete without reading it, pushing past the curiosity, past that fractional part of me still desperate to know what he was thinking and where he was. Instead, I rerouted my mind away from him and onto Depesh.

After he'd come out to his parents, we'd started talking on the phone almost every evening, and had spent countless Saturday or Sunday afternoons walking along the lake or drinking coffee at trendy cafés he'd discovered near campus. Others in the Indian community were starting to find out that he had a boyfriend, and it was only a matter of time before everyone knew. He wanted to know what it would be like to stand face to face with someone who didn't accept him, and I tried to find the words to help.

Each time we spoke I also wondered if it was the right time to tell him the truth, but those were the words I never seemed to find. He needed someone to talk to, didn't he? How could I come clean, push him away at a time like this?

Often we spoke only about Caleb, who Depo swore was his perfect match. Caleb had had an entirely different upbringing – his parents liberal and aloof – and while Caleb couldn't understand all of what he was going through, Depo claimed their relationship challenged him, made him think about the world and himself in a different way.

He also spoke a lot about his parents. They hadn't thrown him out of the house, and the berating, the chastisement slowly eased up, morphing into a status quo where Depo lived among them like a room-mate. I thought it was a sign of adjustment, of a family finding its new normal – but Depesh didn't see it that way. He wanted acceptance, a return to the way things were, and it pained me to think how long he might have to wait.

I dialled Depesh's number on impulse, and let it ring ten times before I ended the call. Suddenly I realised that we hadn't spoken the evening before – or the evening before that. It had been days since he'd called or messaged, and I glanced at my calendar. His university exams would be over now. I tried calling again, and a mild dread washed over me when he still didn't answer.

Alice was out of town, so I took Zoey as my date to the party. The lounge was typically urban: chic decor and angular sofas, a DJ in the far corner playing classics from the 1980s and 1990s. We perched at a back table and watched Shay flutter from guest to guest as each one arrived. Zoey went to the bar to buy our second round, and I finally worked up the courage to open an email from Bill that had been sitting in my inbox for hours.

Zoey had warned me the email was coming: Bill was concerned about my performance, and about my commitment to the team. Why didn't my job seem to matter any more? Hadn't I cared all my life about what people thought of me, and measured my happiness on how well I was doing in school or at work?

I reread the message twice, and then threw my phone back into my bag. I looked up and scanned the room. Julien had arrived and was standing in the corner, seemingly arguing with Shay, and Zoey was waiting at the bar with Serena. But then when I glanced back towards the entrance, I saw Asher.

His jeans and faded leather jacket had been replaced by khaki trousers and a white button-down shirt, like he'd been dressed by the brunette beside him; she was petite and very thin, and wore a white silky dress that stopped just below the crotch. They stood in the entrance talking to one another, her hand on the base of his spine, and as she leaned up and whispered something in his ear, he caught my eye. He smiled at me, and I waved in return. He started to walk towards me, and the girl grabbed his hand and trotted along next to him.

I tried not to look at her too much as he introduced us; how she constantly flicked her fringe out of her eyes, and the way her lash-covered cow eyes made her look stupidly young.

I bored *Rebekah* instantly, and as her eyes skirted the room, I wondered how old she was.

'Rebekah is also a teacher,' said Asher, as if he knew I had my doubts.

'I teach music,' she said, rifling through her bag. She pulled out a fat tube of lip gloss and began to smear it onto her pout. 'Orchestra band, jazz band,' she smacked her lips, 'and what else, sweetie?'

I winced.

'Choir, *right*. I run the choir.'

I nodded. 'That's great.'

'She's also a musician,' said Asher.

'And do you play basketball too?'

She shook her head. 'Too short. Always been more into singing.'

I smiled, trying to look earnest. 'Good for you. I sing terribly.'

'So do my students,' she laughed, and then tugged twice on her ponytail. 'So …' She turned to Asher. 'Should we get some drinks?'

'Sure.' Asher glanced at me. 'Raina, would you like anything?'

'Mine's coming, thanks,' I said to them both, although Rebekah had already started to walk away, pulling at Asher's sleeve behind her.

They disappeared into the thick press of bodies at the edge of the bar and I watched Asher's head, a foot higher than most, bob above the crowd. It was dark, and I tried to make out whether he was smiling, and to whom he was talking.

'Who's that?'

I hadn't noticed Zoey reappear, and she pressed a drink into my hand. I took a long sip through the straw, just as Asher stooped out of sight. '*That*, is Asher.'

The night passed painfully slowly, and I only had the chance to speak with Shay again briefly as she darted between cousins, friends and co-workers all pawing at her like a scratching post. Zoey and I chatted with the groups we met – friends of Julien's from the hospital, local sports teams, and then a whole crew from Quebec who'd hired a bus and driven in that day, and who, now drunk, indulged me as I tried out my remedial French. But I kept seeing Asher and Rebekah everywhere; standing in the queue for drinks; and again at the bar as she played on her phone, sipping her sixth cocktail; and then later at the edge of the dance floor, Rebekah bobbing her head up and down as Asher and Victor talked, it seemed, about the Raptors play-off game.

What did he see in her? Maybe Rebekah was the kind of girl Asher briefly thought I was. One who was passionate and talented and followed her dreams; one who could stand in a crowded room, suck on her fingers and not care what anyone else thought; because even though she was *Rebekah*, she knew exactly who she was and didn't give a damn who cared or judged her for it.

I left Zoey at a table with two chatty residents Julien worked with, and joined the queue for the ladies'. Half a dozen girls were lined up on the far wall – texting, applying lipstick, whispering – while the other wall, leading towards the gents', was empty.

I took my place at the back, and a second later I saw Asher appear in the far doorway. He smiled, and gave me a big, goofy wave as he walked towards me.

'So, she's a teacher,' I said, the words coming up uncontrollably.

'Yeah.' He nodded. He seemed almost embarrassed. 'She's a teacher.'

'She seems nice.'

'Rebekah can come across a bit … I don't know.' He shrugged. 'But she's really good with the kids. Even if she isn't exactly *passionate* about the job.'

'I see.'

'I think so many people end up teaching because they don't know what else to do.'

I shrugged. 'It happens, doesn't it? I'm not passionate about my job; not sure I ever was.'

'What are you passionate about, then, Raina?'

The way he said it made me stop short, and I wished I had an answer. I wished I knew what I was passionate about.

'I don't think I've ever felt about anything the way you feel about teaching.'

'What did you want to be when you were little? Astronaut? Fashion designer?' He grinned. 'National basketball player?'

I slapped him lightly on the shoulder. 'Hey. I could have been in the pros.'

'Yeah?'

I was about to joke back, but then I shook my head. 'No, I couldn't. It would have been too risky.'

'Risky, why?'

'My grandparents were really ... poor. They were immigrants. They worked hard, and after my Mom never amounted to anything in their eyes, there was so much pressure on my uncle Kris, and then me, to really ... become something. To get jobs that were, I don't know, impressive. Stable. That earned a lot of money.'

'So you always wanted to be an investment analyst,' he said softly.

'I never knew what I wanted to be.' I shrugged. 'I suppose I never had a chance to figure it out.'

'It's not too late,' he said after a moment. Then he winked. 'You're not that old.'

'I'll be thirty next week.'

His mouth dropped open, and I fake-shoved him again. I loved the creases around his mouth when he smiled.

'What does your gut tell you?'

I drew back. 'About what?'

'About your passions. About what – and who – you want to be.' He ran a hand through his hair. 'Although look at me. It took me eight years to figure out that my first instinct was right. I really did want to teach.'

'My gut instinct about what to do has never been that helpful,' I said, suddenly thinking about Depesh. 'It's been misleading, actually.'

'That's not your gut you were listening to. That was your fear. You see, you have to listen harder, go further down.' He palmed his stomach. 'And then you'll hear it.'

Was he right? Was it just fear that had led me here? An ex-boyfriend I was too afraid to let go of? A grandmother I was too afraid to disappoint?

I caught Asher's eye, and an incredible sadness washed over me.

Was it fear that had made me too afraid to tell him I wasn't gay? That, really, I wanted to be with a man, and that maybe – maybe that man was Asher?

My body was trembling, and my arms, crossed and shivering, recoiled away from him. 'I need to tell you something.'

'Yeah?'

I made myself look at him. What was stopping me? I took a deep breath. 'Asher, I'm—'

'*There* you are.'

I dropped my arms and turned towards the voice. Rebekah wobbled towards us, a scowl on her face. She walked up to Asher and put an arm around his waist.

'Hi, Becka.'

'What are you guys talking about?' she asked him, not looking at me.

'The wedding,' Asher said quickly. 'Raina's in the wedding party.'

'Is she?'

'We have to be there early for the ceremony,' he turned to me, talking quickly, 'don't we? What time again?'

'The ceremony starts at ten – so, five a.m., maybe six?'

'That's *early*,' said Rebekah.

'It's customary for us to get married in the morning.'

'Well, can I come too?' she said to Asher.

'It's only for family and close friends. I'll be with Julien and his dad and brother,' Asher glanced at me, 'and all the women will be helping Shaylee get ready.'

'I like Indian clothes,' she said.

I pressed my lips together.

'I'll talk to Julien,' he said.

She folded her arm through his. 'Thank you, baby.'

I winced, and then, as quickly as I could, I excused myself and went back to the party.

Chapter 33

Shay and Zoey found me hiding in the cloakroom. They tried to console me, but when that didn't work, Shay insisted I go home so I didn't have to watch Asher and Rebekah together. Jokingly, Shay said she didn't want a miserable *middle-aged* woman ruining her party anyway. Zoey offered to drive me but I refused. I could tell she was having a good time. They hugged me goodbye, and a few minutes later I found myself walking home alone along Yonge Street.

It was official. Asher had a girlfriend. He'd moved on from whatever we'd shared. And he'd chosen *her*.

But had I given him a chance to choose me? Would I have wanted him to?

With Dev, I'd been jealous of anyone who got to spend time with him: his colleagues, his housekeeper, even his own mother. But this felt different, and just thinking about Rebekah made my lungs burn.

Asher was nothing like anyone I knew, and so unlike Dev. If things had been different, could I even have had a future with him? And what about Dev? He still called, and every time a faint impulse in me tempted me to answer. Didn't that mean a part of me still believed in *him*?

I tripped over a crack in the pavement, and caught myself before I fell. My head was spinning, and I leaned against a lamp post and let my chin fall to my chest. My eyes closed, I could hear the cars whizz past, the pedestrians – high heels and leather soles clacking – the slow thud of music from a nearby bar.

I felt a low vibration coming out of the pole, up through my leg and body, and it took me a moment to realise it was my phone. I found it in my coat pocket, and took the call when I saw it was Depo.

I held the receiver to my ear. 'Hello?'

'Raina!' I heard him laugh, and a chorus of voices laughed in the background.

'Hey, what's up? I—'

'I've been meaning to call you back.' He laughed again, and then shouted into the phone, 'I'm going to Europe!'

'That's amazing! Where?'

'London, baby! Caleb's brother used to live in Brixton – is that good? Should we go there?'

'Wait a second. You're going to London? When?'

'Tonight!'

My stomach dropped.

'We booked a last-minute flight, heading straight to London. Then Berlin, maybe. Who the hell knows? But I'm doing it. Exams are over, and I'm going to Europe. Like, me and Caleb and a few other guys. We're going!'

'Since when?'

'Since I got a full scholarship, Raina. I got the highest marks of all the first-year students in my college.'

'Depo, wow. Congratulations, but—'

'So I'm leaving. My summer job starts in ten days, but who knows, maybe I won't do it. Maybe I'll just stay in London and take a year off—'

273

'A *year*?'

'Before doing the whole medicine thing. Caleb is thinking about taking a gap year.'

I could feel the panic rising. 'Please, slow down.'

'I've always done the right thing. I've always been a good boy – but maybe I don't want to be that boy any more. Maybe I want to be like Caleb. He's free. He does whatever the hell he wants. He's his own person, you know?'

'Following Caleb is not being your own person.'

He didn't hear me. He was talking rapidly, excitedly, and he wouldn't let me speak. He was following a boy he barely knew across the world? He was leaving with him for a year?

Without knowing the truth?

'Raina, like, thank you *so* much – for, you know, everything.' He came up for air. 'I couldn't have done it without you.'

'Wait a sec. I need to tell you—'

'Can we talk later? The flight leaves in a few hours, and I have to pack.'

'Please, just think about this—'

'But text me, OK?'

Before I could say another word, he rang off.

I was frozen in my tracks. The pavement was giving way beneath me. The street was spinning. I couldn't do this. There was no more delaying, no more waiting for the right time. Depo was leaving, and he deserved to know the truth.

It took me less than a minute to find a taxi, and within forty-five minutes I was at the airport. I waited near security in the international terminal. After an hour of checking

274

and rechecking the departure board, wondering whether I'd missed him, finally he appeared.

I watched him from afar as he checked in for his flight at the kiosk, laughing with three other boys his age, small backpacks slung over their shoulders. And by the way he was looking at one of the boys – rosy cheeks, black glasses, platinum-blond hair – I could tell which one was Caleb.

Depo looked so happy, a lightness to him that I hadn't seen since he was kid. When he saw me, he gave me a big smile and waved. He walked towards me, dropped his bag by my feet and enveloped me in a hug.

Tense, I hugged him back. My heart pounded, and I could feel sweat forming on my face.

'You didn't have to come and see me off.' He pulled away, grinning, and then looked towards security. 'Sorry; I told them to go through. I should have introduced you to Caleb – should I go and get him?'

I shook my head. 'Another time. I need to—'

'That sounds good. Like, when we get back – or if we stay a while, maybe you can come and visit. Do you ever go to Europe for work?'

I shook my head.

'You're all dressed up.' He smiled. 'You look really pretty.'

'Thanks,' I whispered. 'I was at a party for Shay and Julien.'

'Ma's pissed off I won't be home for their wedding.' He laughed. 'Despite everything, she still wants to show me off – tell everyone about the scholarship.'

'Of course she does, Depo. Your Ma and Pa – they're both proud of you.'

He shrugged and looked at his feet. 'We still barely speak. Today Pa didn't even hug me goodbye.'

'Depo, your courage…' I put my hand on his arm. 'I'm so proud of you. I really am, and—' I hesitated. 'I also…'

'What is it?'

'There's something you need to know. Before you leave.'

'Yeah?'

I looked him in the eye. I could feel myself shaking. 'Depo, I'm straight.'

He didn't respond. His face – it didn't flinch.

'I needed you to know before you left.' I shook my head. 'I'm not gay. I didn't mean to trick you. If it was something I could take back, I would, I promise you. If I could go back a year – a few years, even – I would do it differently.'

He still didn't move.

'I'd do a lot of things differently. I'd try and be a better person; I don't know. But one thing I don't regret is our friendship. I'm so happy we got to know each other this year, and I – I don't regret that. I really don't. I wanted to be there for you. I still do. And this stuff with Caleb – it's happening so quickly, and I get it. I get how you're feeling right now, and if you want to talk about—'

'*Talk?*'

I watched his face, his muscles perfectly tense, unflinching. But then he blinked.

'You *bitch.*'

It was dark by the time I pulled into the driveway. The taxi drew up beside Kris's car, and the driver turned off the ignition. My legs and spine were frozen to the seat. Finally I paid and then forced myself out of the car.

I had made light of something I had no right to joke about. Now, months later, it was time for me to do the right thing. I couldn't control how and when and why I disappointed Nani, but I could control this.

What would she say? I shook my head. It didn't matter; I had to face it – I *wanted* to face it.

It was late, but for some reason the front door was unlocked. I stepped into the house. The hallway lights were off, the house coated in silence; no television or kettle whistling, no Nani humming or singing or snoring in the background like white noise. All I could hear was the discerning tick of the cuckoo clock as the hands tapped their way round.

I stepped out of my shoes and crept into the living room. It was empty, and as the pale light of the muted television ghosted through the room, I noticed a full mug of tea abandoned on the coffee table.

'Hello?'

I turned, drawn by a noise in the kitchen, a sliver of light beneath the doorway. And when I pushed through, the door swinging wildly open, there they all were, sitting at the kitchen table. Space and time, backward and forward; my childhood playing tricks, playing out right in front of me. Nani and Kris in their usual spots, jaws tensed, shoulders slouched. And across from them, seated cross-legged on my chair, there she was.

'Hi, Raindrop.' Chin resting on her palm, Mom grinned at me. 'So I hear you're a lesbian.'

Chapter 34

20 May 1994

Nani surprises Raina with all her favourites: thick yogurt, mango chutney, an aloo paratha with extra butter. Raina sits at the kitchen table eating her breakfast, sipping her glass of apple juice from the table without touching it, her top lip curled over the glass, her greasy hands held up as if in surrender. She eats carefully, tearing a piece of the paratha off with one hand, how Nani taught her, dipping it and then bringing it slowly to her mouth. She has covered herself with three paper napkins. It is hours until her party, but she is already wearing her new dress. Manavi reappeared with it – a belated Christmas present after a trip to Las Vegas last year – and only now has Raina grown into it. It is lavender, the same shade as the pillows on Raina's bed, and she admires herself as she chews: the white and violet frills on the cuffs, the hem that skirts around her knees.

Her feet do not touch the ground, and she swings them as she eats, kicking a ball across an imaginary field. Raina is only part way through her breakfast when the murmurs from downstairs become louder. Staccato and sharp. She slips quietly off her chair and tiptoes towards the door that leads down to the entertaining room. She slides onto her knees and presses her ear against the door, trying to make out the sounds.

Before, Kris used to take Raina to her room, turn on the radio. If that wasn't enough, he'd press her hands over her ears and tell her to keep them like that until they stopped. But these days Kris is rarely home, so when they yell, Raina tries to listen; she is curious to understand why everyone seems to be so angry all the time. They yell about the mess of long hair Manavi left in the plughole, or the door she slammed too hard, or the boy who dropped her off. About the right way to teach Raina to tie her shoes. Raina listens hard, but this time their voices are too muffled, as if they know she might be listening.

Raina hears a thumping up the stairs and she bolts back to her seat, reaches for her glass of juice. Manavi swings the door open, followed seconds later by Nani. Manavi crouches down beside Raina and tugs on one of her plaits.

'Do you want to go to Wonderland, Raindrop?'

Raina's eyes widen. 'Wonderland?' Her face breaks into a smile. 'Really?'

'Manu …'

But Nani stops short when Manavi snaps her head in Nani's direction.

'Yes, Raindrop.' Manavi turns her head slowly back to Raina and blows her fringe from her face. 'Let's go. Get your coat.'

'Now?' Raina slumps forward. She wants to go, but not today. Today is her seventh birthday, and there will be a party at the new restaurant. 'But there's going to be a magic show!'

'Raina, come *on*.' Manavi leans back, balancing on her heels. 'I got us tickets for today.'

'Please, Manu.' Nani is now standing at the kitchen sink,

her hands leaning against it like she's trying to catch her breath. She turns to them and says, 'Please, not—'

'I *told* you, they're only valid for today!'

'Did you even remember it was her party?' Nani's voice is strained, and Raina looks down. Her eyes start to water when she notices that, despite how careful she's been, a fat droplet of juice has found its way onto her dress.

'So, are we going?' Manavi snaps. 'I haven't got all day.'

Raina's eyes are locked on the stain, and after a moment, she says, 'Can we go tomorrow?'

'Tomorrow?'

'But today is—'

'No, we can't go tomorrow,' Manavi growls. She stands up in one fluid motion. 'I'll go with my friends.' And with that, she grabs her leather jacket off the hook and marches out, mumbling inaudibly until the kitchen door bangs heavily behind her.

The new restaurant is bigger than the last one, Nani says, although to Raina it looks very much the same. Raina and her friends sit around two of the long restaurant tables pushed together. Nani and Nana have decorated them with white plastic tablecloths and gold confetti, and pink and purple helium balloons. They have set out supplies like it's art class, with every colour of cardboard craft paper, pipe cleaners and lolly sticks, cotton balls and glue. The expensive magic markers.

Raina makes her crafts sitting next to a boy from her soccer team, and an Indian girl named Shaylee that Nani keeps inviting to the house. When the magician arrives, they are all herded towards a makeshift stage in the corner.

Raina sits at the end of the row, and when the magician makes a rubber duck disappear into a hat, her friends gasp. Raina thinks she knows how he did it: the hat is wide and long, and surely the duck is being hidden inside; in a secret pocket, perhaps. She thinks about raising her hand, or leaning over and telling Shaylee how it happened, but she doesn't want to ruin the trick. So she doesn't say anything.

Next, the magician pulls out a deck of cards, and Raina blinks hard, trying to memorise the sequence, trying to unlock the secret of this trick, too, when she thinks she hears Manavi's voice behind her. She turns round, and is excited to see that Manavi has decided to come to her birthday party. Nani is whispering to Manavi, and although Nani is smiling, keeps flicking her eyes towards Auntie Sarla and the other adults at the back, Raina can tell that her Nani is angry. They go into the kitchen, and silently, swiftly, Raina follows.

Inside, she can hear their voices, and she ducks behind a rubbish bin, carefully peering round the side.

'I don't care—'

'Shh!'

'What the *fuck* they think about me.'

'Manu—'

'And don't shush me.' Manavi stamps her foot like a child. She is crying, and her words are slurred. Raina has never seen her like this before; at least, not in the middle of the day.

'There is party happening, *nah*? Sarla is here. You must settle down.'

'Who cares about *Sarla*?' She grabs a frying pan from the stove and tosses it between her hands. For a moment,

Raina thinks she might hit Nani, swing at her with it like a baseball bat, but after a few catches, Nani lunges for it. She knocks it out of Manavi's grasp and it clatters to the floor. Nani reaches down to get it, one hand on her lower back, and then puts the pan back on the stove.

'Never could let me have a little fun, could you?'

'You've been having your fun for a while now.'

'It didn't start out that way, did it, Ma?' Silence. Then Manavi says, 'I'm moving out.'

'You've been saying for years. Go ahead. Move out.'

'And Raina?'

'She will stay with us.'

'You don't have the right – you think *you* have the fucking right to decide that about her?' Manavi laughs. 'I dare you. I dare you to stop me.'

'You are not taking that girl with you.'

'I'll take you to court.'

'Take me wherever you like,' Nani takes a deep breath, 'but you will not take my Raina.'

'She's *my*—'

'Boozing, men, doing God knows what. You coming, going – we never know. Raina never knows. You think you can be her mother?'

'I *am* her mother,' cries Manavi, black tears rolling down her face. '*I* am her fucking mother!'

'You are not a mother. Grow up. Stop being a child. Start acting like you care about Raina, that you want to *be* mother to her—'

Manavi cries harder, slams her fists against the counter.

'Always blaming others. Never your fault, *nah*? Never taking responsibility—'

'I *hate* you, you self-righteous *bitch*.' Her words pour out in chokes and gasps, and Nani turns her head.

Manavi inches closer to her, and from the way Manavi is leaning against the counter, sobbing, their shoulders nearly touching, Raina has the feeling that if only her Nani would turn round, there wouldn't be so much yelling.

But she doesn't turn round, and after few minutes, Manavi stops crying. She grabs a roll of paper towel, uses the whole of it to dry her face. Nani is motionless, still facing away. Manavi inches towards her again – and then she retreats.

'You want her?' Manavi stares at Nani's back, and a moment later, whips the roll at her head. 'You can *fucking* have her.'

Chapter 35

'Hey, get up.'

I rolled over, and slowly opened my eyes. It was still dark, just a hint of light coming in through the window. I felt something tug on my ankle, and as a reflex, I kicked.

'Ouch!' It was Mom's voice, and then the light came on. 'You *kicked* me.'

'Sorry.' I fell back onto the pillow and closed my eyes. 'What time is it?'

'Seven thirty.'

I groaned.

'Let's get out of here.'

'Mom, it's Saturday.'

'Come on. Before Ma wakes up.' I felt her tug on my foot again. '*Please?*'

I grabbed the keys to Nani's car and left her a note, and then Mom followed me out to the car.

We drove around aimlessly, up and down the side streets of the neighbourhood, through the car parks and back alleys behind the shopping centre. Still she hadn't told me why she'd come; what had happened or what she wanted to do. All she'd said was that, just for a while, she wanted to get the hell away from Nani.

We reached the end of a cul-de-sac. I looped around, and

then stopped at the end of the street. I looked over at Mom. She seemed older than the last time she'd been home; her waist and neck were thicker, and despite the concealer, I could still make out the bags beneath her eyes.

'Why'd you stop?'

'Where are we going?'

She shrugged, and pulled her legs up onto the seat.

'Are you OK?' I paused. 'You look tired.'

She laughed.

'Is that a *yes*, you're OK?'

'Yes.' She flicked her head towards me. 'I'm OK. I'm fine. Drive to the school. I want to see it.'

I parked the car outside the auditorium doors. The car park was empty except for us, and she rolled down the window. The cool morning air spilled in, sharp with the scent of grass, of chlorine from the nearby pool, and she leaned back against the seat.

'A friend of mine teaches here now.'

She didn't answer. I looked over and saw that her eyes were closed. She was breathing heavily as if she was asleep, her belly steadily rising and falling.

What was she doing here? In Toronto? At our old high school? I'd stopped asking Mom questions long ago, as she seemed incapable of giving me straight answers. Perpetually vague, she talked to me like I was a demanding passenger in economy class – she, the ever-patient flight attendant. After a few minutes I thought I heard her snoring; bored and restless, I turned off the ignition and the radio cut out.

'I was listening to that.'

'I thought you were asleep.'

She yawned and stretched her arms behind her, evaluated

the car as if it were an inspection. And then she turned to me. 'So your friend teaches here?'

I nodded, and said, 'Maybe I should have been a teacher.'

'Bankers make more money.'

'I'm not a banker.'

'I could have been a pilot, you know. Roger's a pilot – he says I have a knack for it.'

'Is Roger here with you?'

'I could take flying lessons, next year.' She sat up in her seat and drummed on her thighs. 'I'm not too old, you know.'

'Never said you were.' I started the car, and the radio flickered back to life. 'Where do you want to go now?'

She laughed. 'A gay bar?'

'Funny.'

I glanced out of the window. A car pulled up directly beside us and a trio of high school kids filed out of the back seat. They ran, backpacks and shopping bags in hand, up to and through the auditorium doors. Maybe they were here for the Spring Play. The drama club used to practise every weekend from the day the snow started to melt up until the last day of school, when all the parents, or grandparents, filed into uncomfortable rows of wooden chairs and watched that year's production of *Mikado* or *King Lear*. *West Side Story*. In our senior year they'd put on *Bugsy Malone*, and Shay and I had sneaked into the dressing room and run around the hallways after dark in two of Blousey Brown's flapper dresses. We got caught, and that was the first and last time either of us ever got detention.

'I'm sorry I didn't know.' I heard Mom sigh, and I looked back towards her. 'You know I'm not in touch with anyone here. If I'd known you were … going through something like that, I would have called more. I would have come home sooner.'

I snorted.

'I'm serious, Raina.' She nodded earnestly. 'Kris called me the other day. He's been having a tough time since Serena broke up with him.' She shrugged. 'Anyway, he told me you'd come out. And I thought … I thought that maybe I should come home.'

Her voice trailed off, and I didn't respond. Had Mom come home to make sure I was OK? This time, had she just shown up out of the blue for *me*? And not because she needed something?

'Anyway,' she folded her arms across her chest, 'I want you to know I'm proud of you. This is really cool.'

My cheeks burned. 'Mom, it's not *cool*.'

'Of course it is.'

'No it isn't. Because I'm not actually gay.' I turned off the car and curled my feet into my lap on the seat. 'I made it all up.'

'Why the hell would you lie about that?'

'Nani was setting me up a lot, and then I found this online marriage ad.' I shrugged. 'I freaked out.'

'An *ad*?'

'An ad.'

'That woman.' Mom groaned loudly, pointing her middle fingers at the roof in exaggeration. 'She fucked you up too.'

'Don't blame her, OK? She didn't lie. It was *my* choice to lie, and now—'

'And now you're fucked.'

287

The car park was filling up, kids getting out of cars and into the school by the handful.

Was I *fucked*? Depesh knew now, and here I was, still lying. The evening before, while sitting at the kitchen table with the only family I had, would have been the right time to come clean.

Instead, I'd made everyone tea. I'd pushed through everyone's bad moods and defensive fronts and tried to find common ground between us. I'd held Nani's hand under the table, steadied her each time Mom said something that made her fingers tremble.

If I wasn't able to tell Nani the truth then, when would I be?

Mom said she was starving, so I took her to the Scuz round the corner. I hadn't been there since a bouncer had confiscated my fake ID, and from what I remembered, the few seconds Shay and I had been allowed inside, it hadn't changed. A diner by day, a bar by night, there was still a jukebox in the corner and a section of pool tables, tattered, like someone had run a straight razor along the felt. The place smelled sour, of slightly stale beer, and I followed Mom as she crossed the room and collapsed into a booth.

'This place still exists,' she said. 'You know, it was around in my day too.'

I wiped the crumbs off the seat and sat down.

'What is that?' Mom watched the waiter as he trekked past with a plate of brownish-grey food. 'Is that supposed to be omelettes?'

'We don't have to eat here.' I watched her pick up a

menu, and a second later, put it back down. 'We could go to my place, pick up groceries on the way.'

'What, you want me to cook?'

'No. You can't even make rice.'

'And you can?'

I shrugged, and reached for her discarded menu.

'Let's invite Shaylee,' she said after another moment. 'Let me guess. Is she gay too?'

I rolled my eyes. 'Her wedding is this week. I doubt she has time to eat with us.'

'Just call her, would you?'

I fished my phone from my bag and sent a message to Shay. I put the phone on the table, wiping dried beer off the wood with my sleeve first, and then looked up again. Mom had taken her sweater off, and was fanning herself with a stack of napkins.

'And?'

'I texted her.'

'Did she reply?'

'It's literally been ten seconds.'

Why did she want Shay to come so badly? Was she afraid to eat a meal alone with her own daughter?

I glanced around, looking for the waiter, and then back at Mom. Again it struck me how tired she looked. 'How's Roger? What's he like?'

'Oh, you know.' She shrugged. 'He'll do.'

'He'll do?'

'I'm kidding, Raina. He's great – he's away on a job right now.'

'When do we get to meet him?'

'Whenever. I didn't know you wanted to.' She grabbed

another stack of napkins, folded them up and patted the back of her neck. 'My God, it's hot.'

'It's not that hot.' My phone buzzed, and I glanced at it. 'Shay is on her way.'

'Good.' Mom wiped her face, and when she lifted up her arm, I saw the sweat stains, jagged across her armpits.

'Are you having a hot flush?'

'I am *not* menopausal.'

'Are you sure?'

'Raina, I'm not, trust me.' She pulled a black elastic from her wrist and tied her hair back in a bun. Then she leaned forward onto the table. 'I can't be. I'm ... pregnant, actually.'

I laughed. 'No, you're not.'

'Raina.' She sighed, and, stretching her arms behind her, said, 'I'm not kidding.'

I was frozen to the seat, and only my hands were moving. Shaking.

'Did you hear me?'

'I – I heard you.'

'Are you going to say anything?'

'Is that even safe?'

'Oh, come on.'

'You're forty-*six*, Manavi. Are you out of your mind?'

'Knock it off, would you? I have a good doctor—'

'And they sort everything, don't they?'

'Jesus, kid, you sound just like Ma.'

'What? Was it an accident? You just forgot to use a condom again?'

She didn't reply. She picked up the menu, and as she turned it steadily in her palms and pretended to read, it hit me.

'You planned it.'

'IVF.' She nodded. 'First try, too. You see, Roger doesn't have kids. We're planning to stay put in Philadelphia. Roger's got a sister there, and his dad's in a nursing home. It'll be good.' She paused, putting the menu down. 'And you know, it's only a quick flight from here, an hour and a half. You could do it in a weekend.'

'Now you want me to visit?'

She frowned. 'I've always wanted you to visit.'

'Have you?'

'Of course.'

'Shouldn't you be the one visiting me? Your *daughter*?'

'So you won't come then,' she snapped. 'You won't come and see your baby sister and be a part of the family.'

'You weren't a part of my family.'

'What am I supposed to say, huh? That this is how I thought *my* life would turn out? That I got what I wanted out of life? No. Not even close. But, like I said, Roger never had any kids, and…'

And *what*, Mom?

You didn't really come home to make sure I was OK, but to tell your old family you'd started another one?

You weren't that different from us 'good Indian girls', and wanted a marriage and children all along.

You just didn't want me.

Without answering her, I left her there, sitting in that disgusting booth, and drove away.

I found myself on the highway, and kept driving west on the 403 until, much later, I realised I was an hour past Hamilton. I pulled into a petrol station car park, did a

U-turn and then headed back to Toronto. The announcer between songs began to annoy me, and I smashed the dashboard until the radio stopped playing.

Mom was pregnant. Again.

She was starting a *family*.

This time she'd get it right: she'd order baby furniture from IKEA and paint the room *sunshine yellow*, take her vitamins and rub oil on her belly so she didn't get stretch marks. She'd do things the right way, with *Roger*, with her perfect new daughter.

I wanted to scream, but every time I tried, nothing came out. All my life it had taken so much energy to feel *anything* for her – love or hate, apathy or just plain amusement.

This was my mother? She was the woman who hated her own mother so much it ruined her life, so maybe it was destiny for me to hate mine too.

But I didn't hate her. Did I?

Hours later, I finally made it back home. All the lights were off, the curtains drawn. I was starving and I crept through to the kitchen and flicked on the light.

Kris was sitting at the table. He squinted at me and raised his hand in slow motion, shielding his eyes.

'Jesus, Raina.'

Kris's eyes were puffy and red, and I sat down in the seat across from him, just an empty glass and a whisky bottle between us. I let my bag fall off my arm and drop to the floor, and after a moment, he pushed the bottle towards me.

I shook my head.

'It's reserve label.'

'Reserved for what?'

He grinned at me stupidly. 'Special occasions.' He raised his glass, and, realising it was empty, put it back down.

'Where's Nani?'

'Upstairs, resting.'

'Did Mom…' I paused. 'Did she get home OK?'

'Shaylee drove her,' he lolled his head to the side, 'to the airport.'

'She's gone, then.'

'Cheers to that,' he said, and then belched.

'You're drunk.'

'And Manu tells me you're not really gay!'

'Shh!'

He laughed loudly, and I reached across and hit him on the shoulder; Nani's room was above the kitchen. He collapsed forward onto the table, his face on his hands, and giggled like a toddler. I grabbed the bottle from him, and I felt the liquid burn my tongue, my throat, as I swallowed. My eyes watered, and when I finally opened them, Kris was staring at me. He looked so old, suddenly; worn and restless, and almost exactly like Manavi.

Sometimes I forgot that she was his sister, and that they'd grown up side by side. The same parents and upbringing, and the same lethal mix of genes: Nana's nose and Nani's mouth. Big, wide eyes that, when they shone right at you, it almost hurt.

'I need to tell Nani the truth, don't I?'

He didn't answer. His eyes were half-closed now, and I wondered if he'd even heard me.

'I need to tell her. I keep meaning to tell her.' I nodded to myself. 'She just wanted me to be happy, like she was, and get married and—'

293

He started to laugh again, and I pushed the bottle of whisky back towards him. '*What?*'

'You know,' he hiccuped, 'until you were born, she slept in your bedroom.'

'Who did?'

His smile faded.

'Kris,' I whispered, leaning towards him. 'Nani and Nana? They slept in separate bedrooms?'

'Until you. *Their* little Raina.'

Chapter 36

20 May 1988

'Make a wish, my sweet.'

Raina sits on her Nani's lap, her chubby legs dangling. One of her socks falls off and Nani reaches down to retrieve it.

'I can do it, Ma.' Manavi lunges for the sock and her head bangs against Nani's with a loud thud.

'*Oy!*' Nani turns to Manavi as she sits back up, plucks the sock from her hand. 'Clumsy girl.' Nani massages her head with the back of her palm, shifts Raina on her lap.

Raina giggles as her Nana brings out a tray of brownies. He slowly cuts them into squares, and the chocolate drizzle drips onto the kitchen table as he places a thick slice on a small white plate.

'Mine!' Kris licks his lips as he eyes the brownie. He reaches out and digs his finger into the icing, and Nani swats it away.

'First the birthday girl,' Nana says, gently scolding. He cuts more slices and passes them round. A cassette of Ravi Shankar plays in the background as they sit and chew the warm cake, as Raina squirms in delight, her pudgy cheeks drooping like jowls. She is still teething, and smacks her lips together often, dark brown crumbs falling out of her mouth, and after each bite, her Nani licks a napkin, dabs the stains from her chin.

'Just leave it until she's finished,' says Manavi. 'Babies get dirty.' But it's as if no one has heard her, because nobody answers.

Raina no longer likes eating baby food. She likes unspiced aloo gobi, rice and daal mashed together, spoon-fed from Nani's fingers. She drinks apple juice and mango juice, bottles of fresh whole milk. She knows only the scent of a heated home and a warm bath, the beige and wood-panelled walls insulating her existence. She knows only love and security. Abundance and affection.

Raina's skin is lighter than the rest of her family's; and this seems to be something that excites her Nani. Her hair sticks out in two short pigtails above her ears, and saliva bubbles out of her lips as she tries to blow out a candle.

Nana focuses the lens of the Pentax. 'Say cheese!'

Everyone else is smiling, and so Raina smiles too.

'Good girl!' Nana sticks out his tongue and Raina giggles. She claps her hands together as if the performance is just for her.

'Can I hold her now, Ma?'

'Manu, clear the table.'

'Ma, I want to—'

'Table.' Nani shifts Raina to her other knee. '*Now.*'

Manavi gets up from the table, a load of plates piled on her forearm. She turns back to Nani, and whispers, 'May I at least put her to bed tonight?'

'Did you finish homework?'

Manavi breathes loudly, sharply, and then turns back to the sink.

*

Raina has chocolate frosting all over her face, in her hair and on her clothes. Nana and Nani carry her upstairs to the bathroom and fill a warm bath with strawberry bubbles. Later, they carry her to bed, envelop her in a baby-blue sleep suit and tuck her into her cot.

Raina is drifting, her eyelashes batting, when the door opens and light cuts into the room. Raina opens her eyes and sits up in the cot. Manavi is in the room, and Raina squints as she watches her tiptoe across the carpet and sit down on the floor beside her. Manavi reaches her hand through the bars and strokes her hair, brushes her fingers along her face.

'Say *Ma-ma*,' whispers Manavi.

Raina whimpers.

'*Ma-ma*?' And when Raina says nothing, no noise comes from her lips, Manavi stands up and lifts Raina out of the cot. She squeezes her tight, presses their cheeks together. Raina struggles to pull free. She squirms, tries to unfasten her body from Manavi's grip, and when she is unable to, starts to cry.

'Oh, baby. Please don't cry,' begs Manavi. She rocks Raina back and forth, pats her on the back lightly the way Nani does. But Raina keeps crying, marble-sized tears rolling down her cheeks, and she presses her tiny fists against Manavi. Pounds them, trying to push her away.

'My Raindrop, please—'

'Manu!' The light flicks on and Nani sweeps into the room. She pulls Raina into her arms and cradles her. 'Manu, look what you've done.'

Raina is quickly soothed. She basks in a warm light and

the soft touch of her Nani. Comforted, firm in her Nani's grasp, she stops crying; and the sharp voices drowning out around her, she drifts safely towards sleep.

Chapter 37

I stayed with Kris well into the afternoon, and in the evening Nani still hadn't come downstairs. We called a taxi and slipped out without disturbing her. Along the way, the driver dropped Kris off at his house on the outskirts of town. I watched him as he fumbled with his keys, groggily wave goodbye before stumbling inside, and then we continued on to my place.

Was it only the night before that I'd been at Shay and Julien's party? Drinking with my friends, and watching Asher dance with another girl? I'd barely seen him in months, but suddenly I missed him fiercely – as if just his presence would bring my family back together.

But it wouldn't. Kris was as he had always been – miserable, detached – and Mom was pregnant with a baby the rest of us would probably never know.

And Nani?

The distance between us seemed impossible. I had let myself drift so far away; and owning up to her about everything was the only way back. But could I really tell her the truth now? After Mom had come home, shattered her and then disappeared again?

Sometimes after Mom left us, Nani would stay in her room for days. Nana would cook, and he'd take her half-burnt aloo and tea, shutting the bedroom door behind him – only to return an hour later with the plate of food untouched. Days would pass, the house consumed with silence, and then, as if nothing had happened, Nani would re-emerge, smiling.

I spent the night cleaning my apartment, ironing my outfits for Shay's wedding, paying my bills. I was restless. It wasn't the right time to tell Nani; not with the wedding coming up, not with Mom's bombshell news. She wasn't ready, and neither was I. But there was one thing I *was* ready to do.

Bill was already at the office when I arrived. It was Sunday morning, when he should have been at home making breakfast with his kids – when he should have been doing a thousand other things that used to make him happy. He sat beside me on the sofa in his office, and, staring out of the window, the first pink touches of light hitting the lake, asked me if there was anything he could do to change my mind.

I could have made it more dramatic, but I didn't. There was no point. I handed him my letter of resignation, and said simply that my priorities in life had changed.

But they hadn't changed, not really. Family. Friendship. Love. These were the things that had always mattered. And now, eight years after first accepting a passionless job that was only ever meant to fill in the gaps, I was more than ready to leave.

Shay's wedding week started in a blur. Serena, the twins and I were recruited for countless errands: picking up and dropping off relatives, lugging wedding decorations to and from the venues, helping Shay manage Auntie Sarla's demands. There were dinner parties with relatives, with family friends who had travelled to Toronto, and then the Ganesha pooja: a religious ceremony performed to remove obstacles and ensure the successful completion of the wedding.

I sat down near the back of the temple with Serena and looked around the room. It was a workday, and many people hadn't come – including Asher. Up at the front, Nani and Auntie Sarla were assisting the priest as he carried out the ceremony. Shay and Julien were sitting cross-legged with their eyes closed, and as the priest resumed chanting, I closed mine too.

I'd never really tried to understand Hinduism. For most, it conjured the image of Ganesha's trunk and bright colours; bronze statues and bathing in the Ganges; and my knowledge – my understanding of it – only went a tad further.

Its belief system was supple. Its rituals and traditions had been blended and nuanced over thousands of years, and from one region to another. But surely, at its core, there was nothing about it that decreed its believers to be intolerant. The *Kama Sutra* encouraged homosexual relations, and so did the holy book, the *Rigveda*. Shay had mentioned that there were even transgender characters in the *Mahabharata*.

But then why did so many traditional Hindus, like Depesh's parents, like Auntie Sarla, vehemently disapprove? When had all that started? Why had we been taught to fear, to discredit everything but our own perspective?

Whatever the belief system, we were all in charge of our own values. Depesh had been brave to challenge them, to stand up to his own family and community. And now, for a while at least, he was gone. As much as it hurt, as much as I didn't want to let him go, I knew that he would be all right without me.

Two days before the wedding, Auntie Sarla hosted Shay's mehndi – a ladies-only ceremony held to decorate the bride with henna. The entire evening, Shay was stuck in the middle of the living room as two artists painted her hands, wrists and feet with the black ink. I wanted to thank Shay in person for driving Mom to the airport, tell her about quitting my job, about Depesh, and to see how she was coping with the wedding stress, but someone always seemed to be within earshot. When I saw her slip into the kitchen, I followed her and found her standing in front of the sink limply scraping off the dried henna.

'Are you OK?'

She didn't reply, and in silence I watched as she rubbed her hands together. Her eyes were fixated on the black paste as it crumbled down the drain, leaving a sprawl of bright orange on her palm.

'Here.' I reached for a platter of samosas. 'You must be hungry.'

'No, not hungry,' she said quietly. Suddenly she looked up through the glass in the kitchen door. 'Shit.'

A moment later, Auntie Sarla burst in, glaring at Shay. 'I *told* you – you must leave that on all evening.' Auntie Sarla lunged for Shay's hands. '*Aacha*? It is all ruined! The colour will be gone by ceremony!'

'Ma, it doesn't matter.'

Auntie Sarla whipped towards me. 'And Raina has taken hers off too. Of course. Follow *her* example.'

'I needed to call Julien. I can't use the phone with this stuff on my hands.'

Auntie Sarla launched into a tirade in Rajasthani. I kept trying to interrupt, but Auntie Sarla ignored me, and after a few moments even Shay told me I should leave. I wasn't going to, but I felt my phone vibrate, and when I pulled it out from under the strap of my bra, my heart stopped. It was Depesh.

I nearly tripped over my sari as I raced into a quiet room at the back of Shay's house. Deliberately, I clicked answer and held the phone up to my ear.

'Depo?'

I heard heavy breathing, faint music thumping in the background. I checked my watch. It was the middle of the night in London.

For almost a minute, he didn't speak, and I listened to him breathing and tried to work up the courage to say something.

'Where are you?' I finally asked.

'I'm in Hack-*ney*.'

I nodded into the phone. He sounded drunk, his words slurring, and with every ounce of me I prayed that he was safe.

'Are you OK?'

'Tell me why.'

'Remember the British guy I used to date?' I pressed my hand over my face. He didn't answer, and I continued. 'It was for him. I was under pressure to get married, and I still wanted him.'

'A *guy*? An ex-boyfriend?'

'I know it doesn't make any sense. It *still* doesn't make sense. I have no excuse—'

'I came out – I fucking came out to my parents because, because of *you*, because I thought you—' He broke off, and I could hear a garble through the phone.

'Depesh, I don't expect forgiveness.'

'Good.'

'But I'm always going to be here for you,' I said slowly. 'You can hate me, but I'm here.'

'God. I'm not – not some baby bird that needs taking care of, OK? I don't need you.'

'Depo…'

'And you don't need me either, Raina.' He laughed. 'Apparently all you need is a *boyfriend*.'

My ears burned.

'Sorry,' he said after a minute. 'Sorry, I'm *drunk*.'

'No, it's OK. I deserved that.'

The music started getting louder through the phone, and I heard shouting behind him.

'I should go.'

'Depo, are you being safe? Do your parents know—'

'Yeah, OK? They know where I am…' He paused, and I heard a voice beside him. 'I have to go.'

'Wait, please. Just one thing.'

'What?'

'I know you don't need me. I know you're hurt. But just – just know you can call me any time.'

He didn't respond.

'Tell me you know I'm still here, Depo.' My voice cracked. 'Please.'

A moment passed. And just before he rang off, he said, 'I know.'

*

304

It took me a while before I could go back to the party. Most people had left, and I couldn't find Shay anywhere. I came across Nani at the front door. She'd asked a friend to drive her home, but I told her that I was ready to go too.

She seemed tired, and on the way back in the passenger seat she kept her eyes closed, her short legs tucked into the lotus position. I could hear her breathing, steady and meditative, and I drove home along the clean, dark streets that separated Shay's home from mine.

Was now the right time to tell her about Depesh – about me? Depesh knew I was straight, and so what was stopping me from telling Nani?

A cold gust blew in through the window. I shivered, and I knew exactly what was stopping me.

Every time Mom left us, Nani refused to talk about her. She'd smile, and she'd cook, and she'd fill the house with as much noise as possible – people, music, movies – trying to drown out the silence Mom always left behind. Nani would turn her attention to me, making sure I was fed, that I was happy and safe and felt loved. She counted on me to be the daughter Mom never was. She counted on me to smile, and to tell her that everything – our small, imperfect family – was OK.

But I wasn't OK. We, Nani and I, weren't OK.

'Did you have fun?'

I looked over. Nani had opened her eyes. She reached across and brushed a flyaway hair out of my face.

'It looked like all the girls were having a fun party.'

'Yeah.' I nodded. 'It was fun.'

'You could have called Zoey to come.'

'Zoey and I are just friends,' I said, trying not to sound irritated. 'I've told you that. Many times.'

'But she seems like nice girl.'

'So two nice people should date and get married, just because they're both nice?'

'Marriage is not about finding *nice*, or being perfect. It is about finding a good match. A good partner.' Nani reached for my hand. 'Zoey is also working at bank, she also likes' – Nani scrunched up her face – 'cottages, and these party things you go to. She would make a good partner.'

'Before it was a husband, now it's a *partner*? Why are you so hell-bent on playing matchmaker?' I dropped her hand. 'Why don't *you* remarry and find a "partner"?'

Nani laughed. 'Because I am *old* woman now, and I am finally having some peace. I am *happy* as things are for me. And you – well, *you* will find someone to make you happy. Not Zoey, then, but another. I know this.'

I gripped the steering wheel, trying to ignore the queasy feeling in my stomach. The anger rushing up.

'I may not have your Nana ...' She paused. 'But I have a lot, Raina. I have something I never had when I was young like you. *Freedom.*'

I swallowed, trying to steady my breathing.

'I spent *thirty-six years* taking care of your Nana. Working, and at home always cooking, cleaning, washing his stinky-stinky underwear.' She plugged her nose with her fingers and winced. 'You remember how he smelled after work. Now, I only wash my underwear!'

She wanted me to laugh, but this time I didn't. It wasn't funny.

'So you deserve your freedom, but I don't? I need some-one to be happy, but you don't?' I snapped. 'Is that it?'

'*Nah,* I am saying—'

'What, you got married like you were supposed to, pushed out some kids, and that way earned your freedom?' My voice was louder now, and I felt it crack. 'Now you're allowed to be happy however you want – now that your husband is dead?'

'Raina, I just want your happiness—'

'And that means I can't be single?' I stared straight ahead at the road, and I could feel the tears, welled up, finally pouring out. 'We women can't be happy or good enough unless we have a partner? But what kind of *partner* did you have? A man you didn't even want to sleep in the same bed with?'

'*Beta*—'

'Were *you* happy? Did you even love him? He didn't do a thing for you. You took care of Kris and Mom, and Saffron and *me* – but still you think that we women are nothing without our *partners*?'

'Raina,' I heard Nani say. 'You must listen. I just want your happiness. You are my child, and I wish you the best—'

'No, Nani. You're a hypocrite. You say you want me to be happy, but actually you want the perfect Indian daughter you never had. But I'm not her. I'm a screw-up, OK? Just like your other children. Just like *you.*'

The car was quiet. I could hear my heart pounding as I turned onto our street and then pulled up onto the driveway. Silently, she unbuckled her seat belt, and without a word, slid out of the car and closed the door behind her.

Chapter 38

I woke up early and went for a run, but when I got back I felt even worse. I showered quickly and drove home, racing past the commuters stalled in traffic on their way into the city.

I'd never spoken to Nani like that before. I'd never been so disrespectful, and I couldn't believe that I'd yelled at her, let her go inside and then driven away.

I slowly opened the front door, hoping I'd find her sitting on the sofa, waiting for me. But the living room was empty. Her tablet was lying on the coffee table, her yoga mat neatly rolled and stood to the side. I walked into the kitchen, but she wasn't there either. I made two cups of tea and trekked up the stairs. She wasn't in her bedroom. I checked my room, the bathroom and even Kris's old bedroom, but they were all empty. I took a deep breath, went across the landing towards the last unopened door. Slowly, I turned the handle and pushed my way in.

Nani was sitting cross-legged in the middle of the bed. Her pastel-pink trouser suit stood out against the beigeness of the room. Our family photo album was open on her lap, and her palms were resting on the open page. She looked up at me, blinking, and then snapped the album shut.

What had Nani and Nana expected out of their lives,

when they left everything behind and moved across the world? Did they really love each other? Or had their culture, their obligations and their children bound them together?

What had happened in this house before I was born? Or when I was young – too young to remember?

Mom once told me that she wasn't allowed to decorate her room when she was young. Nani had torn down all her posters of movie stars and boy bands, and had refused to cook breakfast until Mom had folded the stiff white sheets perfectly at all four corners of her bed, and aligned the pillows.

But I remembered how her wardrobe poured out of her bedroom door like a waterfall, down the stairs, her handmade jewellery and shoes flooding the cupboards, scarves washing up on the end tables. She was different to everyone I'd ever known. She was beautiful and interesting and oddly insightful. But Nani had never seen that side of her; she hadn't wanted to see it.

Was that why Mom left? I couldn't remember, and every time I tried, all I could picture was the room spinning around me. I was sitting waist-deep in a pile of her clothes as she slowly plucked them one by one from around me and stuffed them into bin bags. Nani was holding her tea, looking in from the doorway where I was standing now.

Was she crying?

I closed my eyes, clutched the scalding mugs in my hands. Still I couldn't remember. There was sun, and the window was open. It smelled like grass and pollen. It must have been summer, but I wasn't sure. All I knew was that it was the only day they hadn't fought. The only day I hadn't fallen asleep with my pillow over my head, praying it would all stop.

Nani cleared her throat and I opened my eyes.

How had we got here? How had I got us here?

I took a deep breath. I sat down beside her on the bed, put the mugs on the bedside table. It was time to tell her the truth, wasn't it?

'Nani, can we talk?'

She pressed her lips together, her hands folded tightly over the album.

'I'm really sorry for yelling at you. For last night. I—'

'It's fine,' she said curtly. She inched away from me and threw her legs over the far side of the bed. 'I need to stop bugging you.'

'That's not what I meant. I need to tell you that …'

The cuckoo clock started chiming downstairs, echoing through the house.

'That … I, um—'

The cuckoo clock kept going, one chirp after the other.

I took another breath. 'I …'

That clock. That damn cuckoo clock that Mom made, and nailed to the wall, and left behind.

'Not now,' said Nani.

The clock stopped.

'We must not be late for Shaylee's sangeet.' She stood up from the bed. I caught her wiping her eyes, the tears forming on her lashes.

Her heart was broken.

Quietly, I followed her out of the room, and as I shut the door firmly behind me, I knew I was breaking it all over again.

Serena picked me up a few hours later, and we dropped off our armoury of saris, jewellery and make-up at the hotel. Our room was next door to Nikki's and Niti's, and a few floors below Shay's suite, where we'd all get ready together the next morning. It was the eve of Shay's wedding, and the final pre-marriage celebration – the sangeet 'music party' – came well stocked with dinner and dancing, live music and an open bar.

We changed quickly and then made our way into the main ballroom downstairs. Dozens of waiters in uniform bustled around the room fussing with chair covers and centrepieces, scattering rose petals and pouring wine. In the corner Auntie Sarla, clipboard in hand, was instructing another group of waiters.

The guests started to arrive, and Serena and I took up our posts at the entrance and handed out programmes. I smiled and made an effort with Nani's friends that I recognised, and while I expected many of them to be distant with me, most weren't. Some I hadn't seen in months, even years, and they seemed genuinely pleased to see me.

Shay acted strange all evening, and, watching her at the top table wedged between Auntie Sarla and Julien, a fake smile painted on her face, I could tell something was wrong. It was more than stress; she looked miserable, even though she should have been the happiest woman in the room. The moment dinner was over she pushed back her chair and raced out of the hall. No one seemed to notice. Everyone was moving towards the dance floor, watching the band take centre stage. I looked back and saw that Julien had slipped away too.

When the band started and they still hadn't returned, I went outside into the foyer to look for them. Both Shay and Julien's phones were going straight to voicemail. I searched the lobby, the back rooms, but I couldn't find them anywhere.

I went back into the hall, scanning the crowd. Half the guests had abandoned their seats for the dance floor, and the live bhangra was in full swing. From across the floor I spotted Asher, his head poking up above the crowd. I felt my stomach flutter. He caught my eye and waved. I waved back, and tried not to wonder where Rebekah was. The band was loud, and it seemed like everyone was bouncing along as the female lead singer belted out Punjabi lyrics.

Shay and Julien were missing their own party. I motioned to Asher to check his phone, and then I texted him.

Where are S & J??

A moment later, he replied.

I don't know. Want me to help you look?

I texted back.

You check his room. I'll check hers.

I put my phone back in my bag and turned round. The crowd was thick around me, and I pushed my way back into the foyer. I was sweating by the time I reached the lifts. I reached forward to press the button, and as I was waiting I felt a hand on my waist.

'Darling.'

I whipped round.

'You look *gorgeous*.' He pulled me in for a hug. 'I've been looking for you everywhere.'

I couldn't breathe. What was he doing here? At Shay's wedding? Back in Toronto?

I suddenly remembered that it was Friday by the coloured tie he was wearing. His hair – light black and bristly, a few wisps of grey – was typically parted and in place.

'Took me ages to track you down, and *wow*. And to think I've never even seen you in a sari.'

I was speechless. He tried to reach for me, and I pushed him away. He dropped his arms, studying me as if suddenly I'd become a complex graph; a banking equation it was his mission to solve.

'What happened? I flew in yesterday, *finally*, and Bill said you—'

'Quit.' I crossed my arms. 'Yes, I quit.'

He sighed, putting his hand around my waist. 'Tell me this isn't about us.'

'Us? There isn't an "us". We haven't spoken in a month.' I tried to shrug off his hand, but then he wrapped the other one around me too. 'The thing is, Dev, this is the first thing I've done in a while that has nothing to do with *us* – or my Nani, or anyone but me.'

'Raina, it's been so stressful for me, and on top of that you stopped speaking to me, and it threw me. It's thrown me right out—'

'I don't want to hear it.'

'But I'm staying put at the minute. Don't you see? Don't you see what that means for us? I'll travel, still. But I'm based here. Near *you*. Properly now.' He smiled and leaned in closer. 'Really, love. You didn't have to quit.'

'Are you even listening to me?'

'You and I were happy together, weren't we? I love you...'

My head swam, and when he leaned forward to kiss me, I tried to pull away.

'I always have.'

I felt my cheek against his chin, his hands on the back of my neck, my waist.

'Raina, I *think* I'm ready.'

He pressed his lips against mine and I winced. I was breathing hard when he pulled away. I opened my eyes, my vision blurred and my lashes stuck together. Finally, everything became clear. But I didn't see Dev. I saw Asher.

'Asher…'

Dev spun round. Asher was standing just behind him.

'Sorry, mate. Didn't see you.' He extended his hand. 'I'm Dev.'

Asher's hands didn't move; his eyes didn't leave me.

'You a friend of Raina's?'

I could feel Dev shift beside me, and when he tried to put his arm around me, I flung it away. Asher's face was motionless.

My mind raced. This was wrong. It all felt so wrong. I wanted Asher to hold me, Asher to kiss me – the way he had in New York.

'Asher, I—'

He turned on his heel, started walking towards the door and I followed.

'Raina, where are you going?'

But I kept running after Asher, nearly tripping on the hem of my sari as I tore through the revolving door behind him.

'Asher, wait.' I caught up with him, tugged on his shoulder until he turned round. 'Please, don't go.'

I looked into his eyes, pleading with him. Would he forgive me? Could I say anything, *do* anything, to make it right between us? Take us back to New York, back to midnight?

'Look at me, Asher,' I whispered. 'Please.'

A gust of wind tore in from the car park – sharp, sandy – and I wrapped the tail of my sari around my arms.

'I know what that looked like. I know what you must think of me, but let me ex—'

'You have no idea what I think about you.'

'Please, let me explain. My heart was in the right place, I swear.'

'You're in love with that guy?'

I looked at his hands. They were shaking, and I wanted to reach for them.

'I used to be,' I whispered.

'And now?'

'And now ... I'm falling in love with you.' I stepped towards him, but he drew back. One step, and then another.

'I didn't mean it to go this far, I swear. It got out of hand, and I didn't know *what* I was doing.' I paused, willing him to look at me. 'I'm not a bad person, it's—'

'I know you're a good person,' he said slowly. He wouldn't meet my eye. 'I wouldn't have cared for you if you weren't.'

'So you do care?' I asked, hoping. Pleading. 'You still – you *could* still – care about me?'

'I'm a simple guy. This, you, it's too ... complicated. I can't.' He breathed out, and his voice caught. 'I can't do this right now.'

'I'm sorry, Asher. Please—'

'I'm sorry too.'

But he wouldn't look at me, and he kept walking away.

*

I didn't want to let him go. But I did. He disappeared behind the hotel, and after ten minutes I forced myself to realise he wasn't coming back.

Dev was still in the lobby, reclined on a sofa, his legs crossed. Right ankle over left knee, BlackBerry in hand. He looked up as I approached and tucked the phone in his pocket. He shifted over on the sofa, and I sat down next to him. For a moment neither of us spoke.

'Why did you do that?' I asked him finally.

'Do what?' He moved closer to me. 'Darling, who was that?'

'Dev, I'm not your darling. Stop calling me that.' He tried to brush a piece of hair behind my ear, and I pressed his hand down. 'I want you to stop.'

'Raina, then. What's happening?' I didn't answer, and he intertwined his fingers through mine.

How had it taken me this long to get here?

'Weren't we happy?' he whispered.

Maybe he really was ready this time, or maybe he wasn't. But finally *I* was ready, and I knew I could never go back.

'We *were* happy. But being with you ... it's not enough.' I dropped his hand. 'I was just too in love to realise it.'

Chapter 39

The morning arrived, and I was thirty.

I opened my eyes and found Serena snoring in the bed next to me. I reached over and hit the alarm, and then threw cushions at her until she woke up. A few moments later, we crawled out of the room, knocked on Nikki and Niti's door and the four of us, gowned in hotel slippers and robes, our matching bridesmaids' saris draped over our arms, took the lift up to the top floor. It was almost five a.m. We arrived at the suite, but when Nikki knocked no one answered.

'Did she set an alarm?' she asked. She knocked louder, and then Niti joined in, their fists pounding against the hotel door until Serena insisted they stopped.

Serena pulled out her phone, but when she called it went to voicemail, and suddenly I remembered, guiltily, about how Shay and Julien had disappeared the evening before. How after my long, long talk with Dev, I'd gone up to my room and forgotten all about them.

'Maybe she's in the shower,' I said hopefully.

The lift bell rang from down the corridor, and shortly after, Shay emerged. She still had her full hair and make-up on from the previous night, and she was wearing a pair of blue checked pyjama pants and the blouse of her sari.

She drearily turned her head, and then sulked towards us. Her eyes were red, her long-wear mascara bleeding at the corners.

'Have you been up all night?'

She didn't answer, and fished a key card out of her clutch. She jabbed it into the slot. She tried to swing the door behind her but I caught it and pushed through just in time to see her collapse face down onto one of the sofas.

'Shay?' I sat down beside her.

She turned round slowly, wiping her face with the back of her hand.

'What is it?'

She swallowed loudly, and, tears welling in her eyes, she said, 'I think the wedding is off.'

For twenty minutes Shay just lay there, face down on the sofa, her arms splayed out behind her; I couldn't tell if she was asleep or awake, crying or even breathing.

'Are you ready to talk yet?'

Shay groaned, and shook her head into the cushion. I'd instructed everyone else to start getting ready without us, thinking surely Shay would snap out of it quickly, but I was getting worried.

What had happened? The wedding wasn't really cancelled, was it?

'Shay, tell me.'

'I don't want to talk about it.'

'You know what,' I grabbed her by the waist and yanked her up from the sofa, 'I don't care. We're talking about it.'

Somehow, I managed to get Shay into the bathroom. I locked the door behind us, and when I turned back round she had seated herself cross-legged on the counter. I stood with my back against the door, waiting for her to speak, but she just looked at her hands.

'Did you and Julien have a fight?'

I saw the tears pooling in her eyes, and then a fat droplet rolled down her cheek. I wiped it away, and her body trembled as I put an arm around her.

'Where is he?'

'I don't know.' She wiped her face with the backs of her hands.

'Do you want me to call him?'

'He won't answer.' She shook her head, laughing. 'He's *so* angry with me.'

'What *happened*?'

She hopped off the counter and started pacing in front of me, her hands on her hips.

'Shay?'

'Don't be angry. OK? Manavi told me you were angry when you found out she was pregnant.' She paused. 'And, *well*, so am I.'

'Angry?'

'No. Jesus, I'm *pregnant*.'

'Oh my God.' Tears welled in my eyes. 'Shay, you're going to be a mom?'

She shrugged.

I lunged for her, hugged her, squeezed her until she pushed me off. 'This is amazing, Shay. Why the hell are you guys fighting—'

'Because I didn't want it to happen yet, Raina! I've just finished my residency. Just got some semblance of independence. And then there was my freaking circus wedding to deal with. Finally I was about to get some pressure off me, and this happens! I'm having a baby!'

'These things are unexpected—'

'I'm a doctor. I'm on the pill, Raina! This wasn't supposed to happen yet. I'm not ready.'

'You're going to have to be ready.'

'That's what Julien said.' Shay frowned. 'And I got angry and said I wanted an abortion.'

'You *what*?'

'Of course I don't want an abortion. I want a baby – I just didn't want one *now*. And I was angry at Julien because he was *so* excited, but he doesn't have to get stretch marks. He doesn't have to shit out a baby.' She grabbed a load of toilet paper and wiped her nose. 'We've been fighting all week because he wanted us to go to confession before the wedding, ask for *forgiveness* from his priest and get married right then in the church. And last night we almost did go. We were practically in the car, and I was *so* angry – I don't know, hormones – and I know how his whole raging Catholic family feels about it and I just … told him I wanted an abortion.'

'And you didn't mean it.'

She sniffed. 'No.'

'Then apologise, Shay. It's that simple. Tell him the truth, and apologise.'

Was it really that simple? Could every mistake be fixed this way? Falling to one's knees, begging those you've hurt to forgive you?

Shay knocked over the toilet seat lid and sat down. I handed her more toilet paper, she blew her nose and handed it back to me. I stuffed it into the pocket of my robe and crouched down next to her.

'Do you remember the night you introduced him to me?'

Shay looked up, nodded slowly.

'I was going to save this for your toast tonight, but do you know what he said to me the next morning? He came out of your room and I was in the kitchen making coffee, and he wanted to make you breakfast – do you remember that?'

'He was the first guy ever to make me breakfast.'

I nodded and grabbed her hand. 'And I was showing him where the toaster was, the sugar, the milk, and then he stopped and looked at me, and said, "Raina, I'm going to marry that girl".'

Shay's face crumpled.

'Almost six years later, and he still wants to marry you. You two are *happy*, Shay. You've found your person.' I fished my phone out of my robe pocket and handed it to her. 'So stop being so dramatic and call him.'

At eight-thirty Auntie Sarla and a flock of her friends and relatives started arriving, wedging themselves into the love seats and onto the room's surfaces. The make-up artist finished with me and moved on to Serena, and a second later a hairstylist named Claire appeared, grunted hello and roughly started to comb my hair. She angled my chair into the room's corner – so she could more easily reach her curling iron, she said – and I couldn't see anybody.

I heard noises escalating behind me, more and more aunties arriving. Every time I tried to turn my head to see whether Nani had arrived, Claire yanked my head back sharply.

A few aunties came by and said their hellos, offered me tea or juice and then quickly disappeared again. I could hear everyone fussing over Shay on the opposite side of the room, her fake-placatory voice agreeing to every suggestion as they tied her sari, ensured every curl was perfectly pinned to her head. I laughed to myself, and wished Claire would hurry up. I reached up and felt my hair, but only half of it was curled and pinned back – the other half was still in a limp mess by my shoulders.

'Is there a problem?' Claire snapped.

'Just wondering how much longer.' I smiled. 'I still have to put on my sari.'

She rolled her eyes. 'Well, next time tell the bride not to make the wedding so goddamn early.'

'It wasn't her choice,' I said softly, though Claire had already stopped listening.

I could feel the room filling up even more; it was becoming fiercely hot, and I regretted not changing out of my flannel pyjamas and bathrobe before everyone arrived.

'Could someone open a window?' I said to the wall, to no one in particular. The air conditioning was on, but the room felt like a sauna. 'Please?'

An auntie appeared beside me. 'Already open – we have called for fan.'

I thanked her, and she disappeared from my peripheral vision.

I was becoming more restless with each passing minute. I wanted to help Shay get ready, make sure she was still OK, but the progress of my updo had stalled. Claire dropped her hands from my head to grab her coffee, and I took the opportunity to turn round.

Shay's aunties and relatives surrounded her. Her make-up and hair seemed to be done, and she was sitting at the foot of the bed half-dressed in her petticoat and blouse. Auntie Sarla was standing over her, and they seemed to be yelling at each other in Rajasthani. Shay looked like she was about to cry again, and it was as if the aunties around them – steaming her bridal sari, idly primping her hair – hadn't even noticed.

I stood up and walked towards them, ignoring Claire's protests.

'What's going on?'

Auntie Sarla's eyes flicked towards me as she continued yelling at Shay. Then she stopped, and, glaring at me, said, '*Nothing*, Raina.'

Shay stood up. 'Don't speak to her like that.'

'Auntie, did I do something?'

'What *haven't* you done?'

'Ma!'

'Auntie, please tell me.'

'It's fine,' Shay said. 'I handled it.'

'Handled what?' The rest of the room seemed to have gone quiet. They were listening to us.

'Some of my more *conservative* relatives,' Shay said evenly, 'didn't come this morning to help me get ready, and—'

'Because of *you*, Raina,' snapped Auntie Sarla. 'You are ruining Shaylee's wedding—'

'Shut it, Ma.'

'Who would want to be around you, a *gay*—'

'Yes, *shut it*, Sarla,' I heard Nani say. I turned to look. She

323

was sitting in a chair near the window. I hadn't seen her arrive, and I was briefly stunned that she hadn't come over and said hello; wished me a happy birthday.

Nani stood up slowly. 'Are we really going to start again with this now?'

'She is ruining—'

Shay groaned. 'Raina is not ruining my wedding, *you* are, Ma!'

'Me?' Auntie Sarla cackled. 'You have me to thank for this whole wedding—'

'I didn't want this day. I didn't want this whole wedding! You think I wanted some hyper-religious ceremony where I'm not even allowed to kiss the groom?' Shay's eyes filled up again, and her voice had grown hoarse. 'I did this for you, for Dad, and you know that.'

Auntie Sarla snapped an interjection, and her arms flailed wildly.

'English *please*,' I said.

Shay rolled her eyes. 'Oh, she's just mad the attention isn't on *her*.'

'On *you*, Shaylee! This *your* day.'

'Don't you mean *your* day?'

'Ungrateful child,' spat Auntie Sarla.

'*I'm* ungrateful?' Shay yelled. 'I did *everything* you and Dad ever asked of me. I was perfect. I'm having your *perfect* wedding – and still this isn't enough. You want the attention on me? You got it. Julien and I almost eloped last night. How's that for attention?'

'Elopement?' repeated Auntie Sarla. 'But *vhy*?'

'Because this goddamn thing is a nightmare! Because we wanted a small wedding – in a church, in some French

324

town – away from all of this. Because I'm – I'm *fucking* pregnant!'

Auntie Sarla gasped, and echoes of her gasp followed behind her. She collapsed onto the bed, and an auntie started to fan her with a magazine. She started mumbling something incoherently in Rajasthani, and Shay rolled her eyes.

'Ma. Are you OK?'

Auntie Sarla didn't reply, and Shay squatted down beside her.

'Ma? I'm sorry, I—'

'*Pregnant*. Shaylee!' She sat up slowly, unsteadily, her plump face flushed like a plum. 'How did this happen?'

'I sat on a dirty toilet seat.'

I snorted out a laugh. Shay started laughing too. Auntie Sarla stood up and pinned her glare onto me.

'This is *your* doing.'

'Huh?'

'You and your Nani. And that dirty Manavi – whole family *always* causing trouble.'

'Ma, you're going to be a Nani.'

'*You* were bad influence on my Shaylee.'

'Don't blame Raina for Shaylee's actions,' said Nani.

'This is all Raina's doing! Ever since she decided to be lesbian, nothing but hassle, but difficulty for everyone. And I hear now Sharon's boy is gay too. What did you do to him?'

'What did *I* do to him?'

'You're running around with him, making—'

'Hush, Sarla! This is not right time. This is your daughter's wedding, *nah*?'

'When is the time then?' spat Auntie Sarla. 'When all the kids have turned gay? When Raina marries another girl? When there are two bridal saris to tie? I will not be there to help, Suvali. No one will be there!'

I tried to catch my breath, and the yelling around me escalated. Billowed. The dullness in the pit of my stomach, uneasy and sharp, mushroomed, and, my body shaking, I just couldn't take any more. I had to stop it.

'Everyone. SHUT. UP.'

In a moment, the room was silent. Still. And everyone was staring at me. I could feel sweat had started to gather in my armpits, to run down the base of my spine. I glanced at Shay. She smiled at me. Nodded. I took a breath, and finally I said it.

'I'm not gay.'

My fists were clenched tightly, and I loosened them. My vision blurred, refocused. Still the room was silent.

'*What*?' cried Auntie Sarla.

'You're not?' said Serena.

I shook my head and turned to face Nani. Her eyes were on the floor, and she had pressed her hands into the windowsill on either side of her. She was breathing hard, refusing to meet my eye.

'Why would you lie about something like this?' asked an auntie nearby, although my ears were ringing and I couldn't tell which one it was.

'I just wanted everyone to stop telling me to get married, and setting me up with dates.' My voice trembled, and I pressed on. 'It wasn't supposed to go this far. And then I just wanted people to know that – that it was *OK* to be gay. It shouldn't have mattered. I didn't want it to matter.'

'But you're not,' said Serena.

I shook my head.

'Well,' said Auntie Sarla. She was smiling. 'This is good news. *Some* good news.'

'Ma.' Shay rolled her eyes. 'That's not the point. The point is that it shouldn't matter even if she was gay.'

'But she's not!'

'Yes, Ma. I know. But why does it matter one way or the other?'

'Of *course* it matters.'

'Are you kidding me? Wake up, *Mother*, it's the twenty-first century. People screw before—'

'Shaylee!'

'—they get married. People are straight, others are gay. What concern is it to you?'

'She's right, Sarla,' said another auntie. 'My nephew in Winnipeg is of the gay now.'

'Ma, don't you see how backward you are? That you're …'

Again the room became a commotion. Silence was replaced with horrified and bemused looks; Auntie Sarla's intermittent sobs and screams; and shouts from back and forth across the room. It was mayhem, and I looked back towards Nani. The windowsill had been abandoned. And I turned the other way, past the crowd, just in time to see the door slam shut.

Chapter 40

I followed her outside and found her walking slowly towards the bank of lifts. I ran to catch up with her.

'Nani?'

She didn't turn round. She kept waddling, slowly, like she was slightly out of breath. Finally she turned to look at me when I was right beside her, and as she came to a stop I burst into tears.

'*Raina*,' she said, digging out a tissue from her bra. She dabbed it on my face. 'Your make-up will be ruined.'

I nodded, and carefully patted at the corners of my eyes. She pulled back her hands, and I could feel her watching me as I tried to stop crying. Her face seemed pale; the kajal around her eyes, the blush on her cheekbones oddly jarring. Her mouth was open slightly, as if she was about to say something, or didn't know what to say at all.

'I'm sorry,' I said.

Nani's lips pressed together, and she shook her head. 'You are *sorry*.' Her voice trembled. 'Was I not worthy of truth? Am I not strong, have I not shown you love?'

'Nani—'

'Encouraged you? Protected you? And then you tell me – your own Nani – like this? In front of all these people at Shaylee's wedding?' She was panting for air, cowering away from me. 'Why did you lie, Raina? This, you tell me. Now. All of the truth.'

All of the truth. I trembled, looked down at my feet.

'I was tired of you telling me I should get married. Of hearing that I needed someone to be happy. But the *truth* is, that's what I thought I needed too.'

Out of the corner of my eye, I could see her blinking at me, her face unchanged. She was waiting for me to continue.

'I was scared. And alone, and then Dev moved to Toronto—'

'*Dev?*'

I nodded. 'He moved here, and I wanted to . . .' I hesitated. 'I *thought* I wanted to—'

'Reconcile,' said Nani.

'But we didn't. And we're not going to. It's different now. I think I'm different.' I sighed. 'I was so ashamed of him, Nani. Ashamed of myself. I just – just didn't know how to tell you the truth about him. That's why I let you believe I was gay.' Tears welled again in my eyes, and I wiped my face. 'I just wanted you to be proud of me, respect my decisions.' I swallowed. 'I didn't . . . want to be another disappointment.'

Nani's lips were squeezed together. She didn't say anything, and I stepped closer to her. I could smell the talcum she used, her Chanel perfume, and, overwhelmingly, I wanted her back. I wanted my Nani – her sweet strength, her imperfections – back in my life.

Tentatively I reached out and placed my hand on her shoulder. I could feel the weight of her collapse slightly onto me. 'I am very sorry.'

Her eyes were glued to the floor; she wouldn't look at me. She was barely moving.

'Nani, please say something.'

'After Manu,' she said finally, 'I vowed that this time – with *you* – I would be better. I would, this time, not be like my own mother. But perhaps this is all of our destinies. I was just as hard on you as with Manu. I must have been too hard on you if you could not tell me this truth.'

'You were wonderful, Nani—'

'*Nah.*' Tears formed in her eyes. 'I failed many, *many* times.'

'You did your best. That's all we can do.'

'You thought I would blame you for still being in love, Raina. You thought I would *judge*, disapprove.' She smiled at me, a fading, distant smile. 'Love is never easy, Raina. This I know very well. With your Nana,' she sighed, 'it was love, but it was not easy.'

'I wanted to tell you. I was just so … embarrassed.'

'There is no shame in love. We make choices, and then we try and move on the best we can. We try and live with those choices.'

I thought about my choices; how many wrong ones I'd made in the last year. I thought about Dev and Asher.

I thought about Depesh.

'Raina, my sweet. Don't cry.'

'I lied to you. I lied to everyone.' I wiped my nose with my wrist, gestured down the hall. 'Look what I did.'

Nani smiled up at me meekly. 'It is good these people are hassled sometimes, *nah*? It was good for me too. To think about things – think about *these* things.' She looked up

330

at me slyly. 'And that's why I didn't say anything when...
when I figured it out.'

'Figured what out?'

Nani looked up at me like a conspirator, with that vivacious glimmer I hadn't seen in months lighting up her eyes.

'You knew?' I crossed my arms. 'Wait. You *knew* I wasn't
gay? Since when?'

'I figured out past few weeks. I know my own girl.' Nani
smiled. 'You have been behaving very odd, and then after
mehndi, driving home, you were *so* angry – I knew. I knew
that this wasn't my Raina. But that when she is ready – she
will tell me.'

'I wanted to tell you, Nani. So many times.' I pressed my
lips together. 'Depesh is gay, and when he told me—'

'I have heard this.' Nani nodded, cutting me off. 'I am
seeing now what happened. You wanted to help him, *nah*?'

'Yeah. I really did. But I'm not sure it worked.'

Nani pressed her lips together and looked back down
the hall. 'Sarla is a loud woman. But she is screaming for a
reason.' Nani looked back at me. 'She knows she is losing.
Our people are growing, changing, and that *silly* Sarla will
soon be the only left to resist. You *have* helped, my Raina.'

Had I helped? But how could hurting Depesh the way
I had have been worth it?

'Now let's go back and save Shaylee. So much yelling – it
can't be good for the child.' Nani squeezed my hand and
winked. 'I don't think your news will be biggest scandal of
the day, *nah*?'

Beside us, the lift bell rang, and the doors parted. I
looked over, shocked to find Asher standing behind us,
stepping out of the lift. I tried not to stare. It was my first

331

time seeing him in a kurta pyjama. Jet black with red and gold embroidery along the chest and cuffs. A crimson scarf was hooked loosely around his neck. He looked so handsome, and when he caught my eye, it was all I could do not to buckle in front of him.

'Sorry to disturb,' he said slowly. Draco sat in his arms, and he held it out to us. 'Julien wanted me to give this to Shaylee.'

Nani reached up and plucked it from his hands, and stared at it curiously. '*Vhat* is this? A grizzle bear?'

He laughed.

'Thank you, Asher.' I smiled at him and tried to hold his gaze. What was he thinking? I felt him looking at me – my whole face, my neck. His eyes were twinkling. Or was I imagining it?

Nani cleared her throat.

'Sorry, this is Asher. Asher this is my … Nani.'

'Hi, Auntie, I'm Asher.'

'No, handsome. Call me Nani. I am your Nani, too, *nah*?'

'Oh, uh—'

'She says that to everybody.' I shook my head, and Asher grinned. 'She wasn't implying—'

'And how do you know my beautiful granddaughter?'

'*Nani.*'

'I'm Julien's friend.'

'Ah.'

'And you're right,' said Asher, looking back at me. 'Your granddaughter is absolutely … beautiful.'

I felt Nani elbow me in the ribs, and I blushed.

'I must go now and take this thing to Shaylee. You,' she looked at me, winking, 'no rush.'

332

'Nice to meet you, Nani.'

'Nice to meet *you*,' she said, pinching his cheek.

She disappeared down the hall. As she opened the door, Auntie Sarla's pitchy scream emerged, a rise and fall of hysteria, and then it subsided as the door closed.

'What's going on in there?'

'I'm not sure you want to know. It's pretty … *complicated*.' I shrugged. 'And you said you were a simple guy.'

He grinned and stuffed his hands into his pockets. 'I did say that, didn't I?'

'Last night.' I bit my lip and looked down. He didn't want to hear about my past, my excuses – and I realised that I didn't want to tell him. I wanted to move on. I wanted to make the most of the mess I'd created, and help clean it up – help those I'd hurt – in any way they'd let me.

And I wanted Asher. It had taken me too long to realise it, to recognise the simplicity of happiness when it was standing right in front of me. With Asher, I was ready to push past who I'd become, the mistakes I had made. I was ready – really ready to be the woman I knew I could be. A granddaughter, a daughter, a true friend; roles I'd often neglected in the past.

With Asher, I could be the woman who didn't lose herself to love.

'Would you like to have coffee with me?'

A look of surprise swept over his face, and then he smiled.

'I know you're with someone—'

'I'm not with someone.'

I pressed my lips together, trying to keep from smiling. 'Rebekah and I broke up.'

'I'm sorry to hear that.'

'Are you?'

I grinned. 'Will you have coffee with me or not?'

His eyes moved up my face. 'Are you going to wear your hair like that?'

I touched my head. My hair was still half-done – part curled and pinned, the rest of it hanging straight over my ear.

'It's how the kids wear it these days.'

'And those pyjamas, wow.' He nodded. 'Sexy as hell.'

'I like to keep up with the trends.'

He grinned. 'Is that so?'

I nodded. 'I'll take you to this hipster café I know. You'll love it. They're all *stoners*.'

'You know me so well.' He smiled, and crossed his arms. 'On the other hand, I'm not sure I know you as well as I thought I did.'

'You probably know me better than I know myself.'

'I'll have to teach you all about *Raina Anand*, will I?'

'Sure. I hear you're a good teacher. Although not so good at basketball.'

'And where did you hear that?' He stepped towards me. 'If you're not nice, you'll have to buy me two coffees. Three, even.'

'I have to buy them? I don't know, Asher, I'm currently unemployed.'

'So, now who's the drifter?'

'How about … I'll buy you *one* coffee, and dessert. I won't even shove you into it.'

'Really? Dessert too?' He was right in front of me, inches away.

'Anything you want.'

He licked his lips, moved in closer. 'Anything?'

I could feel the heat of his body against mine. Pepper. Earth. Aftershave. I couldn't move. Slowly, he put his hands on my hips, started to lean in.

'So, coffee sometime?' I was breathing hard. 'It's a ... date?'

'A date.'

I closed my eyes, and I felt his breath on my ear. My cheek. My lips.

'I'll have to check my calendar.'

I opened my eyes. He was grinning at me.

'You're terrible.'

'I'm a very busy man, Raina.'

'You're going to make me pay for this, aren't you?'

The lift bell rang, and the doors opened. He got in, slowly turned round and smiled at me. 'Would you expect any less?'

I had to force myself not to jump in after him. Not to rush this. I knew I had a long way to go. With Asher – with everyone in my life. But right now, as I stood face to face with the man I loved, I knew that I would be just fine.

Chapter 41
20 May 2017

Shay's bridal sari weighs nearly twenty pounds. She is made up like a Rajasthani doll, perspiring through the thick garment of a deep-red bandhani design. The aunties adorn her with garlands and heavy gold jewellery; shower her with praise, religious tokens and blessings. While the hotel room is crowded and sickeningly hot, Nani has regained control, subdued Auntie Sarla's sobbing. No one mentions the pregnancy.

At the end of the preparations, Shay looks like a bride – one that could be plastered on the front cover of a Hindi magazine, or play the leading lady in a Bollywood movie. Raina squeezes her hand as Shay takes one last look in the mirror. Shay looks nothing like herself – her style bent to the will of her mother, her face made up to the point of artificial beauty. Any other day, Shay and Raina would have laughed at the image, ridiculed the excess and extravagance of it all, but today they decide against it.

The ceremony takes place in the lavish hotel hall, the bride, groom and their families seated on a crisp white dais at the front of the room. Shay and Julien are perched on the carpeted surface on either side of the priest, who is performing the rituals in Sanskrit before a small sacred fire.

With few exceptions, this is the way Raina has always

seen marriage – couples binding themselves to one another with the exchange of dark red and ivory flower garlands, measured laps around the flames. Raina watches attentively with renewed intrigue as the couple carry out the rituals. They pour water over a rock, then make offerings of rice to the flames. The priest ties Shay's chunni to the end of the thick, amber-red scarf draped over Julien's shoulders, a pledge of their love for one another. A literal nuptial knot.

Then he instructs them to stand up and take seven symbolic steps. Food, strength, prosperity, wisdom. Progeny. Health. And then the seventh step: friendship. After that, Julien dips his thumb into a small clay bowl and dabs red powder – the sindoor – above Shay's brow, marking her as a married woman.

Raina's face crumples. Shay and Julien are married, and she is deeply happy for them.

The couple move to the front of the platform. The flower girls have passed around wicker baskets brimming with rose petals, and the guests – all one thousand of them – line up to shower the happy couple with blessings. It is a more communal ending to a wedding ceremony than a kiss, but it is tradition, and the guests come forward to toss the petals as Shay and Julien hold hands: plastic figurines on a wedding cake. The last wave of guests makes its way to the front, and the steady stream of petals dies down. Shay and Julien look at each other, as if unsure what comes next. But then, in one swift motion, Shay's eyes twinkling, she kisses him.

For a moment the hall is soundless. Someone gasps, and then giggles emerge from the back of the hall. Raina's eyes flicker towards Auntie Sarla, who appears to be in physical pain, both of her hands folded over her mouth. Raina looks back at the couple. They are still kissing – passionately, eagerly – and without hesitation Raina starts to clap. She cheers, and lets out a whooping roar, causing some of the guests to turn and stare. But Raina doesn't stop. She hears Asher's voice join in, and in quick succession there is cheering from the rest of the groomsmen, from Serena, Zoey and Alice. Others follow, and then more, until at least half of the guests are thundering with applause. Julien grabs Shay by the waist, dipping her in front of the entire room as he kisses her.

And just like that, they have created a ripple. More fodder for their guests' gossip, morphing a tradition and making it their own.

A light lunch, and then the wedding party is herded into limos, shuttled from one photo shoot location to another. Shay and Julien in front of St Basil's church; a family photo in the college grounds; and then another in the shade of Falconer Hall. Julien and his groomsmen posed beneath arches; on the railway lines at Union Station. The last shot of the day: Shay and the bridesmaids perched on benches at Toronto Music Garden. Afterwards, as she's about to stand up, Raina feels two large warm hands cover her eyes, and instinctively she leans back against his stomach, breathes him in. Then Asher peels away his hands, and a piece of chocolate cake – stabbed through with fistfuls of thin pink candles – has appeared on her lap.

'There's thirty of them,' says Shay, smiling down at her. 'And I'm a pregnant woman. You have to share.'

The evening reception has already begun by the time they return to the hall. The hours blur together: food, drinking, music and dancing. Raina is quickly immersed, but her mind, her heart, are not fully present. She notices her Nani circling the room, obscured behind a fake smile, hiding how much she misses her daughter. She sees Auntie Sarla seated beside Shay at the head table, staring at her hands, as if the perfect wedding she's created is still not enough. She sees Depesh's parents avoiding everyone's glances, rushing through their meal and then leaving the reception early.

Raina also sees the gossip. It's hard not to. The rumours have already spread, and everyone knows Depesh is gay, and that Raina is not. Among the cocktails, the perspiration steaming off the dance floor, the samosas and papdi chaat are the whispers. The lingering stares. Emboldened by alcohol, many have even confronted Raina. 'What were you thinking?' they ask her, and Raina responds with the truth. She has nothing left to hide.

Some in her community are insulted, furious; while others roll their eyes and laugh. Raina tackles the questions they throw at her standing at the bar, eating dinner or on her way to the ladies'. She finds that most aren't disgusted by homosexuality like Auntie Sarla – but neither are they as modern or as accepting as her Nani. Rather, they treat the news like the latest plot twist in one of their Bollywood movies, gossip that will be forgotten in time for the next episode. Like her Nani said, the community is changing – reluctantly, sluggishly – but it is changing.

The party is exhausting. Raina excuses herself from the table and wanders outside onto the terrace encircling the hotel. The sky is clear; the wind cool yet soft. She walks, timing her breath with her steps. She turns a corner, and is surprised to see she's not alone.

Depesh has his chin in his hands, and his elbows rest against the railing. He is staring out at the view – a car park, a construction site. He's wearing jeans, a checked shirt, and his backpack sits at his feet. Her heart quickens as she steps towards him.

'You're back.'

The slightest sound escapes his lips, and then he shakes his head. Raina studies his face, but he keeps looking ahead. She leans on the railing next to him.

'How was your trip?'

Still he doesn't reply. He drops his arms from the railing and crosses them.

She knew it wouldn't be easy; she knew facing him again would be hard on both of them.

'Should I leave you alone?'

After a moment, he shakes his head. 'Have you seen my parents?' he asks softly.

'I'm sorry ... they left early.'

He laughs. 'Of course they did. Perfect.' He picks up his bag. 'There's no point me sticking around.'

'I'm sure Shay and Julien would love to say hello,' she says. 'They'll be really happy you came.'

He hesitates, slowly slides his bag over his shoulder. 'You want me to go in there?'

'I think you should. But what do I know?'

'Everyone knows?'

Raina nods. 'Everyone knows – about you. And about me.'

'Well, congratulations are in order for you, too, hey?' says Depesh, his voice edged. 'You're straight again. I'm sure someone inside has a good match for you with a nice Indian *boy*.'

She presses her lips together. Raina knows he's angry, hurt – and he has a right to be. She doesn't know what to say, so she doesn't respond.

Depesh drops his bag. 'I'm sorry. I'm being a jerk.'

Raina shrugs. 'It's OK.'

'Caleb and I are over.' He turns away from her, pushes himself against the railing. 'We broke up this morning.'

Hesitantly, she reaches out for him. When he doesn't flinch, she rests her hand on his shoulder. 'Are you OK?'

Again he laughs.

'You didn't want to stay and do a gap year?'

'That's what Caleb wanted.'

'And you?'

His mouth quivers. 'He's just a boy, right? It's not the end of the world. It's – it's for the best.' Depesh nods earnestly, as if convincing himself 'And who knows, maybe we'll get back together down the road. When we're older. When I've figured things out.'

'You're strong, Depesh. Stronger than I ever was.'

He shrugs.

'I'm really proud of you.'

'You keep saying that, but I don't even know why. I study hard because I care about my future. I was with Caleb because I love him.' He grimaced. 'I came back because I love my parents. I'm just living. I'm just doing what I want to do. It's simple. So what's there to be proud of, huh?'

'Gay, straight, Indian, not Indian.' She moves closer to him. 'Not everyone is brave enough to be themselves.'

He doesn't answer.

'There's a lot to be proud of.'

They stand there, leaning against the balcony, eyes searching the jagged skyline. Bhangra music pulses louder behind them. From the noise, Raina discerns the joyous cries of Shay and Julien celebrating to the music; the children dancing, playing; aunties and uncles chattering.

It is the sound of their community, of their family.

'What's it like in there?' Depesh asks.

'Auntie Sarla's inside,' Raina answers. 'But so is my Nani. So is everyone else.' She tries to catch his eye, wills him to understand.

Slowly, he reaches down for his backpack and looks over. 'You're sure you're ready?'

He nods, and together they go back inside.

Acknowledgements

First and foremost, I want to thank my parents Anita Chakravarti and Parm Lalli. You have been my rocks from day one, and I couldn't have asked for more wonderful, loving and supportive people to call Mom and Dad. Thank you for showing me what it means to live with an open heart and open mind, for encouraging me to chase after my dreams, and for believing in me even when I didn't believe in myself. Any achievement to my name is not mine, but ours. None of this would have been possible without you.

I am overwhelmed with gratitude for my grandparents Maya and Aninda Chakravarti and Surjit and Bikkar Lalli, whose sacrifice and bravery brought our families to Canada. Thank you for instilling in us the values of our culture, while supporting us when we chose our own path. Thank you, Nani, for your grace, love and selflessness; Dadima, for your generosity and laughter; Papaji, for teaching us strength and kindness; and my gentle and loving Dadu, who is with me in spirit every single day.

Thank you to my brother Jay Lalli, for challenging me to be my best self; my sister Anju Sohal, for teaching me about the real world; our baby sister Georgia Lalli, for your unconditional love; my new sister Heather Lalli, for bringing so much joy into our family; my lovely Buaji,

Meena Lalli, for your patience and everything you do for our family; and my uncle Baljit Lalli, for your kind-hearted and free spirit.

To Federica Leonardis, my agent, therapist, friend and saviour: thank you for believing in *The Arrangement* as much as I did, and for sharing it as a passion with me these past few years. Thank you for never letting me take the easy way; for inspiring me and my characters to be and do better; and for your care and hard work in the realisation of this novel.

Thank you so much to my fantastic editor Katie Seaman, Jen Breslin, Lauren Woosey and their colleagues at Orion Fiction for taking a chance on me, for your brilliance and enthusiasm, and for turning a story I had to tell into a real-life book.

Many thanks to Kathleen Grissom for a telephone conversation that changed my life and taught me that a woman from Saskatchewan can be a writer; to Martha Webb, for your insight and wisdom; to my City, University of London creative writing tutors, gurus and friends Clare Allan, Julie Wheelwright, Lesley Downer, Bea Pantoja, Stephanie Reddaway and Lin Soekoe; and to my mentors in both life and the law, Terry Zakreski, Ken Norman and Dwight Newman.

I am very grateful to Saskatoon's wonderful Indian community, who have been my second family, and to my earliest readers and dear friends, Annie MacDonald, Beshmi Kularatne, Sasha Kisin, Sofie Riise, Crystal Robertson, Qi Jiang, Anusha Jegadeesh, Kanika Sharma, Nick Vassos, Liz Miazga, Fafa Ahiahonu, Stephanie Hernandez, Mike Fowler – and of course Raina Upadhyay, my heroine's namesake.

Finally, I want to thank my partner Simon Collinson for putting up with me through all the highs and lows of this process. You have brought balance into my life, and have believed in me through every twist and turn. Thank you for sharing this experience with me.

If you enjoyed

the Arrangement

we'd love to hear from you

Leave a review online

Tweet Sonya @saskinthecity and
@orionbooks with #TheArrangement

Keep up to date with all Sonya's latest news
on her website www.sonyalalli.com